"Just for tonight . . ."

Her hands went behind her neck to remove the emeralds.

"Leave them on."

The heat in his eyes was as familiar as her own heartbeat, and in spite of her intent to remain cold and unfeeling it lit her as well.

"Come here."

Lips tight, she walked over. When she reached his side he took her hand. Gently drawing her down onto his lap, he raised her chin so her angry eyes would meet his. She saw a mixture of pain and yearning, and what appeared to be concern before he eased her close against his chest and whispered, "My apology for being so callous earlier."

Billie swore she would strangle herself with her own bare hands if she showed him her tears.

"I'm sorry." He drew back and used a finger to gently trace her cheek. "This is our wedding night, the only one we'll have. Can we pretend just for tonight that all's well between us?"

Romances *by* Beverly Jenkins

BEVERLY JENKINS

DESTINY'S SURRENDER

AVON

An Imprint of HarperCollinsPublishers

This is a work of fiction. Names, characters, places, and incidents are products of the author's imagination or are used fictitiously and are not to be construed as real. Any resemblance to actual events, locales, organizations, or persons, living or dead, is entirely coincidental.

AVON BOOKS
An Imprint of HarperCollins*Publishers*
10 East 53rd Street
New York, New York 10022-5299

Copyright © 2013 by Beverly Jenkins
ISBN 978-1-62490-900-9

Printed in the U.S.A.

For Bette Ford

DESTINY'S SURRENDER

Chapter 1

July 1885
San Francisco

Billie's orgasm tore through her like a lightning bolt. As it expanded and gathered speed, her body shook with echoing thunder and her throat opened on a hoarse cry. The man supine beneath her smiled with tender satisfaction and with his hands guiding her hips kept up his powerful strokes. This was just one of the many orgasms he'd treated her to in the past few hours, and as the resonance continued to buffet her like waves on a storm-tossed sea, she sensed him on the cusp of his own ending, but knew he wouldn't surrender until they both had nothing left. As if reading her mind, he eased her to a slower pace to give her a moment to rest but continued to entice her with tantalizing, languid thrusts.

His long lean body was perfect for this and she loved every delicious inch of it, especially the ones impaling her and making her ride. Spellbinding hands toured up her waist to circle over the hard points of her breasts, pausing a moment to tease and linger before recapturing her waist and upping the pace until the big bed began rocking and groaning again. No man matched him in stamina or in the joy he took in hot, raw lust, and she loved that about him as well. Just when she thought she might faint from the glory, he growled in Spanish and quickly turned her on her back. The erotic assault continued. The heat in the room mated with the heat rising from their bodies. She was covered in sweat. He was as well. He raised her legs, pulled her closer with a hold on her ankles and plunged in and out of her flesh like a scandalous hummingbird seeking the most wanton of nectars. Seconds later, his own orgasm exploded and her body broke apart in shuddering carnal response.

Later, lying boneless in his arms, she was too sated to move. Unlike the other men she entertained he always held her close in the aftermath. She felt the soft kiss he placed against her damp brow.

"Thank you," he whispered.

"My pleasure."

Humor rumbled in his chest. "You are that, Mina."

Her name was Wilhelmina. Most called her Billie but this remarkable man had given her a unique name all his own: Mina. Being addressed as such always opened a space inside her heart that had no business existing because their relationship was based solely on coin, nothing more.

Casting aside the melancholy thought, she slipped from the bed and stepped behind the screen to remove her sponge and to wash. Seeing the tear in the sponge widened her eyes and she hastily looked over her shoulder as if he might be watching. Making a mental note to spend more on her protection in the future because the last thing she needed in her line of work was a child, she discarded it, cleansed herself and went back to stand beside the bed. "You should let me change the sheets."

He raised himself up on an elbow. Andrew Antonio Yates was the most handsome man on earth, and his seductive smile also resided in a secret place in her heart. "We're just going to dirty them again."

"There is that," she replied, taking a seat on the edge of the plush mattress. "With you around no amount of clean bedding is enough, I've learned."

"Has a lot to do with the company I keep." His

hands found her waist and gently dragged her back so she could lie beside him again. "How about a meal? I'm famished."

They were in one of the costliest suites in one of the most expensive hotels in San Francisco. Without his patronage, a girl like her would've never been allowed inside. "That would be nice seeing as how I'm famished, too."

He eased her closer. "And well you should be."

They were from two separate worlds yet when they came together in bed, it never mattered that he was one of the wealthiest men in the state and a lawyer to boot, and she a simple whore. Mutual pleasure and passion was their only concern. Turning over so she could see him, she gently moved aside the damp strands of coal black hair covering the edges of his chiseled face. No man had the right to be so beautiful. His patronage made her the envy of every girl she knew. He could've picked any number of soiled doves, but he'd chosen her, and whatever the future held she'd remember him always.

He traced her cheek. "Penny for your thoughts."

She knew better than to confess. To do so would send him running for the door and out of her life forever. "Just enjoying being with you."

"The enjoyment is mutual. Now let's see about that meal."

He left the bed and padded nude across the room to summon the hotel staff via the bell on the wall. She ran approving eyes over his lean hips and thighs, the powerful shoulders and the reddish, sunburst-like birthmark in the middle of his spine. He was gloriously made.

While they waited for the meal to be delivered, she donned one of the fancy silk wrappers he'd purchased for her and stood in front of the window that looked out over the city. San Francisco was bustling. Newly constructed buildings were sprouting like mushrooms and every day the trains and ships arrived with scores of individuals seeking adventure and a new life. A decade ago, she'd been one of them. Fresh off a train from her native Kansas City, she'd never seen so many people in one place. Her lack of education and domestic training made securing a decent job impossible, so to keep from starving she used the only attribute she had, her well-endowed charms. She had been fourteen, and now called the Barbary Coast home. It was San Francisco's living cauldron of whores, cutthroats, extortionists and opium dens, where any and all vices could be purchased if you had the coin.

With a sheet now girding his waist, he walked over, fit himself behind her and gently locked his arms around her waist. The brush of his lips over the edge of her jaw made her hidden feelings soar like gulls over the Bay.

"I'll be leaving for Mexico City tomorrow. Might be a good seven or eight months before I return. I'll miss you."

"I'll miss you, too." It wasn't her place to ask why he was going, but she hoped he'd return as quickly as he could. It was every whore's dream to be taken out of the cribs and dance halls and set up in her own residence. She'd known Drew going on two years, and although they'd had good times, he'd never proposed officially making her his mistress. She'd convinced herself it wasn't necessary because no matter the amount of time they spent together, be it a few hours or a few days, his presence enriched her life. His talking to her about world events, what was in the newspapers, and the places he visited on his travels helped fill in many of the holes in her education and sand down a lot of her rough edges. He'd taken her shopping for gowns and nightwear that she wore exclusively for him. Upon learning she had a sweet tooth, he often surprised her with expensive chocolates from Gevalia's, the most famous chocolatier in the city. Unbeknownst to her madam, Pearl Du-Chance, he even slipped her extra money, which allowed her to purchase essentials like female supplies and the occasional bauble. He also footed the bill for her monthly doctor visits to ensure she stayed clean and healthy. "While I'm away, I'll leave my carriage and driver at your disposal."

She turned. "What am I going to do with a carriage and a driver, Drew? It's not like Pearl will let me use it, or allow me to go anywhere my legs can't take me. Has the bed play left you so addled you've forgotten who I really am?"

He looked contrite then chuckled. "I think it may have. My apologies."

"No need." That he cared enough to make the offer was endearing. "I would like to go back to the opera when you return though."

"I thought you didn't care for it?"

"I didn't. All that high-pitched singing gave me a headache, but I did like scaring the bejesus out of those old hypocrites."

Memories of that night amused them both. "Had fun did you?"

She leaned back against his solid chest and his hold tightened. "I did. When the judge saw me I thought he'd pitch over and die right then and there."

The judge in question was a member of the state's Supreme Court and one of her regular customers. Seeing her on Drew's arm at the opera widened his eyes and immediately sent him rushing off in the opposite direction.

"He ran away so fast, he almost bowled over

his poor wife. I wasn't planning on approaching him—I know better."

And as that evening at the opera progressed the scene replayed itself again and again because many of San Francisco's movers and shakers had shared her bed. "And when you get married you'll act the same way."

"Never."

"Liar," she countered softly. "No man introduces his wife to his whore, and I don't expect you to be the first. I know what I am, and it doesn't make sense for either of us to pretend otherwise."

Discomfort played over his features but she had no problems handling the truth. Neither of them was well served by viewing their relationship in a false light.

To make them both feel better, she placed a kiss against his cheek. "But until then, we can have as much fun as your money can buy."

That made him laugh. "Remind me to take you back to bed just as soon as we eat."

Wrapping a hand around his maleness, she stroked him expertly until he was hard and thick once again. In a voice as sultry as her eyes, she promised, "Don't worry. I will."

Drew watched her eat. Her table manners had been atrocious when they met initially but now had improved a hundredfold. He had first set eyes on her posed in a window at the Black Pearl. Such tableaus were common in the bordellos of the Barbary Coast, but there'd been nothing common about her beauty. From her sultry eyes and painted mouth to her bared breasts in the opened red corset, to the long legs in the dark thigh-high hose, she'd been the embodiment of a man's erotic dream. He'd wanted to taste her mouth, course his hands slowly up her legs and part them so he could fill her with the erection the sight of her instantly evoked. Wasting little time, he'd gone into the establishment, put his coins in the hands of Pearl DuChance and purchased her services. Since that time, he'd gifted her with clothing, expensive perfumes and whatever else his money could buy. In turn she gifted him with a skill that would make a man sell his soul a thousand times over.

When they first met, he was surprised to learn she couldn't read, and although she still had a difficult time with the printed words, she had a quick mind and was so eager to learn it wasn't uncommon after their lovemaking for him to spend time in bed reading to her from the newspaper while she asked a hundred and one questions so she'd understand.

Later, as dawn lightened the sky, Drew stood before the same window and watched Otis, his driver, hand Billie into his carriage for the ride back to her room at the Black Pearl. Parting from her invariably left him melancholy; a mood that made no sense considering what type of woman she was, but her departures always made him want to call her back. Frankly, he adored her. Not just for her exquisite talents in bed, but she made him laugh, and introducing her to things like the opera, world events, and Gevalia chocolates filled him with a quiet joy. On the outside his Mina was as hard and jaded as a woman of her profession tended to be. Inside, however, she was as green as spring, and just as refreshing. Having to distance himself once he took a wife didn't sit well.

The carriage pulled off and he turned away. But distancing himself was a necessity. He was in his thirty-first year and it was time to find a wife.

Chapter 2

On a rainy, chilly day three months later, a stunned Billie left the doctor's office. She was carrying a child. She didn't waste time wondering who the father might be because truthfully, she didn't know. Her lone concern lay in how to break the news to Madam Pearl. When facing similar circumstances, many of the girls remedied the problem either through a concoction Pearl kept on hand or by paying a visit to a doctor who specialized in such things. The last time Billie *got caught*, as Pearl called it, the solution had been the drink. The foul liquid made her so ill she vowed never to take it again. Undoubtedly, Pearl would want her to down the stuff immediately so the matter would be resolved and Billie could return to the floor as soon as possible, but it wasn't what Billie herself wanted. A child born to her would face a bleak future, so it was her hope that Pearl could find someone to take it in after the birth and raise it away from the teeming cesspool that was the Barbary.

As she hurried through the rain, she saw very few people on the streets. Most of the residents slept during the day. According to what she'd learned from Drew, San Francisco's "Barbary Coast" took its name from an older, similarly named place off the coast of Africa, where danger, pirates, and slave traders ruled. Her own Barbary Coast ran along the streets and alleys of the Pacific from Stockton to Montgomery, then peeled off into Kearney and Grant. She worked at the Black Pearl. Like the other Black and Mexican establishments, it was located on Broadway. Billie considered herself lucky to work there because it was a parlor hall. The Barbary had three types of prostitution establishments, or *bagnios* as they were sometimes known: cow yards, which were combined apartment buildings and brothels; cribs, which were the most crowded and the lowest, dirtiest places a girl could work; and parlor houses, considered the cock of the walk because they catered to a more upstanding clientele. The Chinese parlor houses were the finest, however. All had sumptuous furnishings made of expensive teak and bamboo with silk hangings and soft couches in the rooms. A majority of the girls were enslaved by their owners but always elegantly clad and exotically perfumed.

The Black Pearl didn't come close to rivaling the Chinese houses, but Madam Pearl went out of her way to make sure her girls were clean and well-spoken.

Finally reaching her destination, Billie found the girls inside getting ready for the evening. "Where's Pearl?"

"In her office."

Inside the office, Billie stood silently and waited for Pearl, seated at her big ornate desk, to look up from the papers she was perusing. In her younger days, she'd been a fabled Creole courtesan who'd come to California to take advantage of the gold in the pockets of the forty-niners. In the years since, she'd made herself rich as a queen, but hadn't aged well. The long, lustrous black hair was now graying and sparse; her pale-as-moonlight skin jaundiced and lined. "Well?" she said finally, not looking up.

"I'm carrying."

The eyes slowly raised to her own. "What?"

Billie didn't bother repeating herself.

Pearl's features were a mix of impatience and disgust. "Tell Addy to give you the drink." Her attention dropped back to the papers. "You'll be right as rain in a few days."

"I want to have the child."

"Take the drink."

"No. It made me so sick the last time I thought I'd die. I don't want to do that again. Once it's born, I want you to make arrangements to give it away."

Pearl's eyes rose to her face. "And in the meantime how do you propose to feed yourself and it?"

"By working."

"Where?"

"Here. I can help with laundry, housekeeping, cooking. Wherever you need me."

"I already have help for that." And as if on cue, Addy, the wizened old Black woman who did the lion's share of the house's laundry, cooking, doctoring, and whatever else Pearl needed, slipped in silent as a shadow and placed a steaming cup of tea on the desk within reach. As always Pearl didn't acknowledge her presence and Addy exited as soundlessly as she'd appeared.

Pearl raised the cup to her thin lips and sipped, all the while eyeing Billie speculatively. Billie had been at the Black Pearl for many years and knew Pearl was weighing her proposal. On the one hand there were enough servants to handle the day-to-day work duties, but then again, Billie was one of her top moneymakers. Losing her to another establishment that might take her in until she got back on her feet would cut deeply into the Black Pearl's profits, and profits were as dear to Pearl as breathing.

"Are you certain this is what you want to do?"

"Yes, ma'am."

"Then I'll make the arrangements for the doctor and midwife, but I expect to be paid back with interest as soon as the child is a year old."

Billie agreed. Due to the times, many children died before their first birthday, so Billie couldn't fault her for wanting to make sure the baby lived long enough to justify the investment.

"You'll continue to work for the next few months, and afterward, you'll stay off the floor and out of sight."

Billie found that agreeable as well.

"But get caught again, and you either take care of the matter, or you're out on your arse. It sets a bad example for the other girls. Understood?"

She nodded, hoping there'd be no next time.

"Now get out."

Billie made a hasty retreat.

Up in her room. Billie dressed herself for the evening. In less than an hour, the Black Pearl would be awash with noise, gaiety, and eager-eyed men bent on whiskey and women. For the first time in her life Billie allowed herself to admit how tired she was of it all. At the age of twenty-four she was now the oldest girl in the house. Her career began in the virgin room, duping gullible clients both young and old into believing the extra five cents they were paying was actually for her innocence. Back then, she'd looked young enough and was a decent enough actress to successfully pull off the ruse but those days were long past. Now she plied her skills for those who could pay the most: doctors, lawyers, men of stature whose wives would be appalled if they knew; men who'd never publicly admit to patronizing houses of ill repute, let alone ones with girls of color. *Where will my future lie?* Her choices were limited. Opening her own house could be an option if she had the necessary funds, but on a salary of twenty-five dollars a week, saving any amount of money was akin to teaching pigs to fly. Rumor had it that Pearl had established her place with funds blackmailed from clients back in Louisiana. Billie had no such power over the men she knew and even if she did, she didn't see herself stooping to something so dastardly; she was already a whore, she didn't need to be a blackmailing one. Some of the girls she'd worked with had been lucky enough to marry their way out of the life. She didn't see that in her future either. Being known as one of the best whores in the Barbary seemed to preclude being escorted home and introduced to the folks as a prospective bride.

Taking in her reflection in the cloudy stand-up mirror, she saw a woman wearing a gaudy low-cut red dress that barely contained her breasts, well-darned fishnet stockings, and high-heeled shoes. The face was passable, although it was hard to tell beneath all the paint, but it wasn't her face the men paid for. She placed a light hand over the child forming inside. That she was carrying was still hard to believe. If Pearl did find a good home for it, she'd have one less worry, but the uncertainties surrounding her own fate made her future as cloudy as the old mirror.

Turning away, she cast a critical eye around her small room to make sure it was ready for the evening. Seeing everything in place, she squared her shoulders and went downstairs to start her shift.

At a quarter past five in the morning, her work was done, so she peeled off the dress and stockings now smelling of smoke, drink, and sex and settled into a tub of warm water. It was always the best part of her day. Gone were the men and their demands. The house's raucous atmosphere faded to a quiet peacefulness that brought with it solace and reflection.

When the door opened and Pearl's son Prince entered, Billie didn't veil her disgust. "What do you want?"

Pearl was a delicately boned *mulatress* but Prince was a big hulk of a man. He had skin as bumpy and pale as the underbelly of a toad, and protruding toadlike eyes that stared out of a round, almost feminine face. He had small, always well manicured hands but it was the missing shell of his left ear and the pulled-taut eye and mouth that people noticed the most.

"Mama says you're carrying."

"And?" She didn't bother hiding her nudity from him, there was no point. He made a habit of intruding while the girls bathed.

"She wants to know if you've changed your mind about the drink."

"I haven't." She wanted him gone. "Anything else?"

He scanned her slowly. "Carrying is going to make you fat as a farmer's cow. Once you drop you may have to find work elsewhere, but I can see to it that you stay, for a price."

And she knew what that price would be. "I'd walk into the Bay first."

Malevolence glittered in his bulging eyes. "That can be arranged, too, you know."

She did. Scores of dangerous men slithered through the streets and back alleys of the Barbary and Prince was among the elite. Like a malevolent octopus, he had tentacles everywhere: whoring, gambling, usury. Patrons or girls who crossed him suddenly went missing, or were found floating facedown in the Bay. The police never found evidence linking him to the incidents, but everyone knew the truth and as a result gave him a wide berth. Billie was no exception. He was like a feral dog. Showing fear only increased the odds for attack, so she didn't allow hers to show.

"You always were an uppity bitch."

"Thanks. I'll take that as a compliment."

A few days after Billie began working there, he'd stolen into her room to try her out as he'd done some of the other girls, and she'd bolted awake with him on top of her. Outraged and terrified, her struggles to stop the assault were useless until she managed to grab the derringer beneath her pillow and put two shots into the side of his head. It hadn't killed him, but were it not for Addy's doctoring, he'd've bled to death. Addy had to stretch the skin in order to cover the damage, then stitch it closed, which accounted for the offset eye and lips. He also sported a nasty scar from hairline to chin and was deaf on that side of his head.

He'd never forgiven Billie for being the cause of the disfigurement, and she was certain that one day he'd try and exact his revenge, but she'd replaced the small derringer with a Colt that now sat within easy reach on the stool by the tub, so it wouldn't be then. "Again, if there's nothing else, please leave me."

"One day soon, bitch."

"Just get the hell out."

Slamming the door, he did, and Billie let out a shaky breath in the silence that swept over the room. One more reason to take up life elsewhere.

Chapter 3

By February Billie was in her seventh month and sagging beneath the combined weight of her pregnancy and her chores. Having to spend her days scrubbing floors and doing laundry in lye-laced water left her knees aching and her hands red and raw. Because her condition prevented her from adding to the Black Pearl's ledgers, she'd been moved out of her large bedroom. Although it had been hers for nearly five years, it now belonged to a vain young thing from Denver named Cherry, who'd worked her way up from newcomer to queen bee in less than six weeks' time by making herself available to Prince from the day she arrived. Billie and the other girls would've warned her that no woman held Prince's interest for long, but she was so full of herself they decided to let her learn her lesson on her own.

Billie now slept on a small thin cot in the basement. She didn't complain about the poor accommodations or the backbreaking work because it wouldn't change things, nor would anyone care, so she got up each morning before dawn, had breakfast, then sought out Addy to be given the tasks for the day.

But on this particular morning, Prince stopped her on the way. "Mother wants to see you."

She had no idea what Pearl might want, but from his smug, ghoulish smile guessed it would be yet another challenge to her severely tattered existence.

Pearl was in her office standing in front of the windows.

"You wanted to see me."

"Yes. I've made arrangements with Addy to take you in until your brat's born. It's bad luck having a woman in your condition on the premises. You'll leave with her this evening."

Billie had no desire to move in with Addy. The old woman with her silent ways and ever watchful eyes was unsettling. "But—"

"No discussion. Just do it."

And when Pearl said nothing else, Billie knew she'd been dismissed.

Addy was midwife to half the Barbary's population and roots woman to the other half. Those who couldn't afford the patent medicine hawked on street corners, or the pricier stuff prescribed by the city's physicians, patronized Addy instead. Very few people crossed her or ducked out on their bills because of her reputation for revenge. Lurid tales were told of people walking into the Bay while asleep and of others setting their own houses afire after not showing the old woman the proper respect.

Billie sat on the hard seat of the listing wagon while Addy held the reins to an ancient mule named Jessup. The persistent cold winter rains left the streets rutted and full of mud so the going was slow. She had no idea where Addy lived but from the direction they were heading and the tang of the Bay filling her nose, she assumed near the docks.

And she was right. After passing the ship-building docks, then skirting ones where whale carcasses were rendered into oil—prompting her to pull up her cloak to shield her nose against the foul smells—they finally turned onto a narrow street near the area where hundreds of tons of hay were imported to feed all the horses used in the city. The old woman pulled back on the reins in front of a small house that stood out from the tumbledown shacks and weathered lean-tos on either side of it like a shiny nugget in a miner's pan. The sturdy, well-constructed outer walls were painted blue and there were no holes in the roof that she could see. The place sat back from the street inside a matching blue picket fence anchored by a wooden gate.

"Surprised are you?" Addy asked, uttering her first words since leaving the Pearl. Due to her advanced age, she had very little hair and even fewer teeth, but the black eyes were sharp as a raven's.

"I am." Billie had no idea what she'd been expecting but it was not the neat-as-a-pin place they were in front of now.

"Thought you would be. Go on in the house and light a fire. I'll tend to Jessup here and be there directly."

"Yes, ma'am." Billie picked up her old weathered carpetbag holding everything she owned and headed for the entrance.

Inside, the place was cold and filled with shadows of the fading day. Slowed by her advanced pregnancy and chilled to the bone beneath her damp black cape, Billie set her carpetbag on the floor then lit the logs in the grate and prayed warmth would spread quickly. As the flames grew and offered a bit of illumination, she spied a lamp on a table. Lighting it, she peered around. There were Chinese rugs on the floors beneath a few pieces of serviceable furniture that appeared to be as aged as their owner but well cared for.

A glance to the far side of the room showed Addy watching her and Billie jumped with alarm.

"Get out of that wet cape and put this on."

Only then did she notice the claret red robe in Addy's gnarled hand. "It'll keep you warm while the heat rises up."

Grateful to get out of the cape, Billie exchanged it for the robe. By its shoe-brushing length, she assumed it had been owned by a man at some point in its past. The soft fabric went a long way in ridding her of the chill. "Thank you."

"You sit there and I'll get you something to eat."

Unaccustomed to being waited on, Billie wanted to help with the food but before she could voice the offer, Addy melted back into the shadows and disappeared.

Later, the two of them sat on a bench in front of the now roaring fire and consumed the best fish chowder Billie ever tasted. Fat, succulent pieces of fish and small squares of potatoes were the prizes in a rich, creamy soup that was so excellently seasoned and smooth it could have been served to a queen. "I could eat this forever."

"Fish will help the child form."

Billie had no idea if that was true, but was disappointed when she finished the last spoonful in the bottom of the wide white bowl.

"More?" Addy asked.

She did, but was afraid she might be eating the woman out of house and home so she declined. "No, but thank you. It was very good."

Addy took the bowl from her hand and left the room, only to return with it filled again. "Eat."

Billie smiled inwardly and ate.

When she'd finally had her fill, she handed the empty bowl to Addy. "Thank you."

"You're welcome."

Sated and a bit sleepy, Billie nonetheless pushed herself to her feet. "If you show me where, I'll wash up the dishes."

"You will sit and rest."

"But—"

Addy paid her no mind and stood. "I'll handle the dishes."

Billie sighed her frustration and watched Addy leave the room.

Alone by the fire she mulled over the old woman. Her kindness, cozy home, and the sump-tuous meal were a sharp contrast to the Addy she'd known at the Black Pearl who rarely spoke and whom Billie assumed lived an impoverished hand-to-mouth existence. The skirt and blouse Addy changed into upon their arrival there, though humble, was of a finer quality than any clothing Billie had seen her dressed in before. It made her wonder if Pearl knew anything about Addy's true life.

"Come. I'll show you where you and the babe will sleep."

The back room was small but a sizeable fire crackled in the grate. The air was warm and a lit lamp illuminated a brass four-poster bed covered by a large quilt made of indigo squares. Billie spied a fine upholstered chair the color of caramel that was so well made it would've looked right at home in some of the fancy hotels she'd been in with Drew. For just a moment his face flitted across her mind's eye. She wondered if he was still in Mexico and what he might think of the condition she found herself in. Pushing away thoughts of him, she turned her attention back to Addy and found herself being watched with that same unsettling intensity. "I wish you'd let me earn my keep in some way."

"You can help me with my deliveries."

"How about the wash and cleaning? I can help with that also."

"No need. Only me, you, and the babe here. Won't be a lot of mess. Sit."

Billie took a seat in the caramel chair. Weariness materialized out of nowhere and she was suddenly so tired, she thought she might fall asleep then and there.

"If you want to sleep do so."

"Are you certain there's nothing you need me to assist you with?"

"I am."

"What about tomorrow while you are at the Pearl?"

"Not going back there. Today was my last day."

Another surprise.

"You and the babe lie down as long as you need to. There's more chowder if you have a hankering for it when you get up."

Billie wanted to be able to thank her in some way but Addy seemed intent upon denying her the means to do so. It occurred to her that the aged midwife might have a hidden motive for being so nice but Billie was too tired at the moment to dwell on the possibility. All she wanted was to take the woman's suggestion and sleep.

She awakened later with no idea where she was. The room was fully dark but for the fire burning brightly in the grate. As the fog of sleep faded from her mind, memory returned, so she left the bed to find her benefactor.

Addy was in the front room seated before the fire. A tray on her lap held tied-up bundles of herbs and a mortar and pestle. Without looking away from whatever she was grinding, she asked Billie, "Did you sleep well?"

"I did. What time is it?"

"A bit past midnight. Would you like more chowder?"

"I'm fine for now."

Abby nodded. "Sit with me if you've a mind to."

Wrapped in the voluminous claret robe, Billie sat and watched the woman separate some of the herbs and place them into small drawstring bags. The powders went into glass jars.

"Where'd you learn your doctoring, Miss Addy?"

"From my grandmother, who taught my mother, who taught me. We were all captives in South Carolina back then." She paused and stared into the fire. Silence filled the room for a long moment before she added quietly, "Nobody left but me, now." The dark eyes questioned Billie. "What about you, any family?"

"Not that I know of. My mother was a whore in Kansas City and one night she didn't come home. Been on my own since. Never knew my pa."

"How old were you?"

"Ten. It was so long ago, I have trouble even remembering what she looked like."

"Was she good to you?"

"Not particularly, no." Billie's entire life had been one of hurt, pain, and no love to speak of.

Addy was again staring into the fire. When she finally spoke her voice was soft. "Had a daughter and one night, she didn't come home, either. Fishermen found her a few weeks later washed up on the banks of the Bay."

Ice filled Billie's blood. "I'm so sorry."

"So was I."

The sparks and pops of the fire punctuated the silence.

"Was she your only child?"

Addy nodded. "Gone ten years now." Focusing on the undulating tongues of red and orange, she remained quiet for a few long moments, then asked, "What do you see?"

The question stumped Billie because she wasn't sure what the woman meant.

Addy explained. "When you look in the grate. What do you see?"

Still confused, Billie shrugged. "Flames."

Her response evoked a soft smile. "I see flames, too, but I also see life and death, the past, and the possibilities of what might come to be."

The hairs stood up on the back of Billie's neck.

"Women in my family are seers. My grandmother read the wind. My mother saw the channels of life in the moon. My gift is fire. Hurricane took my grandmother's life. My mother met her death beneath a full moon. Mine will come by fire." She turned her head and looked into Billie's face. "The night I buried my daughter I saw you and the babe in the flames."

Billie's heart pounded.

"I had no idea who you were until the night you shot Prince DuChance and Pearl called on me to save his life."

A long-buried memory surfaced. "You came to my room."

"I did. I wanted to see the woman who shot my daughter's murderer."

"Prince killed your daughter."

She nodded.

"How do you know?"

"A few months after her death, a man came to my door. Said his wife was very ill. He admitted that he didn't have any money but asked if I'd see to her if he paid me with what he knew about my daughter's death."

Billie listened as Addy related how, on a moonless night ten years ago, Prince entered a wharf-side tavern seeking a boat to hire. The barkeep pointed him towards the man who'd come to Addy's door, and a deal was struck.

"Prince told him the bag held the bodies of his wife's three dogs poisoned by a neighbor, so the man rowed Prince out into one of the channels and they pushed the bag overboard. The next morning when he went to take his boat out, there were bloodstains in the spot where the bag had lain. He assumed it was from the dogs."

Billie waited for her to continue.

"When the bag washed ashore, and word got out that it was my Chassie's body inside, he realized what he'd been involved in. He didn't come to me then because he was afraid Prince would somehow find out and kill him. He also thought I'd accuse him of having aided in her death."

"Then Lady Fate brought him to your door."

"Yes, and although I was angry, I didn't fault him for remaining silent all those many years because a part of me was grateful to finally learn the truth. I do fault Prince and Pearl."

"Why Pearl? How was she involved?"

"My daughter was one of her maids. When Prince began making advances, she went to Pearl and complained but was told she should be honored by his interests, and ordered back to work."

Billie's lips tightened. After her assault, she'd been given short shrift by Pearl, too.

Eyes on the fire, Addy took up the tale again. "The unwanted advances continued, along with threats that had her so scared she left the Pearl and found work at a boardinghouse. It didn't save her however."

"Did you go to the police with the man's story?"

"I did, but they said both Pearl and her son denied any knowledge."

"So you have no further recourse."

"Not with the authorities, no."

There was something in her tone that drew Billie's attention to the herbs and powders on the tray. "So you work for her even though Prince killed your daughter?"

"I had my reasons. I began working for her right after you shot Prince. Neither of them knew Chassie was my child and far as I know they still don't. They believe I'm just an addled old crone, but I've seen their deaths just like I've seen my own."

Billie went still.

"Pearl DuChance is dying even as we speak. Moment by moment, her life is slipping away. Prince will go by water because that was my daughter's gift."

The shock of that statement rolled over Billie and she recalled the dull pallor of Pearl's once bright skin and startling hair loss. Was this old woman responsible? She wondered if she should be concerned for her own safety. "Do you know what she's dying of?"

"Yes."

The certainty in the reply sent a chill over her skin that notched up her wariness and must have shown on her face.

"The only danger here for you are these," Addy responded, gesturing to the herbs and medicinals. "Don't touch them or taste them. Especially this." She held up a short glass jar encasing what appeared to be finely chopped brown leaves. The metal lid was painted bright red.

"What is it?"

"The belladonna lily. *Bella donna* means "beautiful lady," and I put just a bit of it in the special tea I make every day for Pearl to help the pain."

"Is it working?"

"Oh yes," she chuckled softly. "Very much so." A knowing smile curved her lips but the old eyes blazed with such a powerful hatred Billie drew back.

"I think, I'll go back to bed," she whispered, getting to her feet. Even though she told herself otherwise, the old woman had her terrified.

Addy nodded. "Quite all right."

Billie wanted to leave but seemed rooted in place.

Addy wasn't through. "When I saw you in the flames you were seated on a golden throne and wearing a jeweled crown. Your son was seated on your lap wearing a crown, too." She paused for a moment as if needing the prophecy to sink in, then added softly. "Rest well, my dear."

Billie fled.

Chapter 4

"**S**o, Drew, have you found a wife?"

The casually posed question made him glance up from his dinner plate to meet the cool eyes of his mother, Alanza, anchoring the far end of the dining table like a queen. Silent amusement played across the features of Drew's eldest brother, Logan, seated across from him. Beside Logan his lovely and heavily pregnant wife, Mariah, kept her features schooled.

"Well," Drew began, frantically searching for a tale that might make his mother lower her guns. "There was no one in Mexico I felt drawn to."

"Probably because they had their clothes on," Logan drawled, raising his wineglass.

"You're not being helpful, Logan," Mariah quietly pointed out.

"I'm not supposed to be, darling. I'm his brother."

Alanza's gaze never wavered, so ignoring Logan's attempt at humor, Drew plowed ahead.

"I've an invitation to Consuela Anderson's birthday ball next week. Hoping to meet someone there."

It was a lame response at best and everyone knew it. But eligible young women from the old Spanish families always attended Consuela's annual ball, so at least that part of the response held water.

"You will give Consuela my regards?"

"Yes, Mama."

And with that the interrogation ended. He drew in a silent breath of relief but knew his excuses wouldn't be tolerated much longer. She'd been after him to marry for months now. Due to the ever-changing decisions of the California Land Commission, created after the United States war with Mexico, it had become necessary for the old Spanish families to prove in an American court that they indeed owned their land. Because the Yates bloodline was both American and Spanish their claim to the thousands of acres that made up the Destiny Ranch wasn't at immediate risk, but just in case, the easiest way to legally insure the land stayed in the family was to marry and produce an heir. Although Logan held title to the portion of the ranch once owned by their father, Abraham, only Drew's name was on the land deeded to Alanza's ancestors by Spain.

After the meal, Drew and his brother grabbed coats and walked out into the chilly air to enjoy a cheroot, while Mariah and Alanza remained inside to talk.

"Thanks for the support back there," Drew quipped as they took seats at the small table on the expansive patio. "I can always count on you to give me a swift boot in the ribs when I'm down."

"Like I said, just doing my part."

"Good thing Noah's not here. A man can only take so much brotherly support."

Noah was their youngest sibling and captain of a four-masted ship christened the *Alanza*. Last they'd heard he was sailing in the Orient.

Logan asked, "Do you really think you'll find a candidate at Consuela's party?"

"No. I was just hoping to fend off our lovely and persistent mama."

"That's what I thought."

Drew had no idea where to search next. "Logan, I've met women from here to Mexico and back, and not a one was anyone I wanted to spend the rest of my life with. What's left, back east? Spain?"

Logan shrugged. "Your search is the least of my problems. Try sitting around waiting for your first child to be born."

"What's it like?"

"Frightening. Frustrating. Maddening. Did I say frightening?"

"Why frightening?"

"Because I worry if Mariah and the baby are going to be all right."

Drew knew the concerns were valid. Many women died in the birthing bed, as did their infants. "Is Mariah worried?"

"Of course not. She assures me everything will be fine, but what if they aren't? I'll lose my mind if anything happens to her, Drew."

Logan and Mariah married after knowing each other for only a short time, and as far as Drew was concerned it was the most raucous courtship he'd ever had the pleasure to witness. It went without saying that Mariah had his big brother's heart and that Logan loved the ground she walked on. He doubted he'd find a love match but wanted someone as intelligent and fearless in life as his mother; but all the women he'd been introduced to seemed afraid of their own shadows, or were more enamored with his wealth than with him as a man.

"So, you're really ready to cut loose all your women?" Logan asked, bringing their talk back to Drew's quest.

"I am." Although his tone wasn't as firm as he'd wanted.

Logan shook his head and chuckled softly.

"I am," he insisted. This time the words held strength.

"Whatever happened to that piece of love candy you were seeing this past summer?"

"Billie?" As Drew spoke her name he was assailed by a flood of pleasurable memories and he leaned back and exhaled a slow stream of smoke. "Haven't seen her since I left for Mexico seven months ago. Why?"

"Just wondering. You seemed particularly taken with her."

"Can't deny that, but Mama would drop dead at my feet if I presented a whore as my *novia*."

"True."

But Drew continued to muse on the times he spent with Billie—the night rides in his coach, the walks in the parks, the breakfasts they'd shared. As soon as he returned to San Francisco, he planned to look her up and spend a few days with her before attending Consuela's birthday ball. As he'd noted back in July, having to give her up was going to be difficult, but necessary.

Mariah stepped outside and Logan rose to his feet. The smile in her golden eyes was for him alone, and Drew wondered if there'd ever be a woman in his life who'd look upon him in the same loving fashion.

Mariah asked, "Do you mind taking me home now, Logan? The baby and I are tired."

"Let me get the wagon. You sit."

She did as instructed, and while Logan hurried away she asked Drew, "How long are you staying?"

He noted the tiredness in her golden eyes and the effort it had taken for her to settle into the chair. "I'm off to the train in the morning. You said the baby's due in April?"

She nodded. "Only two more months and I can't wait. I feel like an elephant."

"You look fine."

"And you lie almost as well as Logan. Will you be back for the birth?"

"I'll try. Sounds like you're going to need somebody to help Logan keep his wits about him."

"I know. I keep assuring him the baby and I will be fine, but you know your brother."

He did. Logan liked being in control, but because he had none over his wife's pregnancy, he was undoubtedly driving her mad.

"Next time, maybe I'll let him carry the child."

When Logan returned, Mariah struggled to her feet and said to Drew with genuine feeling, "Good luck on your search."

"Thanks. Take care of my brother."

Leaving him with a smile and a nod, she slowly

made her way over to the wagon. Once she was safely aboard they drove off to their homestead on the other side of the ranch.

Alone in the quiet courtyard, Drew sat musing. Yes, he envied the love Logan found with Mariah but again he doubted he'd be so fortunate. Since becoming old enough to claim his own life, he'd been content to discreetly sow his oats from Stockton to the border because he viewed women like a kid in a well-stocked candy store. With so many choices who needed love or the commitments and ties that went with it? Women like Billie were his preference, but now he needed to choose a wife. Logan and Mariah were awaiting the birth of their first child. His mother, Alanza, was ecstatic. She'd been praying for grandchildren since her three sons reached marriageable age. Her love for Mariah was as wide and tall as the mountains on the edges of Destiny's land, and he knew without a doubt that she'd open her heart to his future wife as well. Just as soon as he found one.

Alanza stood in the door and silently observed her son. Logan was her stepson and came to her as a six-year-old little boy when she and Abraham married. She loved all three of her sons fiercely, but Andrew Antonio held a special place all his own because he was the first child of her loins. Both God and Alanza knew that one of her foremost failings was her impatience. Having to raise three boys on her own after Abraham's untimely death had tempered it a bit, but still she found it hard to wait for things to run their course. It had been that way when she wanted Destiny to be profitable, and again when her youngest disappeared during a night out on the town in San Francisco, only to surface months later via a letter to reveal that he'd been shanghaied. Impatience was why she prayed every night for her sons to marry so she'd have grandchildren; a petty want in some minds but she'd already admitted to being flawed. None of the challenges in her life settled themselves easily or quickly and that continued to be the case with Drew. She wanted him to find the woman of his heart, but would he? Where Logan had his feet planted firmly on the ground and focused only on what he could touch and see, Drew was the dreamer. Growing up, he'd wanted to hear stories of the conquistadores and their search for El Dorado. At the age of seven he'd fallen in love with tales of the great Amazon warrior queen Calafia and moped for months upon learning that Calafia, her griffins, and island of gold were only imagined and not real. Since reaching his majority he'd taken up the law and the pursuit of women. The curly-haired toddler had grown into a man with features that made women weep, as one of her aunts had once described him. From the thick black waterfall of hair, which he usually wore tied back, to the matching onyx-black eyes, he was truly something to behold. Because of that, women came to him as easily as the fog to Yerba Buena and she'd despaired that he'd ever settle down long enough to seriously consider taking a wife, but it seemed the time had finally come. However, she worried that because he was so accustomed to flitting from woman to woman like a bee in a valley of flowers that he'd choose casually and not take the time to find love.

She stepped out to join him. "What time does your train leave in the morning?"

"Ten."

"I have to admit that for the past few minutes I've been watching you from inside. You look very pensive. Are you well?"

"I am. Was sitting here realizing I'll probably never have a love match like Logan."

She took a seat at the table. "And why not?" Unlike Logan, Drew had always been open with her about his feelings. That he continued to do so was pleasing.

"I know nothing of love, Mama, only dalliances."

"Life has a way of changing us when we least expect it. You'll find your own Mariah, I'm sure."

"You just want more grandbabies."

His teasing made her laugh. "True. Is that such a terrible thing?"

"No, Mama, but for the moment, you'll have to enjoy the prospect of Logan's and Mariah's child. Might be a while before you pass down all the new baby items to me."

She sighed. "Your brother has threatened to close all my accounts from here to Mexico City if I purchase one more thing for my grandchild." His chuckling made a smile curve her lips. "I keep telling him to wait until he has his own. Only then will he understand."

"So, how are you and Max getting along?"

Because the change in subject was so abrupt Alanza didn't respond at first. It was one thing for her to ask questions about her sons' personal lives but quite another to be questioned by them about her own. "We're fine. He's back East. His sister is ill and he's gone to see about her."

He leaned over and peered into her face.

"What?"

"And that's all you have to say? We're fine?"

"Yes, my nosey son." Max Rudd was an old friend who'd taken it into his head that courting her was what he wanted to do. Her feelings for him were impossible to deny and since his departure back East she missed him terribly, but the reality of opening her heart to another man had her scared half to death. There'd been no other since Abraham.

His knowing look made her echo, "What?"

"Nothing. Just wondering when you're going to admit that you love the man."

She puffed up because it was her way of denying what they both knew to be the truth. "That is none of your business."

"Uh-huh." Getting to his feet, he leaned down and kissed her cheek. "I love you, Mama."

"Go away, you incorrigible boy."

"Maybe we should plan a double wedding. You and Max can get married beside me and my unknown bride."

Laughing, she looked for something to throw but he'd hastily disappeared inside.

Drew arrived in San Francisco late that next evening. The first thing he did after stashing his luggage in his apartment above his law office was to drive to the Black Pearl to see Billie. In spite of the blustery February weather, the streets were beginning to fill with the raucous crowds of men seeking to immerse themselves in the Barbary's three dominant sins: sex, drink, and gambling. Piano music poured out onto the walks from the opened doors of dance halls and drinking establishments. Tourists gathered in front of windows showcasing live, nearly nude women, while on various corners pimps offered the chance to touch a girl's breast for a dime. The Barbary was one of the most hedonistic places in all the world and he admittedly enjoyed the excitement.

Paying a street child to keep an eye on his buggy, Drew entered the Pearl. Sounds of music and the high-pitched laughter of the girls intermingled with the bass-toned voices of men and the clink of glasses. He peered around the packed interior, caught the attention of some of the girls, and nodded a greeting.

"She's not here."

He turned and met the scarred face of Prince DuChance.

"Where is she?" Drew didn't like the man and the feeling was mutual.

"Who knows? Packed up her things a few months back and took off."

"Did you pack them, or did she leave willingly?"

"If you find her, ask her."

DuChance had a reputation for violence. In fact, the first time they met, DuChance had been using his fists on a young whore behind one of the gambling dens; supposedly for not making payments on money she'd borrowed from him. When Drew moved to intervene, DuChance showed his knife. Drew countered with his Colt. The furious Prince backed down and Drew escorted the girl to a doctor. The men had been enemies since.

That night replayed itself in Drew's mind as he took in DuChance's smug smile and toyed with the idea of dragging him outside and using his fists on him in a similar fashion in order to learn the truth about Billie's leaving. However he was distracted by a kohl-eyed young woman who sidled up and slipped her arm into his. "Hey handsome. Never seen you before," she purred. "Introduce me, Mr. DuChance."

"Andrew Yates," he responded dismissively.

"Well, how do, Mr. Yates. I'm Cherry. You want me to show you a good time?"

Drew gently disentangled himself. "No thanks, honey."

She pouted. "You sure? I'm real good. Ain't I, Mr. DuChance?"

Drew assumed the man had been sampling her wares, which immediately rendered her undesirable no matter how good she claimed to be. Ignoring her, he directed his words at Prince. "If you hear from her, let me know."

He didn't expect an answer and those expectations were met. Giving the disappointed looking Cherry a curt nod of farewell, he exited.

On the drive home, he admitted not finding Billie hadn't set well. He'd been eagerly anticipating not only the bed play, but also hearing what she'd been doing during his months-long absence. He'd gotten the distinct impression that DuChance was lying about the circumstances tied to her leaving, but other than beating the truth out of him as he admittedly would've enjoyed, he was left with little recourse as to how to determine her whereabouts. In truth, he had no claims on her and if she wanted to just up and leave for whatever reasons, she had that right. But he had the nagging suspicion that DuChance had a hand in her disappearance and wouldn't be able to banish the feeling until he somehow made contact with her again.

The next day, he made discreet inquiries at some of the other bordellos.

"She hasn't been seen for months," he was told by a madam named Gertie who owned a place across the street from Pearl's. "I like Billie a lot, and if she'd been looking for a new place to work, I'd've gladly taken her in."

"So there's been no talk?"

"Not that I've heard. With Pearl being so sickly these days, Prince is running the operation and he keeps a tight rein not only on the business but on the girls. If they do know something they're probably too scared to open up."

He sighed audibly with frustration. Gertie's take jibed with the other madams he'd spoken with earlier. No one had seen Billie in months.

"Why are you so concerned?"

He shrugged. "Like you, I like her. Her leaving caught me by surprise. Just hoping nothing bad's happened."

"I wouldn't worry. We whores are like cats. We land on our feet."

Exiting Gertie's, Drew saw Prince standing in the doorway of Pearl's. When their eyes met, Prince smiled. Drew didn't and continued the walk to his carriage.

A few evenings later, Drew entered the sprawling mansion home of Consuela and James Anderson and handed his gilt-edged invitation to the doorman.

"Evening, Mr. Yates."

"Henry. How are you?"

"Well sir. Please, go on in."

Inside, Drew nodded a greeting to the familiar faces among the well-heeled, formally dressed crowd filling the ballroom. Consuela's parties were legendary for their size, the excellent food and drink, and the exclusive list of invitees. Making his way to where the Andersons were holding court, he paused to relieve a waiter of a glass of champagne. Moving farther into the room, he spied state senators, railroad tycoons, and members of some of the old Spanish families, talking, laughing, and enjoying the musicians stationed at the far end of the room.

Although Consuela was in her mid-forties the beaming smile she turned his way at his approach was of a woman much younger. "Andrew. How wonderful for you to come."

He bent gallantly over her offered hand and guided it to his lips. "Thank you for the invitation. I'd've been bereft had I not been invited to the birthday ball of the most beautiful woman in Yerba Buena."

She hit him playfully with her fan. "Always the courtier. Your Spanish ancestors would be proud. How're Alanza and your brothers? I hear Logan has married."

"Mother's fine. She sends her regards and yes, Logan has found himself a wife, a spitfire named Mariah. Their baby's due in April."

Clouds passed briefly over Consuela's eyes and he mentally kicked himself for sharing the news of the upcoming birth. Although it wasn't talked about publicly, most of the Andersons' acquaintances knew Consuela had been unable to conceive, and that she was saddened by the lack.

Her smile returned. "I hope everything will go well with the birth."

"As do we all."

Her husband turned away from a guest he'd been speaking with and asked, "Are you flirting with my wife, again, Yates?"

The big burly Anderson was a Civil War hero from famed Massachusetts's 54th and a decade older than his Spanish wife. Andrew had been friends with the couple for years. "I am, but she refuses to have me."

"Always been a smart lady," James noted with love shining in his brown eyes. "Why she chose an old, broken-down warhorse like me is one of the wonders of the world."

She leaned over and kissed his cheek. "Because I prefer old, broken-down warhorses, darling."

James preened in response and said to Drew, "I hear Logan finally tied the knot."

"Yes, I was just sharing the news with Consuela. They were married in October and are very happy."

"Children coming yet?"

"Yes. April."

"Ah." James gave his wife's waist a soft squeeze as if silently offering consolation.

"So when are you going to marry, Drew?" Consuela asked.

"Hopefully, soon."

"We both know that isn't true."

"Ah, but it is. Spent the autumn in Mexico in search of a likely candidate, but so far haven't found anyone as lovely as you, Consuela."

She rapped his shoulder again. "Go on with you. I'm sure there are a number of beautiful *senoritas* available. In fact there a few you might find interesting seated at the far end of the ballroom."

Her husband added, "And guarded by enough duennas to keep even the most persistent wolves at bay."

"Then maybe I shall go over and pay my respects." Knowing his hosts had other guests to greet, he bowed and departed.

After depositing his champagne flute on the tray of a passing waiter and stopping to chat with various acquaintances, Drew found the elegantly clad senoritas perched on the sofas as if they were a gaily wrapped display in a store of sweets, while their dourly dressed duennas watched over them like protective birds of prey. He knew a few of the girls and their duennas from social events he'd attended with his mother, so he stopped and made small talk. However, across the room sat a glowing dark-eyed beauty he was unfamiliar with.

Seeing his interest, she hastily lowered her head, whispered something to the girls beside her, and they all giggled quietly behind their hands. Drew was instantly intrigued. There was no denying her beauty, and to his delight, when she looked up again, she met his eyes boldly, almost challengingly. No shy flower there. But he knew how to play the game. Rather than make a beeline to her side like a besotted youth, he calmly paused to speak with another duenna and her charge that he'd met in the past, and then another before finally moving her way. Having been raised in a proper Spanish household, he also knew the rules, so he turned to the duenna eyeing him with the most interest and introduced himself. "I'm Andrew Antonio Yates, son of Alanza Maria Vallejo Yates."

"I know your mother and her family," she replied pleasantly. "They are highly respected. I am Senora Martinez, and this is my great-niece Rosaline. Her mother, Senora Ruiz, is my niece."

Rosaline. Being named for such a celebrated flower was quite apt. "It's a pleasure to meet you, Rosaline."

"A pleasure meeting you as well, Mr. Yates," she responded quietly, her eyes lowered in the manner well brought up women were taught to employ.

"May I call on you, tomorrow?"

She looked quickly to her duenna, who responded with an almost imperceptible nod.

Rosaline's shy yet beaming smile filled him like sunshine.

Senora Martinez passed along their address, and the time that would be best to call. Armed with that and the memory of Rosaline's sweet smile, Drew bowed. "Until tomorrow." And the very pleased Drew took his leave.

Chapter 5

The next day, Drew took great care with his dress. He assumed he'd be meeting her parents and wanted to make a good impression. The illustrious name of his family helped clear the first hurdle and his wealth would undoubtedly be viewed as a positive as well, but the rest would depend on their assessment of him as a man.

At precisely eleven A.M., he knocked on the door of the address he'd been given by the duenna. A maid answered and ushered him into a quiet parlor filled with statues of saints. The walls held painted portraits of saints and various renderings of the Crucifixion. Raised Catholic, Drew wasn't put off by the religious icons, but they let him know the household took its reverence for the church seriously.

The sound of rustling silk made him turn to the entrance of a short, thin woman dressed in black. A mantilla covered her hair. Her ivory face bore a strong resemblance to Rosaline's but lacked the younger woman's softness. Where Rosaline's eyes held a special kind of light, the ones now evaluating him were cool and brusque.

"I'm Senora Ruiz, Rosaline's mother. Please sit, Mr. Yates." She gestured to the settee. "Welcome to our home."

"Thank you."

"Rosaline will not be joining us. I'd like for us to gain each other's measure first."

"That is acceptable."

"Whether it is or not, it is the way we will proceed."

"Of course. I'd expect nothing less."

"Good."

He wondered how many of Rosaline's would-be suitors had run from this woman as if their saddles were on fire. Seeking a wife elsewhere remained an option, if he decided Senora Ruiz was too much of a dragon to stomach as a mother-in-law.

"Tell me your intentions, if you would, Mr. Yates."

"I'm seeking a wife. If your daughter and I suit, then I shall ask her father for her hand."

"My husband is dead to me and to Rosaline. It's my approval alone that you seek to gain."

"I see." On his way home, paying a call on Consuela might be in order. To understand what he might be getting into, he needed a quick primer on the family's background

For the next thirty minutes she quizzed Drew about his life, work, and family. "Although I was younger than she at the time, I remember the talk when your mother ran off to be with your father. She brought great shame to her family's name. Are you aware of that?"

"I am. My mother has never been one to hide her past from her sons."

"And you approved of her actions."

"I'm her son, the product of those actions. Would you have me dishonor her by being judgmental?"

She seemed taken aback by his tone. "Of course not."

"Your next question then."

"Do you have any bastards?"

Now he was taken aback. "No."

"And your brothers?"

He masked the distaste such personal questioning evoked. "None that I am aware of."

"Good. I don't want my daughter associating with anyone doomed to spend eternity in hell."

At this point, most men would've gotten to their feet and bade the bitter woman a polite farewell, but Drew refused to be intimidated. "Any bastards in your family, Senora Ruiz?"

She startled as if struck.

He waited.

Lips tight, she finally confessed, "My husband has three by his mistress, which is why I consider him dead."

"I see."

"I'll not have her humiliated and shamed."

"I have no bastards and no mistress."

"But you plan to take one after you marry," she stated as if it were fact.

"No. The men of my family are honorable to our name and to our wives."

For a moment she said nothing. He had no idea if she believed his claim, but he reminded himself again that searching elsewhere for a wife was always an alternative.

Her next words came as a surprise. "You have my approval to court Rosaline, but it must be for a year. At the end of that time, if I find you worthy, the engagement will be announced. Until then, I'll permit you to visit her for one hour each day. In a month's time you may take her walking provided my aunt accompanies you. Do you have any questions?"

"No."

"Thank you for your visit. My maid will see you out." And with that she stood and left the room.

A scowling Drew followed the maid back to the door. Climbing into his buggy, he paused to look back at the stately old house and saw Rosaline in an upstairs window framed by open drapes. She nodded. He offered a terse nod in return and drove away.

Drew's knock on the Anderson door was answered by the houseman, Henry, who after a greeting led him into the parlor, where Consuela sat reading the newspaper. At his entrance she looked up "Well, Drew. How are you?"

Henry quietly withdrew.

"I'm well. My apologies for dropping in unannounced, but I needed to speak with you about something."

"Of course. Sit. How may I help?"

"Senora Ruiz."

She sighed audibly. "Am I to assume you've met her?"

"Just a short while ago. I may be interested in courting her daughter."

"My condolences. Emmalina Ruiz is a truly joyless creature."

"Will you share what you know about the family? I'm not asking you to stoop to gossip."

With mischief twinkling in her eyes, she countered. "But may I?"

"Of course."

"Shall we begin with the scandalous husband or the scandalous daughter?"

Warning bells clanged. "There's scandal tied to Rosaline?"

"No, the older daughter, Annaline, ran away with a seaman a few years back. The gossips had a field day. As for the husband. He left her. I suppose he found her too joyless as well. Moved in with his mistress about ten years ago. Has fathered three children, and there are rumors that he gambled away most of the fortune Emmalina brought to the marriage."

"Now I understand why she considers him dead."

"Is that what she told you?"

"Yes."

She shook her head sadly.

"How many of Rosaline's suitors has she run off?"

"A slew. The girl's nearly nineteen. In some corners she's considered past marriageable age, which is tragic because once you get her away from her mother you find that she's pleasant enough."

"Is the older sister still in the city?"

"I've no idea. Are you truly considering Rosaline?"

"I am. She's very beautiful."

"That she is. A bit of a spine as well, which is often missing in young women from the old families. Rumor has it that she helped her sister flee."

He did want a woman with a spine, but did he want a mother-in-law he couldn't abide? The jury was still out. "Senora Ruiz wants the courting period to be a full year. If we still suit, the engagement will follow."

"She prides herself on being very traditional. Did you agree?"

"I have little choice."

She nodded understandingly.

Drew had all the information he needed and so stood. "Thank you, Consuela. I've taken up enough of your time. Again, my apology for the rude arrival."

"None needed. Just keep me informed. Rosaline would learn a lot at the feet of that fierce mother of yours. I will put your quest in my prayers."

Inclining his thanks, he made his exit.

Back in his office, he put the Ruizes out of his mind for the moment and opened the day's mail. Drew had been a practicing lawyer for nearly a decade. He'd inherited his office and many of his clients upon the death of his good friend and mentor Victor Cabrillo, a descendant of Juan Rodriguez Cabrillo, discoverer of Alta California. In amongst the day's delivery were two letters from Spanish families seeking representation for their land claims. Even though he'd been handling such cases for many years the turmoil tied to them continued to draw his ire. After the defeat of Mexico by the Americans, the 1848 Treaty of Guadalupe Hidalgo was signed, giving the government in Washington full sway over the states of California, Texas, and New Mexico. The treaty specifically stated that all Mexican land grants would be honored. The California Land Commission was established to oversee the claims, and in the beginning the Spanish were only required to produce their original land grant titles. Many were able to do so, but others could not—after the passage of three and four generations, items were misplaced, lost in home fires, or damaged by the elements. The Commission appointees didn't seem to care. They wanted what they termed legitimate proof that the Spanish families were entitled to live and farm on land they'd been doing both on for more than one hundred years. Many unresolved cases had been in the courts for close to two decades now while the Commission continued to add amendments that seemed deliberately designed to frustrate the claimants and further aid the government in its ruthless land grab of their ranches and farms.

The first letter asked his help in removing squatters. Drew sighed angrily. Land still in dispute had been added to the public rolls and squatters were moving in and declaring the land their own. They in turn were selling their bogus claims to unscrupulous land developers, who were selling the land at a tremendous profit.

The second letter was from a family facing foreclosure due to survey problems. Currently it was also necessary for Spanish landowners to have their land surveyed to show that the plot lines on their property corroborated what was written on their titles, even though many of the original boundaries were hand drawn. Such families were now being forced to hire surveyors in addition to lawyers and translators, which added to the families' frustration and his.

In his mind the original edicts of the 1848 Hidalgo treaty should be the only legalities applied. And in dreams, Queen Calafia could really fly.

He pushed back from the desk, stretched out the knots in his shoulder and spine and walked over to the windows that faced the city. Thoughts of the queen made him remember his childhood obsession. He wondered if the lovely Rosaline knew of the mighty Amazon warrior and her brave exploits. If her mother raised her as rigidly as he imagined, the answer was probably no. Would such a sheltered young woman enjoy having the stories read to her? Billie loved them. He stilled for a moment as Billie's laughing face filled his mind, bringing with it a familiar warm affection. Where are you, Mina? he mentally queried while surveying the people and carriages traveling on the walks and streets below. Had she found a protector? Had she left the city willingly? Was she safe? The not knowing rose to plague him once more. In truth, with a potential courtship on the horizon, her disappearance couldn't have occurred at a more opportune time, but still, he'd feel better if he had answers to his questions.

By the middle of March, Drew earned the approval from Senora Ruiz to take Rosaline walking. Her great-aunt had to accompany them, but he didn't mind because the small boon was such a relief after being forced to sit in the parlor day after day trying to make conversation out of small talk. Traditionally, the duenna trailed the courting couple a few paces behind, but as he assisted the older woman down from his carriage she smiled and said, "Although I depend on Rosaline's mother for a roof over my head and food to eat, I remember how it felt to be young. You have my blessings to go on ahead."

That earned her a grateful kiss on the cheek

from Rosaline and a bow of thanks from Drew. As they walked down a path in a park not too far from the Ruiz home, she trailed them but left enough distance to allow Drew and Rosaline to have a personal conversation.

"My apologies for all the hoops my mother has made you jump through."

"None needed. A prize worth having is rarely earned without challenges."

"You look upon me as a prize?"

"I do."

"That's sweet," she said. "You are very handsome, Drew."

"And you are very beautiful."

She lowered her eyes as if embarrassed.

"Don't tell me this is the first time you've heard that."

"It isn't but you sound so sincere."

"And I am."

They passed a group of young mothers sitting on a bench while their young children played in the grass nearby. Drew nodded a greeting. They smiled as he, Rosaline and the duenna passed by.

"Do you think your mother will approve of me?" Rosaline asked him.

"I do."

"My mother says she's not a woman to emulate."

His distaste for Senora Ruiz rose again. "And why is that?"

"She said she caused a scandal when she was young and then refused to remarry after her husband died, but my sister Annaline caused quite a scandal, too, as I'm sure you've heard."

"I've heard a bit."

"Mama told her she'd rot in hell if she chose a man she didn't approve of, but Anna replied that being under Mama's roof was a hell all its own. Mama didn't like that."

"Is it true you helped your sister run away?"

She wouldn't look at him, so he sought to reassure her. "I won't think badly of you if the answer is yes, Rosa."

"I pretended to be ill so that Mama would have to sleep in my room that night. When we awakened the next morning, Anna was gone. Mama guessed I'd lied."

"Was she angry at you?"

"Oh yes. I received ten lashes across my bare back and made to recite two hundred Hail Marys on my knees as penance. I also had to go to confession. The priest gave me another fifty Hail Marys."

Drew sighed.

"Mama said you don't attend church regularly. Is that true?"

"It is. I only go on Easter Sunday." It was one of the things Senora Ruiz asked about the first time he came to call. She hadn't appeared to be pleased by the response.

"Well, you'll have to come with me more often then. I'd like to show off my *novio* to all the other girls."

That amused him. "I'll see what I can do."

After driving her and the duenna home again, he said, "I had a wonderful day with you, Rosaline."

"I enjoyed your company as well. What will you do for the rest of the day?"

"I've some errands to take care of and then back to my office. Your mother has invited me to dinner tomorrow, so I will see you then."

"Until then," she said softly and she and the duenna went inside.

A smiling Drew drove away.

Billie helped earn her keep by making Addy's deliveries up and down the docks. Bundled up against the raw winter wind blowing in off the water, she was in her eighth month and the weight of the baby made her feel as if there were fifty-pound watermelons tied around her waist. Frankly she was shaped that way as well. Her cape, once perfect for hiding her condition beneath, now barely concealed her girth. Cold and weary, she was thankful to be heading to the day's final delivery. Old Mr. Arroyo's bootblack shop. His gout was acting up and he swore by Addy's medicine.

Entering the small establishment shivering and trying to warm her hands, she was brought up short by the sight of Drew Yates seated in the chair having his boots shined. He appeared equally as stunned and although her first instinct was to turn and run, she shook off the shock and grabbed hold of her faculties. Mr. Arroyo needed the medicine and she needed to bring his payment back to Addy.

"How are you, Drew?" she asked as if the sight of him hadn't knocked her to her knees.

"Prince said you'd left the city."

She shrugged. "As you can see, he lied. Mr. Arroyo, here's your medicine."

"Thanks, Billie. Hold on a minute while I go in the back and get my coin purse."

His departure left them alone and she'd never been more uncomfortable in her life.

"Is there a reason he lied?" he asked.

"Probably because of this." She opened her cloak and his eyes went wide.

While he sat there looking even more stunned, Mr. Arroyo returned and Billie put the coins into the pocket of her cloak. "Thank you. Nice seeing you, Drew."

"Wait a minute!"

Hurrying out the door she didn't slow. Pity was the last thing she wanted from him, and even though she didn't have a dime to her name she had too much pride to take the money he'd invariably want to offer. She was also embarrassed about her condition and that seeing him reminded her how stupid she was to be in love with him still. He called her name again but she kept walking as fast as her advanced state would allow until he caught up to her and gently made her stop with a hand on her arm. "Talk to me, please."

"What would you have me say?"

"I'm not sure. Do you know who the father is?"

She studied him for a long moment. "No, so don't worry, I won't make any demands on you."

"That wasn't what I meant."

"No? Then if I can somehow tie the baby to you, you'll claim it."

He didn't reply.

She turned on her heel. "Have a good life, Drew." Billie didn't know why she was so angry or so close to tears. He'd asked a reasonable question, she supposed, but she didn't feel reasonable, just tired and frustrated and so uncustomarily helpless, she wanted to drop to the ground and weep. It wouldn't help though. The only thing that would help would be the birth, giving the child over to Pearl, and seeking a new life somewhere else.

A grim-faced Drew watched her go, then solemnly returned to Mr. Arroyo's shop. After quizzing the man, he learned that Billie had turned up on the docks a few months ago, living with an old roots woman named Addy Graves. Arroyo didn't know how long the two had been acquaintances, or the circumstances of their relationship, only that Billie sometimes made the woman's deliveries. He shared Addy's address and when he finished blacking Drew's boots, Drew walked back outside into the cold gray day. His first instinct was to seek out the house to inquire if Billie needed financial assistance, but she hadn't looked pleased to see him again. Rather than add to her distress, he drove home. The answers to his questions had finally been revealed, so why was he left so unsettled?

Chapter 6

The baby was born April 15, 1886. A boy. Addy put him into the weary Billie's arms and the sight of his angelic little face erased all the pain and exhaustion that accompanied the fifteen hours of labor. "He's so beautiful," she whispered through her tears. She hadn't expected to have such an emotional reaction to seeing her child for the first time. Her eyes lingered lovingly over his scrunched-up face, tiny closed fists and the thick down of black hair covering his head.

"Got a birthmark on his back, too," the mysterious old woman pointed out.

Billie turned him over and gently eased aside the soft blanket. The sight of the birthmark put ice in her blood. It was twin to the blurry sunburst Drew Yates had on his back. She'd resigned herself to not knowing the identity of the father, but now. . . . the implications were enormous. Would he want to know he had a son? If he did, would he claim the child and thus complicate the deal she'd made with the DuChances? She calmed her mind. There was no point in drowning in speculation. All that mattered was that she had a beautiful, perfectly formed son, and in spite of the promise she'd made to give him up, she named him. Antonio Andrew Wells.

A few days later, Addy entered the room where Billie and the baby slept. "Someone here to see you."

Before Billie could ask the visitor's identity, Prince DuChance appeared in the threshold.

"Well, well," he purred with silky malice. "Aren't you the perfect picture of motherhood?"

He was so busy gloating he failed to see Addy's unveiled hate. He wasn't someone either of them wanted to see, Billie in particular, not after having spent every night since Tonio's birth walking the floor with him. He wasn't eating or sleeping well and cried incessantly. Addy speculated that there might be something wrong with his insides because Billie's breast milk sent him into tortured screams instead of peace and contentment.

"What do you want, Prince?" The baby in her arms wailed.

"Just stopped by to see how my mother's investment is doing."

"Not well at the moment, as you can hear. He's sickly and nothing Addy and I do seems to make a difference." The cries filled the room.

"Find a cure. We have an agreement. Since he's a boy the parties will pay more."

She wanted to tell him what he could do with the agreement but said nothing.

"And when are you coming back to work?"

"I'm not. The babe's too sick."

"You owe us money."

"I know that," she snapped. "You'll be paid. Don't worry."

Ignoring his toadlike eyes, she began pacing with the howling baby, hoping the movement in tandem with her soft, comforting words would invoke some modicum of calm, but he screamed all the louder. "As you can see I've my hands full. Come back another time."

He didn't like being dismissed, but the circumstances left little choice. "One year. Have him ready or you pay the price." He glanced Addy's way and sneered, "I'll see myself out."

After his departure, Billie cursed him silently then resettled her attention on her poor distressed son. She had no idea how she'd pay the DuChances with the little bit of money she received from Addy and it was one more thing gnawing at her mind.

"Don't worry. Things will be as they're meant to be," Addy voiced prophetically.

Before Billie could ask her to explain, the roots woman left the room.

In the weeks and months that followed, Drew continued his courting of Rosaline Ruiz and Billie the care and feeding of their son. She hadn't seen Drew since the day on the dock and she didn't seek him out. It didn't seem right to suddenly appear at his door and present him with a child he knew nothing about, and again, she'd promised the baby to the DuChances. Thinking back on how she'd once referred to the baby as an it, and how readily she'd intended to give him away, made her realize just how ignorant she'd been about the bonds between mother and child. Her love for her son spread through her being with each passing moment, and when he slept she found herself gazing down at his small, sweet face with wonder. He was hers—from her loins. The feelings brought to mind the ill treatment she'd received at the hands of her own mother—the slaps, the kicks, the cursings. Had there been something wrong with her as a child that caused her mother to not care for her with the same intensity? Nothing in life would ever make her raise her hand in anger to something so precious. Wanting to keep him safe grew as strong as her love.

Addy finally came up with a concoction of herbs and tonics that eased his tender tummy. By the time he turned six months old, he was as healthy and alert as any mother could wish, and when his ninth month rolled around, he was walking and getting into everything he could find. He often accompanied Billie on her errands to the docks, and everyone from the saloon whores to the shipbuilders to the baleen haulers knew him and gave him a smile. A few men even came courting, but she turned them away. With Tonio's first birthday less than a week away, leaving San Francisco had become paramount so tying herself to a man made little sense.

That evening, she glanced over at her peacefully sleeping son. He'd spent the afternoon chasing the gulls on the shoreline, and was so tuckered out, she doubted he'd utter a peep before sunrise. Walking over to his crib, she surveyed the small whirlwind that he'd become and very softly stroked a finger over his cheek. Hell would freeze over before she gave him over to the DuChances. He'd captured her heart from the moment she held him in her arms and she couldn't imagine living life without him, but in order to save him and to save herself, it was going to be necessary to do so. She just hoped he'd forgive her one day. If all went well, they'd be gone before Prince came to collect him. She'd saved up the few coins she'd received from Addy as payment for running her errands. The amount wouldn't get them very far, but with any luck it would be enough to get them where they needed to be. While the baby slept, she turned down the lamp, crawled into bed and hoped her plan bore fruit.

But Prince arrived unexpectedly the following afternoon. "I'm here for the baby."

Swallowing her surprise and fear, she declared as calmly as she could manage, "The arrangement was on his first birthday. I still have a week, Prince." Tonio was playing on the floor. She walked over and hoisted him into his arms. He smiled up at her and settled his head against her shoulder.

She saw Prince watching them and whatever conclusion he'd come to made him made him shake his head. "You've grown attached to the little bastard, haven't you? You always were a stupid whore."

Before she could snap back a reply, Tonio began to wail.

Prince stiffened.

"He's cutting new teeth and not feeling well." She tried to comfort him by rocking him slowly and crooning, but the screams only increased in volume, and as they did, Prince stared on grimly. Billie pressed her advantage and prayed she could somehow delay handing over her child. "How about you come back in a couple of days? The teeth will be in and he'll be much calmer."

She could tell Prince was conflicted. On the one hand he'd arrived with every intention of taking possession of the child, but on the other hand, he clearly wanted nothing to do with Tonio in his present howling state.

In the end, he surrendered, but with obvious displeasure. "I'll be back on Friday. Have him ready. Drug him if you have to. I'll not have him screaming all the way back to town. And don't think about trying to flee. If you do, I'll find you and kill you both."

She nodded tersely.

He stormed out and a shaken but relieved Billie gave her son, whose cries had diminished to whimpers, a kiss on his cheek and a soft squeeze filled with her love.

"Got yourself a few more days, did you?"

She turned at Addy's voice. The glint of humor in the aging eyes was something she'd never witnessed before. "Yes, I have."

"Then let's get you on your way tonight."

Billie had planned on just that, but how had Addy known? "You knew I was leaving?"

"Why would you stay and hand him over to that monster?"

She didn't know what to say.

"Get you something to eat. We'll leave soon as it's dark."

Billie's plan had involved getting her and the baby to the train station and making her way east to Sacramento, but as night fell and she, the baby and Addy walked to one of the waterfront saloons, it seemed Addy had an escape plan of her own design. A fisherman and his small craft were waiting. As Addy held the sleeping Tonio, he helped Billie into his boat and Addy handed over the baby.

"He'll take you up to Stockton and you can catch the train there."

Billie had no idea how much the man knew but her concern was great.

Once again, Addy seemed to read her mind. "He will not betray you. He owes me a lifetime of favors and his silence."

"But what of Prince. What will you tell him?"

Addy waved her off. "Nothing. You go get that crown. May the Spirits be with you."

And then they were pushing off. She wanted to tell Addy how much her care meant and how much she'd miss her, but Billie sensed she knew. She looked down at her son asleep in her arms and when she glanced up to try and make out Addy in the darkness, she saw only shadows.

The man said nothing during the initial part of the journey except to answer her question about what body of water they were traveling on. "San Joaquin River. You get some sleep. We'll be in Stockton directly."

Her mind awash with worries about Addy, Prince, and the uncertain path she'd chosen for Tonio's immediate future, Billie doubted she'd ever sleep again, but she lay down on the tarps covering the deck of the boat and when her eyes opened again, it was morning.

After finishing up Friday's morning deliveries, Addy returned home to find an angry Prince DuChance standing on her doorstep. His angry glare didn't faze her, so she opened her gate and walked to where he stood.

"Where is she?" he demanded.

She didn't bother feigning ignorance. "Gone."

"Where!"

"Don't know. Left here in the middle of the night. When I got up this morning she and the baby were gone."

"Gone where! And don't make me ask again."

She shrugged, and met his eyes. "Ask me as many times as you want. Can't tell you any more than that."

"Or won't?"

Addy supposed she should've felt threatened by him, but her death wouldn't come by his hand, so she asked, "Pearl still dying?"

Startled eyes filled his face.

"She is, you know. Some things in this world are hard to understand, but we all understand death. Got my own lesson when my daughter washed up on the shore of the bay. You probably read about her in the papers. Name was Chassie."

He turned to stone.

She waited.

"Uh, no," he stammered.

"Thought not. Be nice if I could find the one who killed her. Figure I will eventually. Being from Louisiana you know women like me always learn the truth. Christian Bible says an eye for an eye." She enjoyed watching his attempt to mask his reaction even as his hands shook. "Chassie was my only child," she informed him in a matter of fact voice. "Can't decide whether the murderer will die slowly or like"—the sharp clap of her hands made him jump—"that."

A fine sheen of sweat glistened on his nose and brow.

She looked into his scarred face. "Any other questions for me?"

He intimated a hasty no.

"Then you might want to head on back to the city and let me get on with my day."

He left without further word, and as he drove away, she watched him go with a knowing smile on her lips and a blazing hatred in her eyes.

Handling the reins, Prince hated himself for shaking, but she'd scared him badly. All this time, he'd thought her just another old woman, good for nothing but seeing to the occasional sickness, washing clothes, and bringing his mother her tea. Today, she'd let him know she was more, much more, and if his intuitions were right, she also knew he'd killed her daughter. *Why didn't I know Addy was her mother?* a voice shouted inside. Being from Louisiana, he had a healthy respect for those who worked the arts, and in spite of his education, wasn't stupid enough to chalk such beliefs up to superstition. When the girl's body was found, he'd been interviewed by the police, but with no solid evidence linking him to her death, they'd never returned. Why would she reveal her familial ties after such a long passage of time? And was his mother really dying? She certainly appeared to be. Had the old woman been slipping something in Pearl's tea? His first thought was to go back and slit her throat so as to forestall anything she might try to do to him, but he was afraid of what her death might unleash. If she knew he killed her daughter, he felt right in assuming that she'd be looking for revenge, and in light of her startling revelation would the day of reckoning be soon? It was imperative that he locate Billie and the child because the sooner he did, the sooner he could take care of the old woman, even if he had to journey to New Orleans and hire a witch of his own to even the odds.

From the seat of the wagon, Billie studied the massive iron gates with the letters DESTINO scrolled across the top and asked the driver, "This is it?"

He nodded. "Yates been living her for years. House is up this road apiece. Want me to drive you to the door?"

The gates were open as if in welcome, but she guessed Drew was going to wish they'd been locked tight as a virgin's chastity belt once she made her appearance. "How much more will it cost me? I don't have much money left." She'd met him at the Stockton train station. The price he'd quoted to drive her there had taken almost all of her remaining coin.

"Nothing."

"Then yes and thanks."

So he moved the two-horse team forward on the gravel road. Having been a city girl most of her life, Billie found the wide-open landscape surprising. Did Drew's family own it all? she wondered. She knew he was wealthy, but if the expansive vista unveiling itself before her eyes were a true indication, she hadn't known the half of it. There were orchards and outbuildings, small herds of cattle, corrals, horses in pens, and off in the distance mountains still holding winter caps of snow—not that he owned those, or at least she didn't think he did. Dusk was falling as the big house came into view up ahead. The area around it was lit up like a birthday cake. Faint strains of music wafted to her ears carrying with it the sound of happy voices. "Is there some kind of party going on?" she asked.

The driver didn't know.

Anxiety took hold. Every ounce of her being screamed turn around and flee, but she held on to her resolve. No matter what she might find inside the Yates home, it paled in the face of being confronted by Prince DuChance and his knife. By now, he probably knew she and the baby had taken off. She prayed he hadn't take his fury out on Addy.

The driver left her at the front door and went on his way. Billie drew in a deep steadying breath and with the baby awake and peering around curiously from his perch in one arm, she used her free hand on the door pull. A red-haired white woman dressed in the black-and-white livery of service answered the summons. "May I help you?"

Another steadying breath was drawn in. "I'm here to see Mr. Yates."

The woman scanned her slowly, taking in her well-worn dress and wrinkled cape. "Which one?"

She and Drew had never discussed his family, so she had no idea how many other male Yateses there might be. "Drew."

Tonio was doing his best to get out of her arms and down to his feet, but she held him close. The woman eyed the baby silently. "Wait here."

She disappeared.

Standing on the porch, Billie gave Tonio a kiss on his cheek. "Thank you for being such a good boy." The laughing voices of people having a good time came to her with more clarity. Once again she wondered what was being celebrated but the speculating vanished with the return of the servant and a richly dressed woman in a blue gown. Her face, framed by drawn-back, jet-black hair, bore a strong resemblance to Drew. There was gold around her neck and matching earbobs adorning her lobes.

"Hello. I'm Alanza Yates. Bonnie says you

wished to speak with my son. I'm afraid he's unavailable at the moment. Is there something I might help you with?" Her gaze brushed Tonio before moving back to Billie.

Billie wondered how to explain her reasoning for showing up on this beautiful wealthy woman's doorstep unannounced, an explanation the lady seemed to be waiting for, but there was no easy way to go about it, so she went with the truth. "My name's Billie Wells and this is Drew's son."

The woman looked so shocked, Billie thought she just might swoon. "I beg your pardon for showing up this way, but the baby and I need Drew's help. We're in sort of a pickle."

Billie prepared herself to argue her way inside, but the woman stepped back so she and Tonio could enter.

Her eyes swept over the baby again. In turn she received a shy smile but she didn't offer one of her own. She gestured to one of the fine chairs. "Have a seat. Bonnie, would you ask Drew to come inside for a moment please."

The servant exited.

Seated, Billie tried not to squirm in response to the uneasiness churning inside.

"Where did you and my son meet?"

"San Francisco. I'm a whore, ma'am." The way the woman stiffened made Billie whisper, "I'm sorry." Not because she was ashamed of what she was but because of what the revelation must be doing to such a woman of quality.

To escape the show of distress, she put Tonio on his feet. His hand-me-down clothes weren't the best but they were clean. He made a move to take off, but she placed a gently restraining hand on his little chubby arm, which he didn't care for and strained against to escape.

"You can let him go. It's all right," Drew's mother offered quietly.

Free, he took a few steps away from Billie and paused a moment to survey the surroundings. Billie worried that he'd somehow find a way to break all the beautiful costly-looking vases and other ornamental touches in the room, because that's what he did best, but he seemed content to stare around. From beneath her lashes, she spied Drew's mother watching him intently. For a woman who'd been shocked out of her bustle she seemed to be holding up well.

Drew entered and his first glance was for his mother—"Bonnie said you wanted to . . ." Upon seeing Billie his words faded, his eyes widened, and confusion claimed his handsome features. Hair tied back, he was formally dressed in a black suit of Spanish design worn over a snow-white shirt with ruffles over the buttons. "Billie?"

"Yep. It's me."

He then eyed the baby and appeared even more confused. "What are you doing here?"

"I've already apologized to your mother for dropping in like this but I didn't have a choice. This is your son."

"What!" He eyed the baby before pinning her with startled and then angry eyes, but she didn't quake. Her son's well-being depended on how this played out and she refused to show fear. "He's a year old and his name's Antonio Andrew."

For a few seconds he appeared to be speechless. When he finally found his voice it was accusing. "When I saw you on the wharf, you said you didn't know who the father was. And now you show up here and expect me to believe he's mine!"

"It's not about what you believe Drew. It's the truth!"

"A truth you can't prove, I'm betting."

"How much money you got?"

His mother sat up straighter.

Billie supposed he had every right to be upset, and she should've let the sarcasm roll off her back like water off a duck, but if he wanted proof, she'd give him proof.

While the Yateses looked on, Billie hunkered down beside her son and raised the hem of his jumper. She turned him so they could see his bare back. Drew's mother drew in an audible breath of shock and whispered, *"Dios!"*

Drew's face grew stormier. He walked over and rubbed at the spot with his thumb as if it might be something she'd placed there in ink.

"It's real. I might be a whore, but I'm not a conniving one. The baby's yours."

He glared. "How much?"

They were interrupted by a woman so small and beautiful, Billie thought she could have been a fairy princess. From the expensive slippers and gold gown to her rose-tipped nails and exquisite face, she exuded everything Billie would never be. *"Novio,* our guests are beginning to worry." She noticed Billie and paused. "Oh, I didn't know you had a visitor. I'm Rosaline."

"I'm Billie. Nice to meet you."

"Rosaline's my fiancée," Drew informed her flatly.

"She's very beautiful. Congratulations."

The young woman's attention shifted to the baby, who stared up as if as impressed by her beauty as his mother. "And who is this handsome little one?" she asked leaning down to his level.

"My son," Billie replied.

Tonio smiled and tried to grab her necklace. Billie went over and picked him up before he could cause any major damage.

"How old?" she asked and stroked his cheek.

"Just turned a year old." Billie didn't dare look at Drew.

But Drew had apparently had enough and the look on his face must have given him away, because Rosaline asked with concern, "Is everything all right?"

He took her hands in his and kissed the rosy tips. "Yes, my love. Just a bit of business. Nothing to concern yourself with. I'll be right out."

Billie looked away only to be ensnared by his mother's cool scrutiny. What she might be thinking, Billie couldn't tell, but hoped her own feelings were equally masked.

Billie heard the fiancée say to Drew, "I'm holding you to that." She then directed parting words at Billie. "Nice meeting you and your son."

"Nice meeting you, too."

With a rustle of silk she was gone.

Drew didn't waste any time getting back to the matter at hand. "So how much is this little surprise going to cost me?"

"Train fare to Chicago, but just for me." She was about to step into the deepest part of these troubled waters and prayed she didn't drown.

"What do you mean, just for you? What about him?"

"I'm leaving him here."

She saw his mother's eyes widen and flash to the child squirming in her arms.

"How long?"

"Forever."

"The hell you are!"

"I have to!"

"What kind of game are you playing here, Billie?"

"This isn't a game and if you'd shut up long enough to let me explain, you'll see why."

He was furious and she wasn't experiencing much calm herself.

"Then spit it out."

So she told him about her pregnancy and the deal she'd made with the DuChances.

"And you agreed?" he asked, sounding incredulous.

"Yes, because I had no idea I'd love him from the moment he was placed in my arms. Up until then he was just an 'it.'" She looked down at her son seated at her feet, gnawing on the cloth doll Addy'd made for him months ago and her love filled her heart. "I didn't want to let him go. I couldn't."

She saw sadness cloud his mother's eyes.

His angry voice brought her back to the matter at hand. "Do you know who Prince planned to sell him to?"

She shook her head. "I do know he's going to come after us, and if I leave Tonio here with you, he'll be safe. If I can disappear back East, maybe Prince will give up looking for me. If he doesn't and finds me, at least he can't harm the baby."

He sighed heavily. "I have guests to see to. We'll have to finish this up later." And he left her standing in the middle of the room.

She looked over at his mother. "Again, I'm sorry for bringing this here."

"Sounds as if you had little choice. Come, you and the baby can stay here for now. Have you eaten?"

"Not in a while."

"Then let's get you settled. I'll send Bonnie in to help you so that I can go back to my guests. We'll hash this out later."

"Thank you. May I ask what you're celebrating?"

"Drew and Rosaline's engagement."

"Oh." Hearing that made her feel even more like an interloper, if that was possible. She wanted to apologize a hundred times more, but sat instead to wait for Bonnie.

Chapter 7

Drew spent the remaining two hours of the celebration pretending as if all were well. His life had been pushed off a mountaintop, but with Rosaline on his arm, he continued to accept the good wishes and toasts raised in his honor by the wealth of relatives in attendance, he stopped to watch his male cousins compete against each other in dominoes, chatted with some of his uncles and heard the music provided by the small army of hired musicians.

"This is wonderful, Drew," Rosaline said to him. "I like your family."

"And they like you."

One of his great-aunts dragged him to her and planted a kiss on his cheek. In Spanish she gushed about her happiness for them and the beautiful babies he and Rosaline would have, which of course brought to mind the child inside the house. All he could do was smile until his jaws ached.

"Did you get the business taken care of?" Rosaline asked, gazing up at him as they moved on.

"Mostly, yes."

"He's a beautiful little boy."

He nodded his agreement but chose to change the subject. "Would you like more punch or more to eat?"

"No. I'm stuffed."

He glanced up to find his mother watching him from across the patio. It was easy to tell that she was thinking about the drama surrounding Billie and the child. One of her cousins approached, and as they began speaking, she turned away and he continued his promenade with his *novia*.

"You were gone for quite some time," Senora Ruiz pointed out when he and Rosaline returned to her side. "Rosaline said you were conducting some business."

"I was. My apologies for my absence."

"Business with a woman and her child."

He stiffened. He supposed he shouldn't've been surprised that Rosaline had shared the news about meeting Billie. "It was."

Senora Ruiz in her black dress and matching mantilla stood out from the rest of the gaily attired guests like a pale-faced crow in a row of peacocks. She'd chosen to sit away from the center of things as if his fun-loving, sangria-sipping relatives might have some type of contagion she wished to avoid contracting. That she wanted to interrogate him was easy to sense, but he had no intentions of telling her anything until he was ready to do so, though he knew he'd have to tell her and Rosaline everything eventually. Lying might be an option for some men, but not for him.

"Would you like something else to eat or to sip on, Senora Ruiz?"

"No."

He turned to the duenna, who he'd come to like very much. "How about you, Senora Martinez?"

She shook her head.

He bowed. "Then Rosaline and I will see to our guests and return shortly."

Senora Ruiz offered a terse acknowledgment and he squired Rosaline away, vividly aware of the hostile eyes boring into his back.

Later, Drew and Rosaline said their good-byes to their guests. The three-day celebration had come to an end and everyone would be returning home, if not that evening, then in the morning. On the day she arrived, Senora Ruiz made it clear that she and her contingent preferred not to be housed in Alanza's home, so they'd been offered Logan's home instead. He and Mariah and their year-old daughter, Maria, were back East visiting Mariah's aunt. The arrangement worked perfectly because Alanza didn't care for Emmalina Ruiz any more than Emmalina cared for Alanza.

But before driving Rosaline and her mother back to Logan's, Drew invited them to join him in the parlor. Alanza entered and took a seat as well.

"What is this about?" Senora Ruiz asked suspiciously.

"The business that took me away from the guests earlier this evening."

"The woman and the child?"

"Yes. I'll be honest. The child is mine. I had no idea he'd been born until he and his mother arrived this evening."

Rosaline looked stricken and her eyes, searching his, reflected shock. Her mother's lips curled. "So, you've sired a bastard."

Alanza's face tightened angrily.

"The child is mine," was his reply.

"You father a bastard and expect my Rosaline to do what?" Emmalina demanded caustically to know.

"That's up to Rosa. I will tell you that none of this changes how I feel about her. The baby's mother and I will work out an agreement as to his care because that is the honorable thing to do."

"Honor?" Emmalina Ruiz snorted angrily. "You talk to me of honor!"

Drew wanted Rosaline to say something, anything. Instead she sat staring off into the distance, tears coursing down her cheeks. "Rosa?"

"Don't speak to him," her mother warned angrily. "Don't even look at him. The engagement is dissolved. There will be no wedding. Please make arrangements to get us back to your brother's home and then to the station in the morning. You are never to come near her again."

His fury masked behind his manners, he inclined his agreement. "I'll get the coach." As he made his exit, the beautiful woman who until a few minutes ago had been his *novia* silently wept.

In the grim afterwards, Drew sat sprawled in a chair in the parlor while his silent mother looked on. He wondered how long it would take for him to get stinking drunk. He was broken and angry; angry at Billie and the baby, angry at Emmalina and his spineless *novia*, but mostly angry at himself for being so cavalier about sowing his oats he hadn't spared a thought to what might occur if his chickens came home to roost. What a mess he'd made of things. He'd been unfair to Rosaline, thinking of her as spineless. Although he'd wanted her to push back against her mother's authority she hadn't been raised to do so. More than likely she'd never escape her mother's rabid clutches now. Consuela opined that Rosa would learn a lot at the feet of his own mother, Alanza, but that would never come to be. He glanced over and saw sadness mirrored in her eyes.

"Save your pity, Mama. It's all my fault."

"I know, but I still feel your pain."

"Always count on family for the truth," he replied with a bitter smile.

"Glad you can smile."

"What's the alternative?" In reality there was none.

"Do you want me to let the family know the wedding is off?"

"That's probably something I should do. Not sure how though." He could only imagine the gossip that would result and he felt sorrier for Rosaline because she would undoubtedly have to bear the brunt of it.

"A simple note should suffice, but if you don't mind, I'll go ahead and tell the ones still here."

He nodded. He found himself wishing Logan were home so he'd have someone to talk to. "Did Billie say where she was staying?"

"She and the baby are upstairs."

He swung sharp eyes her way.

"Should I have offered them the floor of the barn, perhaps?"

He exhaled a breath of surrender. "No."

"What did you think of her story? Would this DuChance really harm her and the child?"

He nodded and told her about meeting Prince in the alley.

"And his mother was Billie's—madam?"

"Yes." His mind wandered back to the first time he saw Billie in that window. He forced the vision aside and stood.

"What are you going to do?"

"Grab a large bottle of tequila and get myself very, very drunk."

"Drew."

He walked over and placed a kiss on her cheek, and said quietly, "I'm sorry for bringing this to your door."

"Apology accepted but unneeded."

"Thank you. Maybe when I wake up, it'll all have been a bad dream. Good night, Mama. I'll see you in the morning." And he strode from the room.

In the silence following his exit, Alanza reflected on the shocking turn of events. To have a woman appear out of the blue claiming to be the mother of her son's child and then offer such startling proof still made her heart race. Even without the birthmark the baby looked enough like Drew as a toddler to have been his twin. In her heart of hearts, and between her and God, she wasn't sorry about the cancelation of his marriage, although she'd never admit as much to Drew. Maybe if Rosaline'd had a different mother she would have seen the potential for a happy, lifelong union, but with Emmalina in the picture, she'd envisioned nothing but endless interference, and Drew forced to bite his tongue until it bled.

And now, waiting upstairs was a decidedly unconventional woman and Alanza's grandson. She shook her head, and again whispered softly, "Dios."

In a shadow-filled room lit softly by a single turned-down lamp, Billie sat in an old wooden rocker putting Tonio to sleep. He was at the age now where more often than not, she would tuck him in, place a kiss on his cheek, and he'd drift off into dreamland on his own, but that evening, rocking him and having him close made the world a better place. Watching him sleep banished the reality that they had no home and that a man who'd pledged to kill them both was undoubtedly trying to pick up their trail. Moving her eyes over his smooth little face helped her temporarily forget about the forthcoming battle with Drew and his upcoming marriage. Nothing mattered there and then but her love for her child, who in the morning would awaken as he did each day at sunrise and hit the ground running as if he'd spent all night winding himself up so he'd be raring to go. What might he be like when he turned six, or when he grew into a man like his father and married his own fairy princess? She didn't know. What she did know was that she loved him with every breath she drew and that it made her feel beautiful inside.

She looked up and saw Drew's mother framed in the half-lit doorway. She stood there as if waiting for permission to enter, so Billie said softly, "Come on in. He's asleep."

She crossed to Billie's side and peered down at the boy in her arms. "Babies are God's greatest creation," she said. .

"I think so, too."

For a few moments they studied him silently.

"He looks just like Drew at that age."

"Really?"

"Yes."

Billie's eyes moved to the beautiful crib Bonnie rolled in earlier. "Is it really okay for me to put him in the crib over there? Bonnie said it was, but I want to make sure."

"It is."

"Let me put him down then. He's getting heavy."

Billie laid him gently in the crib and covered

him with the soft blanket inside. Bending down she gave him his last kiss of the day and trailed a finger down his cheek in parting. "Sweet dreams, Tonio."

Alanza could almost reach out and touch the love the young woman held for her son; it felt that palpable. There was no doubt in her mind that if the baby were indeed left in Drew's care, she'd grieve for the rest of her life.

"Thank you for allowing us to spend the night here, because I know you didn't have to," she voiced quietly.

"You're welcome."

"And I didn't come here to force Drew to pay me money. I just want my son to be safe and have the life I know I can't provide. If he can live here and have that . . ." She looked away as if overcome.

The honesty pulled at Alanza's heartstrings.

"I know I'm not the kind of woman you'd pick as the mother of your grandchild or even want in your home, but if Drew and I can agree, I promise to never bother him or your family ever again."

Emotions rising, Alanza said simply, "Get some rest. You and Drew can talk this out in the morning."

The young woman nodded. "Thank you again."

Alanza took one last look at the sleeping child and slipped out.

Too wound up to sleep, Alanza grabbed a heavy cloak and stepped outside. Sitting out on the patio in the chilly darkness with the moon and stars overhead, she wondered what the future held. Billie was correct. No woman of good family wanted a whore as the mother of her grandchild; just the thought of it made Alanza recoil, but the reality couldn't be changed. Couple that with the threat posed by the man called DuChance and it made the situation even more complicated. She had no idea what Drew planned, but she wanted what was best for the child. Alanza took her devotion to the church and its sacraments seriously. She didn't take her piety to the extremes like the unpleasant Emmalina Ruiz, but she truly believed in the edicts laid down by the Pope, and knowing the soul of her grandson would be in jeopardy for eternity due to his out-of-wedlock birth was disturbing.

The sound of an approaching rider broke her reverie. She assumed it was Drew returning, but instead Max Rudd walked out of the darkness.

"Evening, Lanz."

The smile in her heart showed itself on her face. "Evening. All done with that house over in Stockton?"

He sat. "Yep. Thought I'd come and let you know I was back."

"Good to see you."

"How'd the engagement party turn out?"

The question brought back her troubled thoughts. "Disastrous."

"What happened?"

So she told him.

For a second he seemed speechless. "That's pretty incredible. The girl's a whore?"

She sighed audibly. "Yes. Emmalina hauled her daughter away so quickly you'd have thought her hair was on fire."

"Where's Drew now?"

"Somewhere getting drunk."

"Can't blame him."

She didn't condone the behavior but she understood. "Billie and the baby are upstairs. Max, he looks so much like Drew there's no way he isn't the father. The birthmark simply sealed the matter."

Max reached out and covered her folded hands resting on the tabletop. "How're you holding up?"

"Better than I should, probably, but worried about what's going to happen tomorrow when Drew and Billie try to strike an agreement."

"It'll work out."

"I hope so. I really do."

She looked into the face of the man she knew she loved but wouldn't admit aloud for her own convoluted reasons. "Glad you're back."

"Hate to pile on when you got so much on your mind, but when are you going to marry me, woman?"

She drew her hands away sharply from his warm hold.

"Tired of being put off, Lanza. If you had a real reason, I'd understand, but you don't."

"So now, you're a mind reader as well?"

"Nope. Just in love with a stubborn, hard-headed woman."

She knew how much he enjoyed needling her and she was certain he could see the tight set of her chin even in the shadows.

"Love getting you all riled up. Be looking for it on our wedding night."

Heat scalded her cheeks. "Go home!"

Chuckling softly, he stood. "Night Lanza." He walked off into the dark. Seconds later, after she heard him riding off, she lowered her forehead to the tabletop and gently bounced it up and down while she prayed for strength.

Chapter 8

The next morning, Billie awakened to the sounds of her son babbling away in the crib. He had no real words yet, but that didn't seem to matter because he had a language uniquely his own. Getting out of bed, she walked over to the short legged crib. When their eyes met, he laughed and held up his arms. She obliged. Snuggling him close, she gave him his first kiss of the day. "Good morning, my little man. Did you sleep well?"

He babbled a response.

"That well, huh? Well, today's the day we find out what your Papa wants to do about us, but first, let's see if we can't find you something to eat." He was squirming to get to his feet so she put him down.

As if on cue, there was a soft knock on the door. She prayed it wasn't Drew because she wasn't mentally ready, so she gathered herself just in case. "Come on in."

It was Bonnie carrying a tray. "The senora sent you breakfast. She says you and the little one can use the bathing room down the hall."

Tonio stood behind Billie and peeked around her muslin nightgown to get a look at Bonnie. When the maid caught his eye, he laughed and hid himself. A second later, he eased his little face around Billie again and when Bonnie laughed, he disappeared once more. It was one of his favorite games. He'd even gotten the usually staid Addy to participate in his fun. Billie shook her head at his antics. The boy had women eating out of his hand and he was just a year old.

"He's a doll," Bonnie told her.

"He's a flirt is what he is," she replied, picking him up. "Come here you. Let's get you cleaned up so we can eat."

Bonnie set the tray down on the edge of the vanity. "Do you need anything?"

"You wouldn't happen to have any clean rags I can swaddle him with, would you? I need to wash out the few I have with me."

"I've plenty. I'll bring them back directly."

"Thank you."

"You're welcome." Bonnie turned to leave, but Tonio began protesting and straining to be freed while holding out his arms. Bonnie stopped. "Aww."

Billie feigned annoyance. "Got yourself a new girl, do you? You know you're making your mama jealous."

Bonnie closed the distance between them and took the baby into her arms. After giving his mama a pleased-as-punch look, he began babbling at the maid, who replied, "Well, I don't know, little mister. What do you think?"

He responded with more "Tonio speak" and Bonnie laughed. "Oh you're a little charmer. That you are."

When she gave him back, Billie asked her, "Do you have children?"

"I do. A daughter. Have a couple of grandsons as well, but they live in Portland, so I don't get to see them much."

Billie saw the sadness there even as Bonnie stroked Tonio's cheek. "I'll get you the rags."

Billie thanked her. "Tell Miss Bonnie bye-bye." She'd been trying to teach him to wave, but so far he hadn't been able to grasp the concept. He babbled instead and tried to get down to the floor.

"He's going to be a handful," Bonnie pointed out.

"Already is. I'm just worn out by the time he goes to bed at night."

The smiling Bonnie made her exit and Billie and her son began their day.

After the meal and a quick washup for them both, Billie dressed her son in his only other change of clean clothing. She donned the plain blue shirtwaist dress she'd worn yesterday. It was all she had. When Pearl made her move to Addy's she wasn't allowed to take anything but the clothes on her back. Everything she owned, including all the lovely gowns and nightwear Drew had purchased for her, Pearl demanded as payment for her room and board. The shirtwaist was one Addy brought back from a church clothing drive for the poor and Billie definitely qualified as that. She had less than twenty cents to her name. She thought about what might happen when she talked with Drew, but rather than speculate on it and worry herself to death, she picked up the baby and secured him with one arm, and with her free hand grabbed the tray to return it to Bonnie.

Tonio didn't make the journey easy. Constantly trying to get at the tray and its beguiling dirty dishes, he kept reaching for them while she did her best to prevent it and not drop either or both. Gentle verbal chastising never worked in situations like these mainly because he was only a year old and because he was the most curious little thing she'd had the pleasure to know. Everything fascinated him, from the gulls overhead back at Addy's place to the trash bin in her kitchen, to litter along the street. He wanted to touch, and lately taste, whatever crossed his path. "Tonio, please," she begged as he bent like a contortionist in a sideshow in an effort to reach one of the shiny spoons. "You're going to wind up on your head."

"Do you need some help?" The question was posed by Drew's mother. She was standing on the landing of the staircase and Billie sighed with relief even as Tonio continued to strain against her hold.

"Yes, please. If you wouldn't mind. Can you take him for a minute. I don't want to drop him or this tray on your beautiful floor."

Alanza cooed, "Come to your *abuela*, little worm. Are you giving your mama trouble?"

He went to her without complaint and viewed her face curiously, but only until he saw the silver hoops in her ears. He made a grab, but she smoothly covered the ear to keep her jewelry out of his grasp.

Billie chuckled. "I should've warned you. He likes shiny things. I think he's part raven."

Alanza laughed and jostled him gently. "Did the two of you sleep well?" she asked.

"We did. Thanks again for taking us in. What's *abuela* mean?"

"It's the Spanish word for grandmother."

"Ahh. So, is Drew around?"

"Not yet. Still sleeping I believe." It was eight A.M. Billie thought how nice it would be to loll around and get up at her leisure. Her last day of leisure was the morning Pearl determined she was too far along in her pregnancy to work anymore. She'd been up at dawn ever since, either being a scrubwoman at the Black Pearl or, after the birth, seeing to Tonio.

"I'm sure he'll be up shortly," his mother said.

They descended the stairs with Alanza now cooing to him in Spanish and Tonio doing his best to get his hands on the silver hoops in her ears. A pleased Billie looked on and carried the tray.

Downstairs, they walked into the kitchen so Billie could drop off the tray. Bonnie showed her where to set it and then spent a moment playing with the baby still in Alanza's arms. Once that was done, they went to the parlor and took a seat, or at least the adults did. The baby, squirming as if his life depended on it, was soon on his feet while his mama watched his every move with eagle eyes to make sure he didn't touch anything breakable which appeared to be everything in the room except for the heavy wood furniture and the paintings gracing the walls.

"Might I ask you a few questions?" Drew's mother asked.

In truth, Billie had been waiting for this, so she nodded a yes.

"Let me begin by saying, I know nothing about the dealings of men and their—" Her words faltered.

"Whores," Billie supplied helpfully. "It's quite all right to call me that. I'm not ashamed of what I do."

His mother appeared embarrassed enough for the both of them, so Billie added, "Whatever you want to know, just ask, Mrs. Yates. I promise you won't offend me."

She showed a small sign of relief. "Were your dealings with my son, just one night?"

"No. Drew and I had an arrangement that lasted about two years."

She looked surprised.

"In fact, he paid my madam extra so that I didn't entertain other men when we were together— sometimes it was just for a couple of days— sometimes as long as a week. He treated me quite special. Bought me clothes, took me places like the opera and midnight rides in his coach." Thinking back to those times brought on a wistful smile. "He'd even surprise me sometimes with chocolates and flowers. Never had a man treat me that way before. I can read much better now because of him, too."

"And your feelings for him."

For a moment, as all the warring emotions rose and swirled she didn't reply. "To tell you the truth, I did something women like me are never supposed to do."

"Which is?"

"Fall in love."

His mother's shock was plain.

"It was stupid of me really. A man like him. A woman like me. No way the two of us would have anything other than what he paid for. Please don't tell him though. He'll probably think I got pregnant on purpose just to hook him, but I didn't."

"I wouldn't betray a confidence that way."

"Thanks."

They spent the rest of the morning getting to know each other. Billie told her about growing up in Kansas City and Alanza talked about her parents and growing up on the ranch. When Drew hadn't made an appearance by lunchtime, they went outside and Bonnie brought them a light meal of sandwiches and lemonade. Around two o'clock, Billie, inwardly snarling over Drew's absence, put her son down for his nap, but an hour later he was up and raring to go.

She was seated in the parlor with his mother when Drew finally graced them with his presence a short while later.

"Afternoon, Mama."

"Afternoon," she replied coolly.

"Billie."

"Drew."

He eyed the baby standing close to his mother's skirts then looked away. "Would you mind if my mother took the baby out for a moment, so we can talk?"

Billie asked her, "Do you mind?"

"Of course not."

"Just keep a good eye on him. He's real quick."

"I will."

"Thank you, Mrs. Yates."

"You're welcome."

Once they made their departure, silence descended. As it lengthened Billie felt the need to say something. "My apologies again for taking you away from your party yesterday. I hope your intended wasn't too upset."

"You mean my ex intended," Drew replied bitterly.

Seeing her confusion, he said pointedly, "Wedding's been called off." He almost added, thanks to you, but kept that unspoken. He was extremely hungover after all the tequila last night, thus the reason for his late arrival. His head felt like there were mules inside trying to kick their way out. "Put yourself in her place. What would you do if the man you planned to marry confessed, 'Oh by the way, that child you met inside is mine.'"

Anger flashed across her features but the mules in his head helped him pay it no mind. "This is what I've decided. First and foremost, I will not be raising the child, I don't have the time or, frankly, the inclination. I'll give you enough money to find a place to live back East or wherever you plan to settle and pay your monthly expenses. I'll also send money for the baby's education and make provisions for him in my will, but when you leave—he goes with you."

Billie wasn't sure why she'd expected more. Maybe because of all the men she'd entertained in her past, he'd treated her the best. She'd even allowed herself to believe he'd cared for her, if only a tiny bit. Obviously she'd been wrong. "I don't want your money. All I'm seeking is a place of safety—for him. I thought maybe you'd care whether Prince finds him or not, seeing as how he's your son, but I guess not."

"Don't dare put that guilt on me. This is your mess."

"My son is not a mess, Drew Yates! And if you're not man enough to stand up and claim him, or care whether he lives or dies, then to hell with you! I'm not going to beg you!"

"But begging is why you're here, correct?"

She stood and eyed him with disgust. "Again, go to hell."

She walked out.

Drew had no idea what her plans were, but his head was pounding even more furiously, so the mules and the anger had him convinced he didn't care.

Outside, Billie found Alanza sitting in a chair on the beautifully constructed patio. Tonio was standing by her side eating a piece of orange. Alanza was enjoying a slice as well, but the fury must've shown on Billie's face because she froze. "What's wrong?"

Billie picked up her son. "The baby and I have to go, Mrs. Yates. Thanks for everything. You take care of yourself."

"Billie!"

She didn't break stride. She had no idea where she could go, but knew it had to be away from Drew Yates. Yes, she felt bad that her showing up cost him his fairy princess, but damn him, her son's life was worth a hell of a lot more.

She took the stairs as fast as the weight of the baby allowed, then gently set him in the crib so she could re-stuff their belongings in her carpet bag. Promising to pluck her eyes out if she shed even a tiny tear, she went about getting them ready to leave. Done, she picked up the baby, then the bag, and sailed from the room.

He was standing at the bottom of the stairs. "Where do you think you're going?"

"Why do you care? You said you wanted us to leave, so get the hell out of the way."

He blocked her path. "Is this more of the guilt I'm supposed to feel? You storm out knowing you don't have a dime to your name, no place to sleep tonight or any other night, just to make me feel badly."

"Listen to me, I don't give a damn about you, your guilt or your called-off wedding! You can go bugger your horses for all I care. Move!"

From there the argument exploded like lit sticks of dynamite. He yelled. She cursed. The house rang with their ugly words.

"You're a conniving bitch!"

"You didn't seem to mind when I was sucking you off!"

Neither seemed to care that the terrified baby was screaming in response to all the shouting and anger, they were too busy getting in their verbal licks.

Alanza shouted, "Stop this!"

But the battle raged on until the sharp crack of her bullwhip set off its own version of exploding dynamite, then silence followed. Even Tonio stopped crying.

Bullwhip in hand and shaking with fury, she stormed, "You two should be ashamed of yourselves. I could hear you going at each other and that baby screaming clear outside." Muttering angrily in Spanish, she gently removed the now whimpering Tonio from the arms of his enraged mother and held him close, soothing him with soft words and kisses. "Since neither of you cares enough about my grandson to settle this like adults, I will. Get married! Today!"

Drew roared, "What!"

"I'm not marrying him!" Billie yelled.

But the sight of Alanza's wintry visage froze them both in mid-protest. "This has nothing to do with either of you, but with his needs. Andrew Yates, how dare you not offer your protection when you know there is someone out to harm him!"

"Mama—"

"Silence! And you," she snapped at Billie. "I've never heard such foulness from a woman's lips before in all my life."

"I'm a whore, ma'am!"

"I don't care. You have a child now!"

Drew and Billie seethed, but Alanza's eyes dared them to say another word. "If the two of you never speak to each other ever again, so be it, but you will be civil in this house and around your child. *Comprendez!"*

Both dropped their eyes and muttered something that sounded like agreement.

With that settled, her tone gentled as she said to the baby, "Come little worm, let's see if Bonnie's made cookies." Baby in tow, bullwhip in hand, she exited. Alanza had no idea where her demand came from. It was as if the words suddenly sprang to life on their own. A marriage between them would be fraught with complications, but she knew Billie cared for Drew, and if Billie had been truthful about Drew's treatment, he cared for her in ways far more heartfelt than he'd ever exhibited with Rosaline Ruiz. That she, Alanza Maria Vallejo Yates had demanded her son make an honest woman out of a whore so the whore could be her daughter-in-law, left her reeling. However when she looked down at the precious child riding in her arms, and his smile touched her heart, she knew she'd said the right thing.

In the aftermath of his mother's forceful departure, Drew dragged his hands across his face and eyed his opponent. His mother's solution was insane of course, but her furious manner told all. She would not be denied, and expected him to marry Billie regardless of his thinking.

"I'm sure your mother let her anger get ahead of her brain. She's not serious."

"Oh, she's serious. Very much so."

"I'm not marrying you."

"Yeah, you are."

"The hell I am!"

He exhaled his frustration and looked away. This marriage was probably going to be unworkable in so many ways, but he loved his mother. When he and his brothers were young and their world was falling down around their ears after the untimely death of their father, she'd gone without food to make sure her sons were fed. She also worked harder than most men to keep a roof over their heads. Only after he was older did he learn from Logan just how dire their lives had been back then, and the full extent of her many sacrifices. Because of her, he'd been able to attend universities in Europe and Mexico and have a life that was both full and blessed. Never once had she asked him to do anything but marry. She'd even been willing to take Rosaline into her life, knowing she couldn't stand the ground Emmalina Ruiz walked on, all because she loved her son. And now. She was asking him to give his name to a child Drew didn't even know existed until yesterday and marry his mother. He could only imagine the gossip and whispering this union would cause, but if she wanted a marriage, that's what she'd have. "We'll leave shortly."

"Where are we going?"

"To get married." And he walked out.

Chapter 9

Billie found Mrs. Yates and Tonio outside seated on a blanket beneath a tree. Her son smiled happily at her approach and threw up his arms. She picked him up, and whispered against his velvety cheek how sorry she was for frightening him. Mrs. Yates still looked upset, which made Billie decide to choose her words wisely, but before she could say anything, she was asked:

"So? What did you two decide?"

Caught off guard, she mentally righted herself. "Drew thinks you were serious and wants me ready shortly."

"Good."

Billie froze. "You were serious?"

"Of course. Why wouldn't I be?"

"I—do you know what a whore does, Mrs. Yates?"

"Sells her body to men for a price."

"And you want me to marry into your family."

"If Tonio is to get the life he deserves, what choice do I have?"

"But the gossip—"

"What about it? The gossips have hounded me since I was fifteen years of age. I'll tell you the story sometime."

Billie found this unfathomable.

"Do you have another dress?" Alanza asked.

Billie glanced down at her worn secondhand dress. "No, ma'am. My madam kept all my clothes. I'll tell you the story sometime," she said, echoing Alanza, who raised an eyebrow in response to the impertinent tone, but Billie didn't flinch or apologize.

"Careful, young woman. Smart-mouthed females are prized here."

That certainly wasn't the reply Billie expected to receive.

Alanza got to her feet. "Come let's find you something more suitable."

Alanza drove Billie and her son across the ranch to a smaller house. "This is my son Logan's place," she explained as they left the wagon. "He and his wife, Mariah, are back East visiting her family. Mariah's a seamstress. If we're lucky she'll have something in her shop that you can wear."

Inside, the home was quiet and spotless. The curtains were a beautiful shade of dark blue. The wood floors gleamed, as did the well-placed high-quality furniture. A lovely glass-faced curio holding small crystal figurines stood in a corner. Billie wondered what kind of people Drew's brother and his wife were, and if they'd be accepting of her or judgmental. She also wondered where she and Drew would live after this farce of a wedding took place.

The shop was in the back and filled with bolts of fabric, notions, and half-completed gowns on dress forms. Brown paper patterns were stacked neatly on the edge of a cutting table and a black sewing machine held court over by the far wall. Alanza opened the doors to a large armoire filled with dresses and began to look through them. She removed her choices and draped them across a nearby chair.

Billie could see her son's interest in all the wonderful items he wanted to get his little hands on, and although he intimated mightily that he wanted to be set on his feet, she refused to play along. "Nope. You're staying right here. Miss Mariah won't be happy coming home to a wrecked shop."

He struggled a few more times, then gave up and placed his head dejectedly against her shoulder. She shook her head, gave him a kiss, and focused her attention on her soon to be mother-in-law holding up a smart-looking green sateen gown.

"What about this?"

Billie found the choice quite lovely, but had reservations. "Your daughter-in-law won't mind?"

"No. Especially once we explain your circumstances."

"But isn't this how she makes her living. She'll expect to be paid."

"Yes, and I'll make sure she is."

"But I can't pay you back."

"Consider it a wedding gift. Now, try it on. There's the screen. Give me the baby."

As they made the exchange, Billie cautioned, "Hold on to him. He wants to explore and that means a lot of things broken."

"We'll be fine, won't we Tonio?"

He was grinning up at his grandmother when Billie stepped behind the screen.

To her delight the dress fit. The bustline was a bit snug and pushed the tops of her breasts up a bit farther than was probably decent for a small town, but such a neckline would've been downright modest back home in the Barbary. She did a slow turn before the stand-up mirror and thought the long-sleeved green gown with its gray underskirt reminiscent of one of Drew's gifts. It was fashionable and finely made. "It's a little tight up top, but you tell me whether it's too much for around here."

She stepped out. By the smile on Mrs. Yates's face she guessed she looked okay. "You look wonderful."

Billie always felt like someone else when she was dressed in finery and she often pretended that she was. Now, the pretense was on its way to becoming a reality. The woman she'd been would be replaced by Mrs. Drew Yates.

Back at Alanza's home, Alanza took the baby. "You go up and get ready. I'll keep Tonio company."

"Is it okay if I take a quick bath?"

"Of course. Help yourself to the bath salts there if you like as well."

For a moment, Billie was so overwhelmed by the woman's kindness and generosity, she had trouble forming the words to express her gratitude. Even taking into account the unwanted marriage, the entire situation could have been so much messier and hard had Drew's mother chosen to act differently; her baby now had a true home and she would owe Alanza Yates for the rest of her life. "I promise you'll not regret taking me in."

"I'm holding you to that. Now go on. I'm going to introduce Tonio to my horses, then we'll return."

Drew pulled out his watch and checked the time. Where the hell is she! His headache had decreased measurably but his mood was still foul.

If his mother wanted Billie to be his wife, so be it. He wasn't going to pretend to be happy about it however.

He heard footsteps and turned to see his mother and the baby. "Do you know where my bride is?" His sarcastic emphasis on the word didn't seem to faze her.

"She's on her way. So, how angry are you with me?"

"Let's not talk about that right now."

"As you wish."

He ran his eyes over the baby. His son. "I'll be returning to San Francisco in the morning. I'll leave you money to buy whatever he needs."

Her audible sigh made him ask, "Surely you didn't expect me to stay here and live happily ever after? He and his mother will have my name and I'll be faithful to my vows, but my office is in San Francisco, so that's where I'll be."

On the heels of that, Billie entered. He ran cold eyes over the fetching curls piled fashionably atop her head, the tasteful strand of his mother's emeralds gracing her lovely neck and the tempting rise of her soft breasts framed by the gown's bodice. When he moved his gaze to her beautiful face now devoid of the layers of paint he'd grown accustomed to seeing, her eyes were a mixture of mockery and challenge. It was as if she knew that seeing her this way would remind him of times together he'd rather forget, and she was correct. "Let's go."

She paused a moment to give her son a kiss on his cheek and to say thank you to Drew's mother before walking with him out to his waiting coach.

Once they were under way, she asked, "Are we going to a courthouse?"

"No. Reverend Dennis over at the church will do the honors."

"Don't we need papers of some sort?"

"Yes, but I'll take care of that when I get back to San Francisco."

Billie noted that he only referenced himself returning. Not that she wanted to return with him and be confronted by Prince. "Where will Tonio and I stay?"

"Here. With my mother. I'll arrange for a house to be built soon. I'll be leaving in the morning."

"And returning when?"

"I don't know."

"I see." So, he wasn't going to live with them. Dismissing the tiny ache in her heart, she supposed the arrangement would be the best. Finding a secure place for her son was all she'd wanted. "In spite of our arguing, thank you for doing this for the baby. I know you don't want to be married to me."

"You're welcome," was all he said. "How'd you find me?"

"You mentioned living near Sacramento, so when I got to the train station, I asked around."

"You took the train to Sacramento?"

"No. One of Miss Addy's friends brought me and the baby in his boat. We left in the middle of the night because Prince was coming to take Tonio that next morning. I'm real worried about what he might've done to her once he found out we were gone. Would it be too much to ask for you to look in on her when you go back?" For all Addy's talk of powers and spells, she was still an old woman and Billie doubted Prince would view that as a deterrent.

"Where's the house?"

Billie described it and the area around it. "Mr. Arroyo, the bootblack, can help if you have trouble locating her place." She studied his hard set face. "So, will you see about her?"

His terse nod allayed some of her worry. "Thank you."

They rode the rest of the way in silence.

When they arrived at the church, he helped her down. The brief joining of their hands set off a familiar spark, but still simmering over the cruel words he'd flung at her earlier, she refused to let the response take root. It made no sense to acknowledge her attraction to a man who held her in such low esteem.

The building was small but sturdy and surrounded by a large open field of grass. The ring of an axe split the silence. Billie couldn't remember the last time she'd set foot in a church.

"This way," Drew said, so she walked with him around to the back where a man with his sleeves rolled up stood chopping wood. He was handsome and of average height and build. Their arrival made him pause. "Drew. What a surprise. Do you need something?"

"I'd like for you to marry us."

He seemed caught off guard. "But I thought you—" He immediately waved off whatever he'd been about to say and turned his attention to Billie.

"Billie Wells," she said by way of introduction. "Real name's Wilhelmina. I prefer Billie."

"I'm Paul Dennis. Nice to meet you, Billie."

"My pleasure."

His confusion continued to show, making her wonder if he'd known about Drew's engagement to the fairy princess and was attempting to figure out why she was standing beside him instead.

"Do you have the license?" he asked Drew.

"No. This came on rather suddenly, so I'll send all the legal documents to you when I return to my office tomorrow."

"I see." His eyes moved to Billie. She kept her features masked.

"Well, come on inside. We really need a witness."

"I'm sure my mother will sign whatever is required after the fact."

"Give me a few minutes to wash up and put on a fresh shirt."

While he was gone they waited in his office. Neither said a word, but the angry gazes they shared spoke volumes.

The reverend returned, and after inviting them to stand before him, began to read the words that would bind them together until death. When he reached the question that asked if she took Drew as her lawfully wedded husband, she hesitated.

The puzzled reverend glanced between them.

Drew drawled, "Well, darling. Are you going to answer him or not?"

In spite of the shadow of annoyance on his face, looking at Drew made her also remember better times, and with them the painful knowledge that they'd never come again. "Sorry. Yes. I do."

When the question was posed to Drew, he answered readily, albeit curtly.

"I now pronounce you man and wife. You may kiss your bride."

He tilted up her chin and gazed down at her

with unfathomable eyes. Never once had he kissed her mouth because whores eschewed such intimate contact, and she was unsure what he'd do. In answer he placed a solemn kiss on her brow and turned back to Dennis. "Thank you, Reverend."

"You're welcome."

Billie offered her softly spoken thanks as well and did her best to ignore the unspoken concern displayed on the reverend's face.

Drew paid the bill and moments later they were on their way back to Destiny.

Seated beside him, she wondered where this would all lead. Truthfully there was nothing about her or in her background that would make her an asset to his illustrious family, yet a few moments ago, she'd been pronounced Mrs. Andrew Antonio Yates. She shook her head at the convoluted twists and turns life could bring. From the Black Pearl to being pregnant to becoming a wife. It was enough to make a girl's head spin but she was determined to find a way to be of value and to make sure Alanza never regretted welcoming her into the fold.

When they entered the house, Billie's first thoughts were of the baby, so leaving Drew at the door, she hurried up the stairs and found Alanza in the bedroom rocking Tonio to sleep. It was a somewhat deflating sight because each night since his birth she'd been the one to shepherd him into sleep, her motherly kiss of love the last act of their day. Hoping he might be still awake, she quietly crossed to Alanza's side and saw that his eyes were closed, as were his little cherub lips. Learning to share him was something she'd have to accustom herself to. Denying him the love his grandmother so obviously felt wouldn't be right.

Both women ran soft eyes over his sleeping form and Billie stroked a whispering hand over his curly head. At the moment she couldn't imagine him grown up and as fierce and tall as his father, even though he would be one day. "How'd he do?"

"He cried after he realized you were really gone, and nothing his *abuela* did consoled him. I sang and rocked him and tried to bribe him with another slice of orange, but he wanted his mama."

Billie caressed his head again, and yes, a part of her cheered knowing his heart hadn't been completely stolen by his *abuela*, at least not yet.

"So I got him ready for bed and then we sat here and rocked and I told him all about the adventures of the brave Queen Calafia, and after a while, the whimpering faded and he fell asleep."

Poor little gent. They'd never been separated for very long, ever. "You should go ahead and put him in the crib. Once he's asleep, a train could roll through and he wouldn't wake up."

"You don't mind me putting him in the cradle?"

"Of course I do, but I need to learn to share him so this will be my practice."

Alanza chuckled softly. "You've strength and heart, Billie. Careful. I'll wind up loving you as much as I do Mariah."

Even though it was nice to hear, Billie didn't believe a word of it.

After Tonio was placed into the crib and covered up, Billie said quietly, "The only thing I will insist upon is being the last person to kiss him good night."

"Then I shall give him my kiss now and step out of your way."

The kisses were placed and both mama and *abuela* were pleased.

While he slept on oblivious to the issues surrounding the adults in his life, Alanza asked her, "And how did the wedding go?"

She responded with a shrug of her shoulders. "We said, I do. We didn't kill each other. We drove back here."

"I hope you forgive me one day."

"No forgiveness needed. I got what I wanted for my son. That's all that matters. I'll live."

"And Drew?"

"He'll live, too."

Amusement curved Alanza's lips. "There's dinner for the two of you in his room. I know neither of you wish to celebrate but I thought you might be hungry."

"Thanks, but I'm not. I think I'll take a walk to clear my mind and then call it a day."

"After we have dinner," countered a firm, familiar voice.

Billie spun to see her husband standing in the doorway. "I'm not hungry."

"Hungry or not, there's business to discuss before I leave in the morning."

"Can't it wait until you return?"

"No."

Her sigh of angry frustration was audible. "Where are your rooms?"

"Backside of the house."

She gave a quick look to the sleeping baby. Alanza seemed to sense her unspoken concerns. "I've some reading to catch up on. I can wait here with him until you're done."

"Thank you." After giving her son and the silently observing Alanza a parting glance, she crossed to the door. Drew moved aside to let her pass and she was escorted away.

Chapter 10

He led her down the hall and around to a section of the sprawling house she'd not yet seen. The large wooden door that he stopped before appeared to be very old. The corners of its face were embellished with vertical strips of scrolled metal held in place by aged silver hobnails. She wanted to ask about its origins but he opened it, stepped back and gestured for her to precede him in. As she did so, she stopped. A beautifully set table covered with a flowing gold cloth sat like something out of a dream in the middle of the room. Tall silver candlesticks held burning candles whose twinkling points of flame played gently over the elegant china, the silver tops of the covered dishes and tableware. She turned to him with surprise.

Again, he gestured her forward. Everything her eyes touched made her heart beat harder—from the table to the large crystal vase of red roses in its center, to the fire dancing in the grate. An archway at the far end of the room led somewhere but she was too busy marveling to give it more than a passing glance.

"My mother went a bit over the top, I'm afraid."

"I think it's very beautiful," she whispered as if speaking loudly might somehow break the trance.

"Shall we?"

She sat down in a lovely upholstered chair, and once she made herself comfortable he walked around to his seat on the opposite side of the table.

To Drew, she was even more beautiful than he remembered, thus the problem. Thanks to the vows he'd made to Rosaline and her mother, he'd been celibate for the past twelve months, and just looking at Billie brought home how long he'd gone without. Every fiber in his being wanted to scoop her up, carry her into his bedroom and make hard, hot love to her until sunrise, even as his mind recoiled in response to the maddening circumstances that brought them together. Outwardly he was hard as a beam of steel. Within, anger boiled like a witch's cauldron. Pushing that aside, he picked up the bottle of champagne standing near the roses. "Would you care for some?"

"No, thank you."

He slowly poured the fine liquid into his flute. Compared to the tequila he'd overloaded on last night, the champagne would be potent as lemonade, but he needed something to take the edge off in order to maintain his control. Sipping, he watched her silently.

"So, what is this business you wanted to discuss?" she asked.

He set down his drink and removed the tops from the dishes to reveal an array of meats and vegetables. "I'm hungry, so let's eat first. What would you like?"

It was easy to see she hadn't enjoyed being put off, but she begrudgingly held out her plate. "The chicken and some rice."

He did the honors and handed back the now filled plate.

"Thank you."

For himself, he forked out a steak and added vegetables and bread.

While they ate in silence Drew mentally recounted the problems he had with this marriage and they were as many as the Sierras were high, least of which being his continuing belief that she'd gotten herself with child on purpose. She'd never impressed him as the scheming type, but what was a man to think when presented with a child out of the blue? Then there was the problem of scandal. Billie was fairly well known in San Francisco, and even if no one in the small towns near

Destiny knew of her background, he doubted it would remain a secret for long. His mother seemed certain she'd weather the storm, but people were cruel. Some in and out of her circle of acquaintances, like Emmalina Ruiz, would take great pleasure in disparaging her because of her infamous new daughter-in-law's past. Another issue high on his list was his personal doubts surrounding the child's upbringing. His own father died when he was young and outside of a few male relatives in Mexico and the presence of Max Rudd, there'd been no influential men in his life. Sure, he could teach the boy to read, ride, and shoot, but everything else of substance had been taught to him by his mother. Did fathers teach things differently? Drew didn't know. He sighed. What a mess, and he'd yet to tell Billie their marriage needed to be consummated in order to insure all the legalities.

Billie was uncomfortable to say the least, and it kept her from fully enjoying the well-prepared food. Although Drew was being polite she sensed the roiling beneath the mask, and it, coupled with her lingering resentment over the nasty argument they'd had earlier, made the atmosphere tense.

"I assume we'll be consummating the wedding." The way he paused and studied her let her know she'd caught him off guard. "Is that why we're here?"

He put down his fork and sat back with his arms folded over his chest. For a moment he said nothing as if trying to gauge her mood. "Yes. You're thinking?"

"What has to be done, has to be done."

His jaw tightened but she didn't care. After all the fun and laughter they'd shared, being called a conniving bitch hurt. "Then let's get it over with so I can return to the baby."

Tossing her linen napkin onto the table, she stood. "Do you want me clothed or nude? Your choice." Her hands went behind her neck to remove the emeralds.

"Leave them on."

The heat in his eyes was as familiar as her own heartbeat, and in spite of her intent to remain cold and unfeeling it lit her as well.

"Come here."

Lips tight, she walked over. When she reached his side he took her hand. Gently drawing her down onto his lap, he raised her chin so her angry eyes would meet his. She saw a mixture of pain and yearning, and what appeared to be concern before he eased her close against his chest and whispered, "My apology for being so callous earlier."

Billie swore she would strangle herself with her own bare hands if she showed him her tears.

Again, he whispered, "I'm sorry." He drew back and used a finger to gently trace her cheek. "This is our wedding night, the only one we'll have. Can we pretend, just for tonight that all's well between us?"

A portion of her heart leapt with joy, but the parts that knew he'd be leaving in the morning doused the joy like water on a fire. "Sure, Drew. Whatever you want."

"You aren't going to make this easy, are you?"

Regardless of the future, she knew she had an array of weapons at her disposal; weapons he'd succumbed to willingly once upon a time. If she wielded them correctly, her revenge would not only be sweet, but could possibly leave him with plenty to think about on the train ride away from her. With that in mind, she asked sultrily, "You prefer I make it—hard?" and she moved her hips slowly and enticingly against his lap. A smile slid into his eyes. As long as she kept her emotions in check, all would be well.

But he began to brush his mouth lightly and compellingly against hers, something he'd never done before. It was so enticing and touched her so deeply, her lips parted of their own accord. His tongue came next, lightly tracing the fullness of her bottom lip, releasing small frissons of need as he seduced the corners and slid it inside to taste her. She needed to stay aloof in order to have the upper hand, but her walls were dissolving. *And this is why whores don't kiss*, complained a small voice somewhere in her head. This was too dazzling, too arousing. The pressure of his mouth, the gentle possessiveness of his hand as he brought her closer, the feel of his lips against her jaw made her senses open like a rose at sunrise, bringing to the fore all she felt for him in her heart and the urge to kiss him back so that he'd be lost just like she'd become.

And she was lost, in the intensity of him, the scent of his cologne, the memories they shared. He lowered his lips to her throat and drank in the flesh above the emeralds while the hot point of his tongue singed the expanse below. She'd always been good at pretending at passion, but this was so real, he could take her right there in the center of the table or on the rug covering the floor, and she wouldn't care. He enjoyed going slowly however. Making her soar to the pinnacle of pleasure with his touch and the placement of his kisses had always been his way, and as they sat in the candlelit silence, tonight was no exception. His hands relearned the lines of her spine and the small of her back, while his kiss greeted the soft skin beneath her ear. He recaptured her lips and as he did, she ran her hands slowly up and down his powerful arms encased in the fine cloth of his coat and bit his earlobe softly.

"*Dios*, I want you."

"Then have me," she whispered invitingly. "However you want, wherever you want."

With a groan, he picked her up and carried her through the archway into his bedroom.

Under the soft glow of the lone lamp, he set her on her feet. Lips locked to hers, he managed to shuck free of his jacket, then stepped back. The sounds of his heightened breathing mingled with hers. She slid her hands behind her to undo her dress but the hooks were unfamiliar and her efforts only resulted in frustration.

"Turn for me," he coaxed softly.

She complied, and as he freed the hooks, his lips slowly toured her bared shoulders and back. Although they'd come together in bed dozens of times before, this felt different somehow. There was a gentle savoring he'd never exhibited before. His caresses lingered. His hand slowly circling her spine touched her as if she were a woman he treasured and adored. She had no idea what it meant but she gave herself over and reveled in it.

Dazzled by sensations, and holding the opened dress close to her body, she turned to face him and took a small step back. His glowing eyes matched the tongue of flame in the lone lamp and the flame he'd put in her blood. Emboldened, she let the dress slowly slide to the floor and stood before him nude as Venus. His stunned face made her laugh softly, "What's the matter?"

"You've been like that all evening?"

"I don't own any underwear as fine as the dress, so I went without. I'd have let you know earlier but you didn't seem much interested."

"Cheeky woman. I should paddle your luscious behind."

"I'm waiting."

He beckoned her with a finger and she sauntered over.

He took her in with hungry adoration. "You're fuller."

"It's from the baby."

"I owe him my thanks." The pregnancy hadn't added much flesh to her frame, but where before she'd had the lean lines of a thoroughbred, there was now a lush voluptuousness in her breasts and hips that made him want to demand she be nude forever. A small voice reminded him that he could now that she was his wife, but he pushed it aside, preferring to concentrate on the present. And what a present she was. He teased a finger over a nipple until it berried then lowered his head to feast. While she moaned softly, he coursed a hand down her belly to her thighs and explored the dark humid place within. He increased the intensity of his explorations until her hips were moving and she widened her stance for more.

"Come for me, baby."

It had been so long since she'd been touched that Billie abandoned her plans to conquer, and surrendered to the wanton workings between her thighs and his mouth on first one breast and then the other. The tugs of his teeth and the hot circling of his tongue made every inch of her body bloom. She sensed the orgasm forming and beginning to rise like swells on a sea and she tried to stave it off so the pleasuring wouldn't end, but he knew how to send her over the edge. Her cry of completion pierced the silence. He smiled and kept up his play until she was twisting and calling his name in a voice made raw by passion. Only then did he lead her to the bed.

He joined her, kissing her, mapping her shoulders and waist while gruffly promising how he planned to love her and for how long. Fitting actions to those promises, his lips traveled over her skin, stopping along the way to feast again on the damp tight buds of her breasts and to smooth his hands over the curves and valleys he'd once known so well. He journeyed lower to greet the small indentation of her navel while his hands spread her legs and caressed them from thigh to knee, and then up to the center of her soul.

Billie had been celibate for over a year and even with the release of her first orgasm she was well on the way to paradise again. Whatever possessed her to believe she could remain immune to a man who knew her body so intimately and who possessed a host of carnal weapons uniquely his own? The soft touches made her moan. The leisurely tasting that followed made her raise herself greedily to his ardent mouth and croon for more. He spent a few scandalous moments concentrating on the small fleshy nubbin that defined her as woman, and when he suckled it in and bit down gently the second orgasm broke her apart with such force, joy sprang from her lips. Her body bucked and stiffened, but as always he wasn't done with her. He continued the pleasuring, holding her in place even as the sensations drove her mad. "Drew . . ." He added his fingers to the overwhelming plundering, making her cry out again and again. Finally when she had nothing left to give, he smiled up over her thighs like a pleased male and withdrew.

Shaking, dazed and so deep in the throes of passion, Billie could do nothing but lie there on the bed and pulse. *God, she'd missed him—this.*

Only he had the ability to make her lose her sanity, and even if the house were suddenly afire, she wouldn't have been able to move, but move she did, because she had to pay him back for such sweet torture.

When he stood to remove his trousers, she whispered. "Let me."

His hands fell away in tandem with his smile. "Whatever the lady wants."

Locking onto his smoldering gaze and wanting him to remember this night and her for eternity, she made short work of his belt and freed the buttons on the placard of his trousers. With a bold move she slowly pushed them down his thighs and took hold of him through his underwear. A slow stroking commenced. His head rolled back. His eyes closed, and he gritted out, "Damn, I've missed you."

Soundlessly, she lowered his underwear and dropped to her knees. "I've missed you, too." And proceeded to show him just how much.

Drew almost came there and then. Her scandalous expertise made his knees buckle and fight with everything he had not to explode like a virgin adolescent. While she kept up her erotic ministrations, he growled his pleasure and leaned forward to slide his palms across her damp satiny back and the tempting flare of her hips. Because of all the pleasure so far, he felt himself tottering on the bright edge of his limit, so he backed out of her hold, breathing like he'd run a race. Her ragged breathing matched his and was manifested in the tantalizing rise and fall of her breasts.

She returned to the bed and beckoned him to join her. When he complied, she wrapped a firm hand possessively around his upright shaft, pushed his shoulders so he'd lie flat, then swung her parted legs over his supine body. She slowly impaled herself and he savored the glorious feel of her warmth and being where he most wanted to be.

As she began to set a slow sultry rhythm Drew hissed out a breath and clamped his hands onto the lines of her waist. He matched her lazy pace at first, but the more she moved, the higher his lust climbed. Soon that same lust had him blind to all else but being sheltered inside her hot slick sheath and the bed became the center of a raging storm. He wanted her everywhere—her mouth, her breasts, the skin of her throat, the flare of her hips, and she let him feed and touch with no shrinking or pulling away because they'd done all this and more. When he reached down between the tight fit of their bodies to get at that bud he loved to suckle so much, she leaned back to accommodate him just as he knew she would. In response to the teasing, her inner muscles tightened deliciously, sending him soaring higher. She leaned forward and offered him her breast, then bent low so his hands could seek and play behind. She arched in response to his carnal dallying and the sight of her lust-filled eyes increased the strength of his strokes and made the tendons in his arms tighten as he began to work her ferociously. Feeling his orgasm about to burst, he quickly put her on her back, thrust into her with passion-fueled strength, and she broke and cried out almost in unison with him as the storm swept them both away.

For the rest of the night, they renewed the sensual bonds they'd forged in San Francisco. Neither chose to think about what would come with the rising of the sun but concentrated instead on pleasure, because in that there was no anger, or harsh words, or hurt, only sensations flamed by passion.

Finally, a few hours before dawn a sated Drew pulled his equally sated wife close and slept. He awakened later hungry for more but when he reached for her, she was gone. Struggling to full consciousness, he sat up and looked around the room. He was in the bed alone.

Chapter 11

Billie was on the floor playing with the baby. She'd quietly left Drew's bed in the wee hours of the morning in order to forestall a painful parting, but now, he was standing in the doorway. From his mode of dress and the brown traveling valise in his hand she guessed he was on his way to the train station. There were circles under his eyes and a weariness in his face that matched her own, but she kept her tone light even as her heart was breaking. "Good morning, Drew."

His mask was back. She'd donned hers as well.

"Morning. My mother has access to my accounts. She has my permission to purchase whatever you and the baby may need."

"Thank you." She waited. His gaze slid over the baby and then back to hers. "Anything else?" she asked coolly.

For a moment he didn't respond, and she wondered if he'd expected her to go into histrionics over his departure, but she had more pride than that. Finally, he shook his head. "No."

"Safe travels."

"Thank you." He turned and left.

She sighed. Shaking free of the melancholy threatening to overwhelm her mood, she refocused her attention on her son.

Downstairs, Drew searched out his mother and found her in her study going over ledgers. She looked up at his entrance. "Good morning. How are you?"

"I've been better. I'm on my way to the station. I let Billie know that she's to come to you for anything she may need." He saw questions in her eyes, but had no plans to entertain them now.

"And you'll be returning, when?"

"I don't know, Mother."

She nodded solemnly.

He thought it best to change the subject. "When will Logan and Mariah be returning?"

"Any day now, I'm hoping."

"Send me a wire when they do so that I'll know they got home safely."

"I will."

"And if anything untoward happens to Billie or the baby, wire me that as well." He walked over and placed a cool kiss on her cheek. "Good-bye."

Watching his departure, Alanza shook her head and returned to her ledgers.

On the train ride back to San Francisco, Drew had much to ponder and all of it centered on his wife. How dare she leave him wanting more. Even now, he could feel her encasing him, recall her scent, and see her dressed in nothing but his mother's emeralds while she rode him hard and put him away wet. He was supposed to have had the upper hand in their marriage, not crave her like a dying man seeking water in the desert only to awaken and find her gone, as if last night amounted to nothing more than a quick coupling, and meant even less. The distance he'd vowed to maintain buckled the moment he took her onto his lap, and vanished completely with their initial kiss. Damn her! The night had been good, so much so that only his pride kept him from saying to hell with the train and riding back to her as fast as his mount would go. However, he'd vowed to leave, and he planned to stay the course, but for the rest of the ride to San Francisco and the days immediately following his return, Billie filled his mind.

In the days after his departure, Drew was on Billie's mind, too, but rather than pine over something that would never be, she concentrated instead on settling into her new home. Alanza had graciously given her and Tonio a suite of rooms in the same wing where Drew's were situated. As they followed her inside, Billie glanced around at all the space and the sunshine streaming in through the wealth of windows.

"Ideally, you and the baby would be with him across the hall, but he's angry enough with me as it is, so we'll put the two of you in here for now."

The large bedroom was connected to a bathing room, and via a door a smaller room that could serve as Tonio's bedroom once he became old enough. A verandah complete with a small wrought-iron table and chairs offered a beautiful view of the countryside. The big four-poster bed with its dark wood looked fit for a queen. There was no bedding on it however. Nor were there any curtains or rugs.

"This was once my son Logan's rooms. I put all the boys in this wing so they could fight and play and do all the other noisy things boys do and not disturb the rest of the house."

Billie knew Logan now lived with his wife so she didn't have to worry about her presence displacing him. "This is very lovely." It was easily twice the size of the room she'd once called her own back at the Black Pearl.

"Our first order of business is to get you some bedding. I'll have Bonnie take care of that, and have Mariah run you up some curtains when she returns."

Once again, Billie wondered how Mariah would react to having a former whore as a sister-in-law. She wanted to ask Alanza if she thought the two of them might get along, but didn't. The woman would either accept her or not. "How old is Mariah's daughter?"

"Little Maria was born April of last year."

"What day?"

"The fifteenth."

Billie shook her head with amusement.

"What's the matter?"

"That's Tonio's birth date as well."

Alanza stared. "Oh, my. Both my grandchildren born on the same day. God works in mysterious ways."

"I guess so."

"Now, all I need is for Noah to have a child on that date."

"Who's he?"

"My youngest. He's a ship captain and is sailing on an ocean somewhere."

Billie couldn't help but wonder how he'd react to her, too.

Bonnie stuck her head in the door. "Senora. Mr. Logan and Mariah have returned. They're waiting for you in the parlor."

"Oh, wonderful!" But the elation faded when she took in Billie. Her voice softened. "Don't worry. You won me over. You'll do the same with them."

Billie knew better than to argue, so swallowing her misgivings, she picked up her son and followed Alanza downstairs.

The man she assumed to be Logan was standing by the windows and looked to be older than Drew. Although he had none of Drew's Mexican features, there was a resemblance and he was just as tall and handsome. His wife, seated on the sofa, had lovely gold-colored eyes in a face that could only be described as beautiful. The baby girl squirming on her mother's lap had cute little gold eyes as well and facial features that were a blend of her parents'. Said parents viewed her and Tonio's entrance with easy curiosity.

Alanza embraced them both, saying genuinely "Welcome home," then promptly picked up her granddaughter and gave her a tender squeeze. "Your *abuela* missed you so much."

The baby giggled and made a grab for the silver bobs in her grandmother's lobes, making Billie believe the two cousins would get along well.

Alanza did the introductions. "Mariah and

Logan, this is Billie. She's Drew's wife and this is their son, Antonio."

Mariah cocked her head as if she hadn't heard her mother-in-law correctly.

Her surprised husband looked Billie up and down. "Where are you from?"

"San Francisco."

The way he stiffened made her think Drew might have mentioned her at some point in the past, so she added, "Yes, I'm that Billie."

His confused wife turned to him as if seeking an explanation, but his blazing countenance was focused entirely on Billie. "And that's my brother's son?"

"Yes."

"You can prove that?"

"Already have."

His mother stepped in. "And to the satisfaction of both your brother and myself."

Billie didn't need her assistance, but let her have her say even though Billie knew it wouldn't be enough to quell his interrogation.

And she was right.

"Since Drew never mentioned having a child, I assume he was unaware of the birth."

"Correct."

"So, you simply waltzed in here one day and made the grand announcement?"

"Logan!" Alanza snapped.

Billie said reassuringly. "It's okay, Mrs. Yates. He's Drew's brother. He's allowed." She and Logan were gauging each other like two prizefighters in a ring. "In answer to your question. Yes. I just showed up, and your brother wasn't pleased."

"I'll bet he wasn't."

Billie resigned herself to being a target for his anger, but she didn't have to like it or him.

Mariah apparently had had enough. "Will someone please explain to me what this is all about?"

Her husband spoke. "This woman is Drew's—" He hesitated as if trying to come up with a delicate way to explain what needed saying.

Billie helped him out. "Whore. I'm his brother's whore."

His wife looked stunned. Hand over her mouth, she ran widened eyes over Billie as if seeking some kind of physical verification of the confession. "Oh my."

Logan glowered. "Why didn't he just send you packing?"

"Because I insisted he do what was honorable," his angry mother replied.

He stared. "What?"

"You heard me. Billie didn't come here to make Drew marry her. All she wanted was to leave the baby with him. There's a man threatening her life and the life of their child."

He gave a bitter chuckle. "Since when are you so gullible? Drew probably didn't believe a word of that cock-and-bull story, and neither do I."

Billie tossed back, "This has nothing to do with what you believe."

He paused as if viewing her for the first time. She thought she saw the ghost of a smile creep into Mariah's gold eyes but it was gone so quickly, Billie decided she'd imagined it. The hard lines of her husband's face weren't imaginary though. He looked fit to be tied.

"What happened to Rosaline?" Mariah asked as if trying to be the calm before an impending storm.

Alanza replied, "Once Drew told her mother about the baby, the engagement was dissolved."

"And Drew?" Logan asked. "Where's he?"

Billie said, "In San Francisco. Giving the baby his name is all he's offering. He's not going to live with us, which suits me just fine. I don't want him as a husband any more than he wants me as his wife."

He seemed startled by that.

"So much for whatever you thought I came here after."

His jaw tightened angrily. Billie looked him

off, effectively conveying how little she cared about that as well. "I'm sure you all wish to talk about your trip. Tonio and I need some fresh air. Nice meeting you both." With her son riding her hip, she turned and headed for the kitchen door, which led outside.

After Billie's departure, Alanza swung her gaze to her son, who immediately came to his own defense. "Surely you don't expect me to act as if this is something I approve of."

"As she said, none of this hinges on your approval."

"How could you condone this?"

"Did you not see the child in her arms?"

"Of course I did."

"According to your brother, the man after them is very dangerous, so much so that she was willing to leave her son with us so she could flee back East with the hope he wouldn't find her. And, she said, if the man killed her it would be okay as long as she knew her son was safe."

He sighed angrily. "She's a whore, Mother."

"Do you think I don't know that? Do you think I don't know what the gossips will say or what my friends might say? My only concern is the child, Logan. His parents get along like fire and dry tinder but he shouldn't have to suffer because of that. It isn't as if he asked to be born into this mess."

Mariah asked, "How long has she been here?"

"Almost a week. As the Fates would have it she showed up the day of the engagement party."

"That couldn't have been much fun."

"It wasn't. Emmalina couldn't wait to get Rosaline away from here."

"So, what's Billie like?"

"Proud. Angry, smart-mouthed, but she loves her son like she loves breathing. Drew's angry, too."

"Then why make them marry?" Logan demanded.

"Because she loves him and I'm fairly sure he cares for her as well."

Logan looked incredulous. "You've done some outrageous things, Alanza, but this is the mountaintop."

"Thank you," she replied sarcastically. "I knew I could count on you to take my side."

He threw up his hands. "She's a whore!"

"So you keep saying!" She shot him a quelling look and turned to her daughter-in-law. "Do you think I'm *loco*, too?"

"I don't know what to think. I've never been in the same room with a woman like her before, let alone have one in the family. I'll admit, I did like the way she told Logan she didn't care what he thought. Reminded me a bit of myself for a moment there."

Logan glared.

She shrugged in response. "Just being truthful. Very few people stand up to you, darling."

Alanza found a modicum of comfort in Mariah's words. "Her son was born the same day as Maria."

Astonishment filled Mariah's face. "Truly?"

Alanza nodded. "Yes. So we'll have a birthday party for both of them."

Apparently Logan didn't care about any of that because he steered the conversation back to the matter at hand. "So, how long has Drew been gone, and when are you expecting him back?"

"He left the morning after she and the baby arrived. He said he didn't know when he'd return. Gave me access to his accounts for whatever she might need and took the train back to Yerba Buena."

Mariah sighed. "On one level this is completely mad, and on other it's very sad. Is Drew planning to confront the man or involve the police?"

"He's not shared his plans, at least not with me."

Mariah looked to her husband and said firmly,

"You may do what you like concerning all of this, but I'm going to try and be a friend to her. Sounds like she needs one."

He shook his head. "I'll not have you dirtied by her scandal."

Her eyebrow rose. "Do you remember what Billie said about you and your opinion?"

His lips thinned.

Mariah got to her feet and picked up her daughter. "Come on, sweetie. Let's go meet your cousin."

Chapter 12

Billie sat in the grass and watched her son chase a butterfly. It didn't matter to Tonio that his little legs were too short or that the butterfly had wings and could easily drift out of reach, he just seemed happy to be out of his mother's arms and playing in the sunshine. Their unannounced arrival at the ranch was akin to a brigantine crashing into a dock for canoes, and the peripheral damage was still unfolding. Logan Yates hadn't been pleased with her or his mother's actions, but she had no idea where his wife, Mariah, stood. Billie was just glad Tonio was too young to understand the whirlwind swirling around his life.

When she saw Mariah coming towards her and carrying her daughter, Billie wondered what she wanted. She hoped it wasn't payment for the dress she'd borrowed for the wedding. As she drew nearer there was a tentative smile on her face, but Billie kept her face impassive.

"I—thought since the babies are cousins—it'd be nice if they played together."

"Your husband probably wouldn't approve of that."

"It wouldn't be the first time. I love him fiercely, but we don't always agree. Do you mind if I sit with you a spell?"

Again, Billie wondered what she wanted, but gestured an invitation. "Have a seat."

She set the baby on her feet and her daughter immediately toddled off to join Tonio. When she reached him the cousins simply stared at each other. "She doesn't have anyone her age to play with," Mariah explained as she joined Billie on the grass.

"He doesn't either."

They were both watching the children when Mariah remarked, "Alanza said they're born on the same day."

"Apparently."

"That's quite the coincidence."

"Yes, it is."

Billie surveyed Mariah's fancy nut-brown traveling ensemble with the snow-white lace blouse underneath and asked, "Not trying to be rude, but why'd you come out here?"

She shrugged. "To try and get to know you I suppose."

"Why?"

"My, you are the blunt one, aren't you?"

Billie waited.

"We're family—sisters-in-law. Just thought you might like to have a friend here. Alanza is obviously championing you and since she's very dear to me . . ."

"You thought you'd come out and see why?"

"Frankly, yes."

"At least you're honest."

"Too honest sometimes, according to Logan."

Billie studied her for another long moment. "Women like you aren't supposed to be friends with women like me, you are aware of that."

"I am."

A born skeptic, Billie wasn't convinced the gold-eyed, elegantly dressed Mariah came out just to offer her hand in friendship. "Are you thinking I'm here taking advantage of Mrs. Yates?"

"Believe me, no one takes advantage of Alanza Maria Vallejo Yates, so the answer to that, my blunt sister-in-law, is no."

Billie let a small smile curve her lips. "You're a lot tougher than you look."

"Thanks."

"Why would you want to be friends with me? You must have friends of your own."

"There's nothing wrong with having more."

"I've never had friends. All the girls I know are competition. Doesn't pay to get close when we're all going after the same prize—if you get my meaning."

"I think I do."

Billie rolled her eyes because she was sure Mariah had no idea of the competitiveness of whores.

"You're all jockeying for customers, is that what you mean?"

That surprised her. "What do you know about that sort of thing?"

"Nothing really. Just a deduction."

"Well, that's pretty good."

The children had discovered a small depression in the ground holding remnants of last night's rainfall. They were happily slapping their hands in the hole and both were covered with splotches of the flying mud.

Billie said, "Maria's getting pretty dirty."

"It's okay. She's just about grown out of that dress anyway, and besides, I don't mind the mud."

Billie had trouble masking her skepticism.

"My mother used to beat me for getting my clothing dirty. When Maria was born I swore I'd let her get as dirty as she wanted as often as she wanted."

Billie viewed her in a whole new light. It never

occurred to her that the beautiful, fashionable woman had been raised by someone reminiscent of her own parent. "Where are you from?"

Little Maria was now smoothing mud on her cheeks as if it were a night cream. Tonio was doing the same. They looked like tiny little mud people.

"Philadelphia," Mariah replied. "I came out here to be Logan's housekeeper. We were married a week later."

"You're pulling my leg."

"No. Seven days. Most overwhelming week of my life. His too, I might add."

Billie chuckled. In spite of everything, she found herself warming to Mariah Yates. It was the first time she'd ever sat and talked with a *good* woman.

"So," Mariah asked. "What's it going to be? Shall we try and get to know each other?"

Billie eyed her. "You sure you're going to be able to stand the heat? The kitchen may get very hot."

"I have no idea, but I'll never turn my back on you, or deny you're my sister."

No one had ever pledged such loyalty to her before. The honesty in Mariah's tone made tears sting the corners of her eyes, but she silently cursed them back to their source. Taking in the woman beside her for a long silent moment, she finally stuck out her hand. The smiling Mariah latched onto it and they shook like businessmen. "Welcome to Destiny."

"Thanks."

"Now, let me find my husband and get Little Miss Mudling home and in a bath. We've been on trains for the past two days and I'm badly in need of a soak myself."

After Mariah's departure, Billie gave Tonio a bath of his own and put him down for his nap. He fought her every step of the way but finally gave in and drifted off.

Downstairs, she went in search of Alanza.

"She's out in the rose garden," Bonnie told her, and gave her directions.

As she walked up, Alanza didn't appear pleased.

"What's the matter?" Billie asked.

"In my mother's day, this whole area was alive with roses. There were pinks and whites and mauves, but for the past few years they haven't bloomed."

The wild overgrown tangle of brown canes and thorns appeared to be dead. Billie surveyed the carpet of small brown leaves littering the ground, then the large trees shading the area. "Do you have a gardener?"

"Some of the hands take care of the grounds but they don't know anything about roses and, frankly, neither do I. I've been more concerned with the plants that add to my ledgers, like the orchards and vegetables."

Billie bent to pick up some of the leaves. "For one, you have black spot." She held out her hand so that Alanza could see the tiny black spots staining the leaves. "And secondly, all these trees are blocking the sun. Roses need lots of sunshine and lots of water."

The utter surprise on her mother-in-law's face made Billie smile. "I used to work at a place called Rose's, owned by a woman named Rose. Guess what kind of flowers she grew."

Alanza laughed.

Billie moved closer to the bare canes and began a slow visual inspection. "Rose taught a few of us girls how to tend them. I helped out in the beginning because it got me outdoors during the day and away from all the bickering and cattiness inside, then I came to really enjoy it." She turned and asked, "Would it be okay if I tended yours?"

"Of course."

Billie dusted her hands off on her dress. "Since I'm pretty sure you don't want to cut down all the trees, the roses should be moved to a sunnier place. You might also think about getting new stock because of this black spot. Sometimes it gets into the soil."

"You decide. They're yours now. Move them, buy new plants, do whatever is needed. I simply want to bask in the beauty and fragrance. Oh, and I want to have the best-looking roses in the valley."

Billie laughed. "You don't ask for much do you?"

"Me? Never."

Billie couldn't wait to get started.

That evening, after putting her son to bed, she sat out on her verandah and let the tension and weariness of the day slide away like the sun slipping beneath the horizon. For the first time in what felt like years, she was relaxed—relatively carefree as well, as long she didn't count having to look over her shoulder for Prince DuChance, or being married to a man who'd given up a fairy princess so his son could have a name. But still, she felt good. There was a peace at the Destiny ranch she'd never experienced before. Were she still working at the Black Pearl she'd be getting dressed, making up her face, and pulling on her cheap stockings. Instead, she was sitting in the silence, thinking back on this new life she'd fallen into. That she'd found a way to be useful added to her peace. Tomorrow she planned to drive around to see if there were any wild roses growing on the property. Alanza assured her there were and Billie looked forward to turning Destiny's roses into the best around. She'd also gained a sister-in-law. Mariah Yates. Billie had been expecting . . . she wasn't sure what she'd been expecting. It certainly wasn't a woman whose pledge of friendship still filled her with amazement and awe. Her brother-in-law Logan left much to be desired, but his wife . . . Billie could only shake her head at what a surprise Mariah turned out to be.

The late evening turned to dusk and dusk into night, and soon she was sitting beneath the stars. The moon peeped out, bringing with it a shooting star, but she didn't make a wish. For once in her life she wasn't holding the short end of the stick. There was no need to ask for more.

The next morning, while Tonio sat in the high chair making a mess of his breakfast of oatmeal, she and Alanza discussed the day's agenda. Billie would be getting her first look at the storage barns to search out items needed to make her suite of rooms more comfortable, and then she'd go rose hunting.

Alanza brought her mind back to the furnishings. "There should be rugs and furniture you might wish to use, along with lamps."

"And I can just take them?"

Alanza sighed in reply. "Yes, Billie. You're a

member of the family. Whatever the ranch has to offer is yours."

Billie nodded.

"May I ask you something that I hope you won't find offensive?"

"Sure."

"What do you think you need to learn to be the new woman you want to become?"

Not offended in the least, Billie mulled over the question for a moment or two before replying, "I need to learn all the things a *good* woman needs to know, like how to run a household and set a proper table—what to do when guests come calling. I know Drew and I are at odds, but when we have to go out together I don't want him to be shamed because my manners aren't up to snuff or I said something wrong."

"Mariah and I can help with that. Anything else come to mind?"

"I know I need to be able to read better, too. Drew used to help. When we first met, all I could do was write my name. He'd read me the newspapers and books, and didn't seem to mind answering all my questions. I learned a lot from him."

Alanza was watching her so intently, she wasn't sure what to make of it. "Should I not have told you that?"

The question was waved away. "It's okay. Hearing about your times with Drew is fascinating to me: the opera, and flowers and clothing. Now to learn he helped you with your reading? You did more together than many married couples."

Billie shrugged. Having not met many married couples she didn't know what they did.

"Drew's been an avid reader all his life—much more so than his brothers. He has a very extensive library. I'm sure he won't mind you borrowing from it."

Billie didn't know if Alanza was right, but she planned to at least look over the books when she had the chance. She doubted she'd ever be as poised or elegant as his fairy princess but was determined to be the best Billie she could be.

When Tonio placed the bowl on his head and the oatmeal began slowly trickling down his face, Billie shook her head and chuckled. She wiped him clean as best she could. "You are going to spend the rest of your life in a bathtub, little man."

She was still mopping up when a man she'd not met before walked up.

"Morning, ladies."

Alanza did the introductions. "Max Rudd, this is Drew's wife, Billie, and their son, Antonio."

Billie took Tonio from the high chair and put him in her lap. "Nice to meet you."

Max leaned down to greet Tonio. "Hey there, fella."

Tonio immediately threw his arms up, and a smiling Max picked him up. The baby began discussing lord knew what, complete with hand gestures. Max laughed. "You're not real shy, are you?"

While this was going on, Billie watched Alanza's face and noted she only had eyes for Max. Were the two lovers? she wondered.

Max handed Tonio back. "Welcome to Destiny, Billie."

"Thanks."

"And since you're now family, you may as well know that I'm trying to get your hardheaded mother-in-law to marry me, so any help you can offer would be greatly appreciated."

"Max!"

Billie was so surprised she wasn't sure if she should respond or not.

"Don't pay him a bit of attention," Alanza scolded.

The mischief in his eyes showed Billie how much he was enjoying vexing Alanza and there was genuine affection in them as well. She made a note to talk to Mariah about this because she wanted to know if he was serious about his suit or just pulling her leg.

Alanza asked him, "Did you come by for a reason or just to bedevil me?"

"Came to see if you wanted to go riding with me."

"Yes, I do, if only so I can box your ears."

"You're on," he replied.

Billie stood. "I'm going to take him in and clean him up." She took the towel and wiped at the oatmeal stains on Max's chest. "Sorry about that."

"It's okay. Looking forward to watching him grow up."

His kindness earned him a smile.

Alanza said, "Billie, we'll look in the barns when I return."

Billie nodded and went inside.

Alanza eyed the man who wanted to be her *novio*. "It wasn't necessary to tell her that, you know?"

"The part about me wanting to marry you, or the part about your hard head?"

Smiling in spite of herself, she stood. "I'll get my mare."

They rode out to the edge of the river where he'd built benches for her to sit upon so many years ago, and while the horses availed themselves of the grasses nearby, she and Max sat companionably in the silence and watched the clear water flow. In spite of the calm face she'd been wearing, the events of the past week had her wound tight as a watch spring and she wasn't sure how to put herself at rest.

He must've noticed something in her manner, because he glanced over and asked, "Something bothering you, *chica*?"

Her husband Abraham had never given her an affectionate sobriquet, but Max had. "A few things," she admitted and found herself telling him all she carried inside. From demanding Billie and Drew marry. Her worries about what damage she may have done to her relationship with her son, to Logan's accusations of her meddling, and her thoughts on Billie's desire to better herself and how impressive she found her new daughter-in-law to be. It all came tumbling out and to Max's credit, he let her talk. He stopped her a few times to ask a question here and there, but for the most part simply listened as if he knew it was what she needed most.

And when she was done, Alanza felt remarkably better. "You've always been easy to talk to."

"You talk, I listen. Works fine."

He'd done so much for her since Abraham's death. "Why do you want to marry me, Max?"

He leaned his head back and gazed up at the clouds. As if searching for just the right words he didn't respond initially, then after a moment, said,

"I've been in love with you since the first time I met you, but you were the wife of my best friend so I put it away because I had to. After he died, I knew you weren't looking for someone to take his place, so I did what I could to help you and the boys. Hoped maybe I could court you once they got older." He swung his eyes her way. "I know I've been brash about wanting you, and if I've been disrespectful, I apologize—but we're getting older, Lanz, and I'd like to spend what's left of my life with you."

"It's a bit scary though."

"What, getting married again?"

She nodded.

"Why?"

"Because as much as I thought I loved Abraham, he didn't love me and I don't want to be in that kind of situation again, nor do I want to turn my life over to someone else."

"I don't want your life, Lanz. Just you."

She allowed herself a small smile. "You're making it difficult to keep saying no."

"Then don't."

Alanza studied the man who'd been in her life since seemingly forever and thought about how nice it would be to have him by her side until God called her home. "You sure you wouldn't prefer someone younger who can give you children?"

He rolled his eyes. "I have your three sons, their wives, and now a little fella who may be the reincarnation of those Spanish conquistadores you love so much, so no, I don't need children of my own."

"Okay. I'll stop trying to put off the inevitable. Max Rudd, I would love to be your wife."

" 'Bout damn time." His smile met hers. "So can we have the ceremony soon or are you going to make me wait another five years?"

"One should be sufficient I believe."

"What?!"

"Just pulling your leg. We can have the wedding come summer. I'd like all the boys to be with us though, so let me see if I can get in touch with Noah."

"As long as we end up husband and wife before the turn of the century, that suits me fine."

She leaned close and he draped an arm over her shoulder. The kiss he placed on her brow warmed her insides.

"Abe didn't love you, but I do. It'll make a difference."

Alanza was sure he was right.

After going through the wealth of furniture Alanza had in storage and picking out the pieces she wanted moved to her suite, Billie prepared to go rose hunting. According to Bonnie there was a large stand on the road that led into town, and although Billie's initial plan had been to search the Destiny property first, the beauty of the mauve damask roses Bonnie described piqued her interest more.

Alanza asked, "Are you sure you don't want me to send a hand with you?"

From her seat on the wagon, Billie replied, "No, I'll be fine." She'd placed a long-handled shovel into the bed for digging just in case the roses were worthy of bringing back.

"Do you know how to shoot a gun?" Alanza asked.

Billie nodded. "I have my Colt in my handbag."

Once again Alanza viewed her with surprise. "Good, but I'll feel better if you have a rifle. Hold on for a moment." She hurried away and returned with a Winchester and a box of shells. "Do you know how to load it?"

"Yes," Billie said, trying to keep the impatience out of her voice.

"Show me."

"Alanza?"

Her mother-in-law folded her arms and waited.

Billie sighed and complied. When she finished, she put the rifle at her feet. "May I leave now?"

"Yes, you may. I'll keep Antonio entertained when he wakes up, so enjoy yourself."

Billie shook her head at Alanza's single-mindedness and set the wagon in motion.

She hadn't had a moment to herself since moving in with Addy, thus the reason for wanting to go on this adventure alone. Granted, she felt as if a part of her were missing not having Tonio along, but they'd be together again soon enough. By Bonnie's estimation the roses were about two miles west, so when the wagon cleared the big metal gates, she headed the mare, who went by the regal name of Duchess, in that direction.

The dirt road was fairly wide and a bit soft in spots due to rain a few nights ago. She maintained a slow pace in order to enjoy the view of the countryside and search both sides of the road for rose canes. Being a city girl she had no idea how to estimate the distance she'd traveled. Alanza assured her that as long as she stuck to the road it was impossible to get lost, so she didn't worry.

After the passage of what seemed like an hour, she spied a large tangle of canes in an open field. The distinctive green color showed they were shaking off the dormancy of winter and ready for spring. Elated, she set the brake and went around to the bed to retrieve the shovel, gloves and pair of stout garden shears. The wild bush was large. When it bloomed the spread would be taller than a man and an equal distance across.

Hiking up her skirts, she waded into the brush, grateful for the old work boots on her feet. They'd belonged to Noah during his youth. According to Alanza he'd been growing so quickly back then he'd only worn them a few months before needing a larger size.

Reaching her destination, Billie bent to give the base of the bush a quick inspection and discovered that there was not one plant, but three. With her old madam's lessons to guide her, she cut back the tops until they were only knee high, then used her foot to punch the edge of the sharp shovel into the still soft earth. It took some time to dig down to the roots, and at one point she wished she'd taken her mother-in-law's advice and brought one of the hands along, but she finally achieved success. Placing the three stumps into a bucket in the bed, she stomped the mud from her boots, removed her gloves and retook her position behind the reins. She knew she should head for home but she wanted to see if there were any other wild roses growing nearby. Aware that Tonio was waiting for her, she mentally promised not to journey far.

As she drove, the landscape changed. Where earlier she'd passed through open country, now, stately cloud-kissing pines lined the road. Knowing the shade wouldn't support the growth of the prizes she was after, she stopped the mare to turn around. In mid-turn, the mare tensed and whinnied and then became so skittish Billie had difficulty keeping her under control, "Whoa, Duchess. Whoa."

Duchess calmed, but her ears were up and the tense set of her body seemed to signal something amiss. Billie took a careful look around, then stood to get a better view of the surroundings. A second later she heard dogs barking, followed by a man's tortured yell. Up ahead a man grappling with the largest bear she'd ever seen came crashing out of the trees. Two angry dogs were leaping and snapping at the bear's limbs while the poor man, his hands covering his head, dropped to the ground. Her heart stopped. She didn't remember picking up the Winchester but suddenly she was firing. The bear's wide back spasmed each time the bullets found their mark, but it seemed more intent upon the man. She kept up her assault, striking the body again, until suddenly, the bear turned her way and raised itself on trunk-sized hind legs. She sent another bullet high up on the torso. It opened its cavernous mouth, showing off huge teeth, and a furious roar shook the heavens like thunder. She kept firing. The bear's giant clawed paw swatted one of the dogs with so much force the animal flew whimpering into the trees. She quickly reloaded and took aim again. The metal barrel of the rifle was hot to the touch but she didn't draw down until the enraged bear screamed once more, dropped down onto all fours again and lumbered back into the pines and out of sight.

She urged the reluctant Duchess forward. When she reached the man she jumped down and ran to his side. He was lying so still she thought he might be dead. The dog keened mournfully and nudged him as if urging the man to rise. She gave the dog a comforting pat before dropping down into the dirt.

"Mister?" she called gently. He was lying on his stomach. His face was turned away but the portion visible sported a nasty trail of claw marks just below his graying sideburn. One leg of his denims was dark with blood. "Mister?" She jostled him slightly.

To her relief the head slowly swung her way. The eyes she met were unfocused at first. In a voice barely above a whisper he asked, "That you doing the shooting, little lady?"

She nodded and said, "Yes. We need to get you to a doc."

He winced and drew in a few shallow breaths.

"Probably right. Name's Tom Foster. Don't remember ever seeing you before."

"Name's Billie."

"You married, Billie?"

She chuckled softly, "Yes sir, to Drew Yates. Let's see if we can get you over to the wagon."

"Give me a minute," he said breathing harshly. "Had sort of an exciting day."

"Okay, but only one. Don't want you dying on me."

He began shivering. "I have a horse around here somewhere, or at least I had one."

Her concern rose. "I need you to try and stand. You're too big for me to carry."

"Wish I could get my Amanda to shoot like that. Maybe I'll have you teach her."

"I'll teach her anything you like, but the wagon first."

With her help he struggled to his feet. "Lean on me." Crushed beneath his nearly dead weight she somehow managed to get him the short distance to the wagon. She had no idea how he was going to climb in.

"Need another minute, Billie."

She waited while he gathered himself. From somewhere deep within he called up the strength to climb in then leveraged himself onto his back on the bed. There was a blanket inside, so she covered him as best she could. The dog joined them and as it began keening again, Foster groused, "Oh, Sierra hush. Take more than a bear to send me to hell."

The other dog never reappeared so Billie assumed it had met its demise.

"The bear get the other one?" he asked weakly.

"I believe so. I'm sorry."

"Don't be. Damn thing's been stupid all its life. Told him a hundred times or more not to chase bear cubs."

Billie wondered if that was what set the near fatal incident in motion, but she couldn't spare the time to ask. She got behind the reins and headed the horse back to the ranch.

From behind her Tom Foster said, "Drew Yates is a lucky man."

Billie appreciated the compliment but the jury was still out on whether Drew would agree.

Chapter 13

Drew parked his carriage by Addy's gate and walked through the light rain to the tiny covered porch. Billie asked him to look in on her. He hoped she was at home. In response to his knock, the door opened and the tiny woman who appeared offered a nod of greeting. "Morning, Mr. Yates. She and your babe arrived safely?"

He was certain they'd never met, so being addressed by name caught him off guard. "Yes. Did she tell you the baby was mine?"

"No, but some things are known."

He wasn't sure what to make of that or of her. "Has Prince DuChance come around to bother you?"

"He has, but his days are as numbered as mine. Tell her not to worry and neither should you."

Because of her odd manner of speaking one might assume her to be addled, but her dark gaze pulsed with a power that made the hair rise on the back of his neck. He made a mental note to learn more about her when he saw Billie again—whenever that might be. He handed her one of his business cards. "If you ever need anything, I can be reached here."

She took the card. "Thank you but we won't meet again, at least not on this plane." In response to his show of surprise, she said prophetically, "The girl is your queen. You will love her until there is no tomorrow. Good-bye, Mr. Yates."

She closed the door, leaving the speechless Drew on the other side.

Driving away, he contemplated her final words. *His queen?!* Billie was no more his queen than he was the Pope in Rome, yet the words seemed to resonate with the same chilling power he'd seen in the woman's eyes. Who was she? She reminded him of the old *brujas* in the fairy tales his mother read to him when he was a boy. *You will love her until there is no tomorrow.* He scoffed. He and Billie shared a love of lust, nothing more. And besides, queens were chosen; they didn't drop into a man's lap out of the blue in the middle of the celebration announcing an engagement to someone else—*or did they?* asked a small knowing voice.

When he reached the center of the city, the visit continued to dominate his thoughts, but he set it aside to stop and pay a visit on his good friend, circuit court judge Wendell Ross. He needed advice on how to proceed with the unsettled land claims of his clients, but Ross's words were far from encouraging.

"The courts have no incentive to move them along quickly, Andrew, and that's a shame. The provisions of the Treaty of Hidalgo might as well have been a government treaty with the Indians for all the weight it's been given."

"But many of these disputes have been languishing for ten years."

Ross nodded solemnly. "I know. We're supposed to be a nation built upon law, but the state's getting rich selling off those disputed lands . . ." His voice trailed off. "And when you throw in the fact that the claimants are all Spanish, well, that doesn't help either. More and more of my judicial colleagues are drawing the color line and refusing to hear cases brought before them by people of color."

Andrew sighed heavily. He knew Jim Crow was rising but held hopes that the law and sanity would prevail.

Judge Ross added, "Some of the jurists back East are barring all lawyers who aren't White."

Andrew knew that as well. The Black newspapers were filled with editorials denouncing the practice and he'd had a few questionable experiences of late as well. "After the decision on the Tape case, I'd hoped California was turning its back on unequal treatment."

"So did I. That the State Supreme Court would support a little Chinese girl's right to attend school made me proud, even though the legislature blunted the victory by allowing San Francisco to create a separate school for her kind."

"One step forward, two steps back," Drew offered ruefully. "So what do you suggest I do for my clients?"

"You're not going to like my advice."

Drew studied him. Wendell Ross had been both a mentor and a supporter. After Drew finished his apprenticeship he'd needed the signature of a sitting judge in order to become certified to practice law. Ross hadn't hesitated putting his name on the line.

"Turn your cases over to someone the court will recognize."

"Meaning someone who isn't Spanish or Black."

He nodded. "Yes."

"No!" he declared hotly. Just the thought of giving in to those with bigoted small minds was infuriating. "Wendell, you know how hard I worked to get where I am."

"I do, but you must put the interest of your clients first—which of course is easy for me to say, not being a man of color."

Drew silently agreed.

Ross viewed him with grim concern. "I don't see any other way out for them, Andrew. Maybe the climate will change in a few years."

"Or a few decades," he countered bitterly.

"I'm sorry."

"This isn't your fault. You've always been a fair man both on and off the bench." Anger warred with the bleakness in his heart. He'd been set on the law since his youth. That the years he'd spent reading case law from England, France, and Spain now meant nothing because of his ancestry made him want to punch something. But he'd known this day was coming. For the past two years, many judges who'd previously welcomed him into their courtrooms were suddenly unavailable. According to their clerks, the jurists' schedules were overloaded or they were out of town. Rather than accusing them of drawing the color line, he'd given them the benefit of the doubt, but now?

"So what are you going to do?" the judge asked.

"No idea."

"If you want the names of some lawyers I know to be honorable, just let me know."

He responded with a terse nod and stood. "I

will. Thank you for taking the time to see me and for the advice."

"Too bad it wasn't better."

"I know."

The two old friends shook hands and Drew walked out into the rain to drive back to his office. On the way he was consumed by thoughts surrounding Wendell's advice. How was he going to represent his clients if judges refused to let him in the door? To surrender to such foulness and turn his clients over to someone else was unthinkable, yet what recourse did he have? His injured pride wouldn't get the cases heard, and although the families had trusted their claims to him for years, he doubted they'd balk if he turned their issues over to someone the courts would look more favorably upon, especially if that person managed to eke out a positive resolution. As it stood now, the families had nothing to show for his efforts but frustration. And if he did bow out, what would he do with his life if he was unable to practice law—rest on his laurels and the fortune he'd received from his grandfather? Due to wise investments, he had no pressing economic concerns. Billie's face shimmered across his mind's eye as if to remind him that he did have a wife and child. Lord knew he didn't want to retire to the ranch and be forced to spend every waking hour in her presence, and he was certain she didn't want that either. Grim, he parked the carriage and went into his office with no clear vision of what his future might hold.

Drew's apprentice was a young man named Cassius Lane, a recent graduate of Howard College who'd come to San Francisco two years ago. He functioned as Drew's clerk and handled correspondence. Drew's decisions concerning the viability of his law practice would impact Lane's future as well. Eventually a discussion on the matter would have to be held.

"Welcome back, Mr. Yates. How's Judge Ross?"

"Doing well. Anything needing my attention?"

"No, sir."

"Then I'll be in my office."

Drew had just settled in when Cassius stuck his head in the open door. "Someone here to see you."

Drew glanced up. Prince DuChance stood beside him. The unwanted visitor didn't help his mood. "Thank you, Cassius."

The young man withdrew.

"I'm busy, DuChance. What do you want?"

"Wondering if you found her?"

"Found who?"

"Billie."

Drew kept his features schooled. "No. Why?"

It was obvious DuChance was waiting for an

invitation to sit down but the offer was not forthcoming. "Just curious. Seems she ran off with something that belonged to my mother."

"I see. Well, I gave up my search months ago. Maybe you'll be more successful." He sat back in his chair and crossed his arms. "Anything else?"

DuChance searched his face as if trying to decide how truthful he was being. Drew let him look.

Finally he responded, "No, but if you see her, I'd appreciate you letting me know."

Considering their previous history Drew wondered why he thought such an agreement would be honored. "I need to get back to work."

Prince's lips thinned. Drew ignored his anger. Prince was dangerous, but so was Drew when provoked and the man knew it, so he inclined his head and exited.

Once he was gone, Drew thought back on the unwanted visit. The *something* Prince alluded to was Tonio and he wondered if it would be possible to make some discreet enquiries in an attempt to ascertain who the buyer might be. *And then do what?* a voice inside asked. He certainly couldn't share Billie's whereabouts, or that the baby was his son. In a perfect world, DuChance would give up the search, but as Drew knew from his meeting with Judge Ross, the world wasn't perfect by any means.

As his driver moved the carriage out into the midafternoon traffic, Prince DuChance sat in the back brooding. He still had no idea where the whore and her brat were. That she'd successfully eluded him continued to fuel an ongoing desire for revenge. He had men watching the old witches' house hoping she might lead him to the hiding place, or better yet that Billie would show up, but all she did was make her deliveries and tend her garden. As of last night, there'd been no visitors. The day after she disappeared, he'd gone to the train station posing as her distraught husband to ask the porters and ticket agents if they remembered seeing her and the child, but that turned out to be a dead end, too. Even the whispered offerings of a sizeable reward to the cutthroats, pimps, and thieves frequenting the Barbary's back alleys for information on her whereabouts had so far proven fruitless. It was as if she'd vanished into thin air. That she might've flown the coop east and was lying low in one of the big cities back East crossed his mind, but he tried not to think about that because if she had, more than likely he'd never see her again. The only bright spot was that the clients wanting the baby believed his tale that the child was ill, and that he was waiting to make sure it survived and fully recovered before making the delivery. He'd promised them news in the next thirty days. As a businessman he had a reputation to maintain. He didn't want to tarnish it by not producing the brat and having to refund their fee.

By the time the driver halted the carriage at his next stop, the rain had ceased, leaving the day windy and gray. Stepping out, he glanced up at the second-story windows just in time to see a curtain fall back into place as if someone had watched his approach. A servant girl answered his summons. After quickly masking her revulsion to his disfigured face, she asked, "May I help you?"

"Here to see Senora Ruiz."

"I'm afraid she's out at the moment. You'll—"

The knife appeared at her throat as if by magic. He smiled at her fear. "I don't think she is. Shall we go in and find out?"

Shaking, she hastily nodded.

"After you." Returning the knife to his coat, he followed the servant inside.

It didn't take long for the illustrious Emmalina Ruiz to make her way into the parlor. As always, she was dressed in black. "Must you terrorize my servants?"

"Only if they lie to me."

"What do you want?"

"Your note is due today. I came to collect."

"I don't have it."

"And when will you?"

She looked away. "I don't know. The business venture I'd hoped would repay you soured. Surely you can wait another few months."

"When you borrowed the thousand dollars, I didn't tell you, surely you can wait a few months."

Anger flashed in her eyes.

"So what was this business venture?"

"My daughter was to marry. I borrowed the money to buy her a new wardrobe, but the wedding was called off."

"Why?"

Her chin raised. "The man had a child and I refused to wed my daughter to a fornicator."

"Maybe you should've remembered your debt before climbing up on your high horse."

She puffed up. "How dare you speak to me that way."

"I dare because with the interest, you owe me an additional five hundred and I want to be paid in full."

He enjoyed the shock she showed. "Have you considered asking that fornicator for what you owe?"

"I told him to never come near my daughter again, so I doubt I'll go on my knees to beg him for anything."

"You might wish to change your mind in order to keep your daughter from working off the debt on her back." He had no idea what the girl looked like, but he didn't care, and neither would the men she'd be servicing."

"No!" she threw back.

"Men have lost their lives for less than you owe, Senora Ruiz."

"I should never have done business with the likes of you."

"But you did. What about your husband? Can he cover your debt?"

"If he could I wouldn't have come to you in the first place."

"Is the man your daughter was to marry wealthy?"

"Very, and after the wedding I was going to get funds from him."

"Who is he?"

"Andrew Yates."

He went still.

"Do you know him?"

"Yes. How old is the child?"

"According to my daughter about a year or so. I didn't see the bastard."

"And she did? Where?"

"At his mother's ranch."

A grin split his battered face. "Call your daughter in here."

"Why?"

"I'd like to ask her a few questions. If this woman is who I think it is, she's wanted by the police for theft."

Her eyes brightened. "Really? Oh wouldn't that be splendid if she were arrested and jailed. I'd enjoy the shame that would bring to him and his family."

While she hurried away, Prince's mind began to race. Was Billie really at the Yates ranch? If so, did that mean Yates was the father of the child? In thinking back on their relationship, he decided it was highly possible. That being the case, getting the child away from him might be a huge problem, but . . .

Senora Ruiz returned with her daughter.

She had such innocence and beauty all he could think about was stripping her bare, throwing her on a bed and taking her in all the many ways a woman could be had. "Good afternoon," he said.

She gave him an almost imperceptible nod in response.

"Mr. DuChance wants to ask you something," her mother said.

"And that is?"

"You met a woman and a child at the Yates ranch. Describe her for me, if you would."

The girl hesitated.

"Answer him!" her mother snapped.

And from the description the daughter gave in her quiet voice, Prince knew it was Billie. He thanked the saints for their grace.

Senora Ruiz viewed him with excited eyes. "Is it the same woman?"

"Yes."

Rosaline looked between the two and asked, "What is this about?"

Her mother answered, "The woman who bore Andrew Yates's bastard is wanted by the police for theft." She looked so elated Prince thought she might actually jump up and down with glee.

"Is there anything else?" the girl asked.

"No."

She exited.

Her mother didn't seem to notice. "You will see that the police know where she is?"

Prince turned from watching the space where the girl disappeared. "Yes, just as soon as I leave you." He wanted her daughter. Badly. But that desire had to be set aside for the moment.

Senora Ruiz said, "So, shall we discuss an extension on my repayment?"

"Of course."

"What are the conditions?"

"Your daughter. I want her in my bed for a month. That should be ample time for her to work off your debt."

"No!"

"I will be back within the hour. Have her ready or have what is owed."

"You will roast in hell."

"And by the time I'm finished with the girl, she'll be right beside me." He bowed. "Until my return . . ."

Laughing, he exited.

Chapter 14

Drew and Cassius were just readying to close the office for the day, when Rosaline Ruiz rushed in. "Oh, Drew, you must help me!"

His surprise at seeing her was immediately replaced with concern upon seeing the fear she exuded. The duenna Senora Martinez, mirroring a similar fright, stood in the doorway.

"You must help me get out of the city!"

"Whoa. Hold on. What's happened?"

In a rush she told him a story that left him cold. Not only had her mother revealed Billie's location to DuChance, the man was demanding Rosaline as payment for some sort of debt her mother owed. "I was listening on the other side of the door after I left them. Oh, Drew, please. Where can I go?"

He looked to Cassius. "I'll need you to take the carriage and drive the women to Otis. Tell him to drive you to San Jose and catch the train to Los Angeles. I'll give you money for the tickets." Otis sometimes functioned as Drew's driver and as Drew spoke he was writing frantically on a piece of paper, which he handed to Cassius. "When you get to Los Angeles, you're to go to that address. It's my cousin Alfredo. Rosaline, tell him the story and have him take you and your aunt to my great-aunt Felicity in Monterey. You'll be safe there until you decide what you wish to do next."

Cassius asked, "Should I come back here?"

"No. You go home to your family in Virginia. I don't want you anywhere near San Francisco when DuChance finds her gone, because he'll come here first."

"But—"

"I'll be closing the office."

Rosaline said, "Drew, I'm so sorry that you have to close your office because of me."

"Has nothing to do with you Rosa. Billie isn't wanted for theft. She's wanted because DuChance wants to sell our son."

Her eyes widened.

"One last thing," he said to them. "If you run into problems along the way, defer to Otis. He was with the Ninth and he's good with a gun."

They nodded.

They looked scared, but he had no remedy, nor could he accompany them. His duty lay with protecting his son. After pulling money from the safe, he handed it to Cassius. "Get going. Rosa, send a wire to the ranch when you get to Monterey."

She nodded.

Senora Martinez had tears in her eyes. "How will we ever repay you?"

"No payment is necessary. Just take care of yourselves."

Rosaline placed a kiss on his cheek. "Thank you, Andrew."

"You're welcome."

They departed.

Drew locked the office, climbed the stairs to his apartment and began packing for the journey home. What in the world possessed Emmalina Ruiz to deal with a snake like DuChance? He had no answer but was furious that she'd exposed Billie's location. Lips tight with anger, he hoped DuChance wasn't already on his way to Destiny. Anyone wanting to harm a member of the family would have to go through Logan and Alanza first; a formidable duo, but he wouldn't be able to relax until he arrived to offer his own guns. Speaking of which, he took down his gun belt and strapped it on. He fed both Colts then shoved them home. Cursing Emmalina again, he carried his bags back down to his office. He needed to get his client files before leaving.

He'd just tucked them away when he heard

what sounded like someone trying to kick the door in. Quickly closing the bag, he drew one of the Colts and waited. Seconds later, the door crashed in, followed by two men wielding knives. Drew calmly shot them both.

Logan arrived on the heels of that. He took one look at the men writhing on the office floor, then another over at the grim set of Drew's face and said, "Guess you don't need my help."

"Not at the moment."

The men moaning and bleeding from their bullet-shattered knees yelled at Drew to get them a doctor but he wasn't in the mood.

"Who sent you?" he demanded, walking over to where they lay.

They spat curses.

Drew's Colt barked again. Screams rose.

"Did you not hear my question!"

One of the men cried out, "He'll kill us if we talk!"

"So you want me to kill you instead? Last chance." He drew the hammer back and the men shouted in unison, "DuChance! It was DuChance! Oh God, please! Get us a doc!"

"Why'd he send you?"

"To bring back the Ruiz girl and to dispose of you."

Pleased that they'd finally told the truth, Drew

now wanted them gone. "More than likely some-one nearby heard the shots and has summoned the police, so I suggest you leave if you don't wish to go to jail."

"But we can't walk, you bastard!"

He shrugged. "Roll, slither, crawl—up to you. I'm letting you live, surely I don't need to help them exit as well, do I Logan?"

"No. I think they're big boys, they can probably make it on their own, but they should tell their boss to come himself next time and not send little girls."

Suddenly, Mr. Volga, Drew's landlord, rushed in armed with an old hunting rifle. He was a big burly man from the old country, as he often de-scribed himself. "I heard shots! Are you all right, Mr. Yates?" He suddenly noticed the men on the floor eyeing him with fright. "These vermin shoot at you?"

"No, I shot them. They came to rob me."

His eyes widened. He then saw the door. "They did this!"

Drew nodded.

"I should shoot you, myself. Look at my door!" he cried.

The men cowered and tried to slide away.

"Did someone go for the police?" he asked Drew.

"I'm letting them go. I think they've learned their lesson. I'll pay you for the door."

Mr. Volga didn't appear satisfied, but nodded. "I'll get the missus to take care of this mess on the floor, too."

"Thank you." Drew turned his attention back to DuChance's thugs. "Time to go, boys, if you want to beat the police."

If eyes could curse, the air would've been blue, but the men managed to stand. Faces creased with pain, they hobbled as best they could past the angry Mr. Volga and out into the hall. Next came the sound of thumps followed by cries and moans as if one or both had taken a tumble down the long flight of stairs. Drew walked over to the window and looked down at the street in time to see them being helped into the bed of a wagon by a third man who quickly drove them away.

"Are you sure you are all right?" Mr. Volga asked again.

"I am." Drew reached into his pocket and peeled off enough bills to handle the door's repair and a few extra for Mrs. Volga as a thank-you for mopping up the small show of blood.

After the money was exchanged, Drew added, "I'm going to be gone for a few weeks. My grandmother in Mexico has taken ill. Would you be kind enough to collect my mail?"

"I will. I wish your grandmother a long life."

"Thank you."

Mr. Volga took one last look at the door. Muttering under his breath and shaking his head, he departed.

Logan cracked, "Never knew the life of a big city lawyer was so exciting."

"Bastards," Drew groused and in a somewhat lighter tone asked, "What are you doing here?"

"Alanza sent me to fetch you. She's been putting off the birthday celebration for our children until your return and she's grown tired of waiting."

Drew's lips tightened. "How's Billie?"

"Fine. Has Alanza and Mariah wrapped around her finger. Tom Foster, too."

"Tom Foster?"

"Yes. Saved him from a bear."

"What?" He waved off further response. "Never mind. You can tell me on the train ride home."

Logan looked confused. "What? Wait. I just got here. I wasn't planning on going back until tomorrow."

"Sorry, but I was on my way home when those thugs showed up. Thanks to Emmalina Ruiz, their boss now knows Billie and the baby are at the ranch and he's probably on his way there."

"So the story Billie told us about someone being after her is true?"

"Didn't believe her, I take it?"

Logan shook his head.

"Well, we can rehearse your apology on the train. Let's go."

At the train station, Drew kept his eyes open for DuChance or anyone else who appeared overly interested in his presence while he purchased the tickets. When the train arrived, he and Logan boarded. Opting for the smoking car, they chose a table in the back to give themselves some privacy. Once the whistle sounded to announce the departure from the station, they relaxed, purchased a drink, and Drew filled his brother in on the eventful day. When he finally finished, he cracked, "So yes, this lawyer's life has been very exciting—not that I'm going to be a lawyer for much longer."

"What's that mean?"

Drew told him about his visit with Judge Ross.

Logan sat back and let out a sigh. "Do you think this country will ever live up to its Declaration of Independence, especially the clause that states: all men are created equal?"

"Probably not in our lifetime," Drew replied. "But my future with the law isn't an issue right now. My main concern is DuChance."

"As well it should be. Sending Rosaline and her

duenna to Alfredo was good thinking. I'd like to wring Emmalina's neck. Any idea why she borrowed the money in the first place?"

"No." And in the scheme of things it didn't matter. Rosaline was on her way to safety and he hoped his help in its own small way made up for the embarrassment and hurt she'd no doubt suffered over the cancelation of their engagement. It was also his hope that one day she'd find a man who truly loved her instead of settling for her as he'd done. He hadn't settled for Billie however; she'd been sent by the Fates, or better yet as a laugh from *Tlazolteotl*, the goddess of lust and sexual misdeeds. Their coming together had been akin to lightning sparking dry grass, but he didn't want anything to happen to her or the baby, especially not at the hands of Prince DuChance. "Now tell me about this bear?"

And when Logan ended the tale, Drew stared in speechless amazement.

Logan said, "It was touch and go with Tom for a while. He lost a lot of blood, but he's on the mend now. He's been singing Billie's praises all over the county. Everywhere I go, people are talking about your sharpshooting wife, and the more the tale spreads, the bigger the bear gets. One of the ranch hands said he heard the grizzly stood fifteen feet tall."

Drew found this incredible.

"And in the meantime, she's giving shooting lessons to some of the women, Mariah included."

Drew's confusion climbed higher.

"Tom wanted her to teach Amanda how to handle a rifle. Some of the other ranchers wanted their wives to learn, too, and it took off from there. Tom thinks so highly of your wife, I swear if he wasn't already married he'd be challenging you to pistols at dawn for Billie's hand."

Drew's drink caught in his throat and he began to cough.

Logan leaned over and slapped him on the back. "It's been an interesting ten days, to say the least."

Billie was so bone tired on the drive home she could hardly hold on to Duchess's reins. She'd spent the afternoon planting eight rosebushes on the church's property and the work had taken its toll. The plants were sent over courtesy of Tom Foster. As his way of thanking her for running the bear off, he had his hands scouring the country-side for rosebushes. The three he'd sent her a few days ago were planted near Alanza's patio. The two that arrived yesterday were put in by Mari-ah's front door. She knew he was grateful, and she appreciated the gifts; however, when eight new bushes were delivered by one of his hands that morning, she'd told the man to tell Mr. Foster, no more please. She'd had her fill of digging holes, manure, and being bitten by thorns for the season.

Tomorrow another shooting lesson was planned. She didn't mind helping the women learn how to handle a gun; being able to protect themselves was a necessity, but she dearly hoped it rained all day so she could stay indoors and let herself be worn out by chasing Tonio instead.

The opened gates of Destiny were a joy to see, and each time she drove through them she felt welcomed home. For a woman who'd spent her formative years living hand-to-mouth on the hurly-burly streets of Kansas City, the reality of all the ranch represented—permanence, safety, family, caring—had been foreign, but it hadn't taken long for those ideals to work their way into her blood. She felt a part of it now. Who knew that shooting at a bear would result in her being embraced by the community. The *good* women of the valley were not only seeking her out for rifle lessons but asking if she'd stop by and look in on their roses as well. She supposed because the place was so small, news traveled fast, but the story about her and the bear seemed to have spread like wildfire. Even people at Alanza's church in Sacramento had heard about it, and Mariah said the incident was a burning topic with her customers as well.

Billie shook her head. This was something.

As she drove to the stables, she mused on the only real problem in her life. Drew. He continued to be a different type of thorn. So far, he hadn't come back from San Francisco and she hadn't been pleased to learn that Alanza had dispatched Logan to make him do so. Billie agreed that his presence was warranted at his son's first birthday celebration, but she was certain he hadn't known about the event. If he had he may well have returned of his own volition. Now, all she expected was polite distance and resentment.

When she reached the stables she stopped the wagon and climbed down on sore legs. Handing off the reins to one of the stable hands, she started towards the house. Seeing Drew standing silently and watching her approach caused her to slow and then stop. She took in a deep breath to steady her wildly beating heart and resumed her steps. "Hello Drew."

"Billie."

Physically he was still as devastatingly handsome as he'd always been, but necessity had prompted her to store her feelings for him in the cellar of her heart and that's where they remained. "Thanks for coming back."

"Alanza didn't give me much choice."

"You could've chosen to ignore her."

"Agreed, but he is my son and I was already on my way here when Logan arrived."

She wanted to think that it was because he decided to try and make a go of their marriage but she doubted that had anything to do with his reason.

"Logan told me about the bear and Tom and about the gun lessons, but why are you dressed that way?"

"I've been planting roses over at the church." Billie was wearing a pair of snug-fitting denims. "They used to belong to your brother Noah. They're easier to maneuver in when I'm planting and I don't want to ruin the skirts and blouses Mariah's been loaning me to wear."

His face was so unreadable she couldn't tell whether he approved of the attire or not, not that it mattered. When they reached the door, she stopped. Although she'd told herself she wouldn't ask, she had to know. "You mentioned you were already on your way here when Logan arrived. Why?"

"Prince DuChance."

"What about him?" she asked warily.

So he told her everything.

And when he was done, her eyes were blazing. "If he comes anywhere near my son, I will kill him with my bare hands. Did you get to see Addy?"

"I did. She's fine. She's a very odd old woman though."

"I know, but she took me in and I'll owe her for the rest of my life. Thanks for coming all this way to let me know about Prince. Are you going back to San Francisco after the birthday dinner tomorrow?"

"No. I'll be staying here."

"Why?"

"Because whether you like it or not, you're my wife, and husbands protect their wives and children."

"You don't have to get all testy, Drew. It was a simple question. And you don't like being married any more than I do."

He didn't respond to that, but said instead, "Logan and I will alert the ranch hands and tell them to keep an eye out for strangers."

She faced him with her arms crossed. "Okay."

"And I'll need you to stay close to the house."

"You'll get no argument from me. I know how dangerous Prince is, but I put two slugs in his head, so he knows how dangerous I can be, too."

He paused and studied her for a moment. "When did this happen?"

"A few years before you and I met. I had a problem waking up with him on top of me and tearing at my clothes, so I shot him. That's why his face is such a mess and his ear's missing. Addy sewed him up and kept him from bleeding to death."

He stared.

"So thanks for coming back, but I can take care of myself." And she resumed her journey to the door.

Watching her walk away, Drew wondered what was wrong with him. By all accounts he should be irritated by her thorny and prickly manner. Instead he wanted to call her back so they could talk about how seeing her again made him feel, and why in the world she'd been out planting roses, and how relieved he'd been to find her safe and not in DuChance's clutches. The rose planting must have included manure because she stank to high heaven, yet all he could focus on was the snug fit of her thighs and hips in Noah's denims.

The family gathered for dinner and as they shared the meal, they spent a few moments talking about the threat DuChance posed.

"Do you really think he'll come here?" Alanza asked.

"Without question," Billie replied.

Alanza said, "Hopefully, he'll realize his quest will only result in his death and we can go on about our lives."

Wine goblets were raised in agreement.

"And on a brighter note," she said, "Max and I will marry later this summer."

Grins spread around the table.

"I want to hear from Noah before we set the date."

Applause broke out, followed by cracks of "about time" from her sons, and words of congratulations from her daughters-in-law.

Mariah said excitedly, "I'll begin working up sketches for your gown right away."

After putting Tonio to bed, Billie sat on her verandah as had become her custom each evening. She was very happy for Alanza. Although Billie had only met Max once, she'd liked him and decided he had to be a very special man for Alanza to want to be his wife, but her happiness was dampened by her own reality. Prince knew where she was. The news wasn't surprising but it was unsettling. She'd been serious about using everything in her power to keep him away from her son and she was certain Drew's family would, too. Drew's arrival coupled with his declaration that he'd not be returning to San Francisco was also on her mind. Parts of her wished there was a way to banish the distrust and distance between them so that at some point down the road they could be happy together, but she knew pigs would fly first. That he'd helped his fairy princess escape Prince's clutches was admirable, and it caused her to wonder if Rosa still held his heart. She assumed that to be the case so she decided not to think about it.

Drew was on his way to his room to soak in a tub and hopes of ridding himself of the harrowing day but found himself knocking on his wife's door instead.

She opened it.

"Are you busy?" he asked.

She scanned him as if unsure about his motives. "No. Do you need something?"

They hadn't been alone since the encounter before dinner. "Thought maybe we could talk. May I come in?"

He sensed her reluctance, but to her credit, she stepped back and let him enter. "I'm outside," she explained. "Join me."

"Nice evening," he said once they took seats.

She stole a glance at him, then turned back to the dusk descending over the fading day.

"Are you settling in okay?" he asked.

"I am. Your mother and Mariah have been very kind. I'm working on my reading and other things to improve myself." She paused before adding in an honest tone, "If we have to be married, I don't want to shame you."

Drew wasn't sure how to respond to that but found the confession very moving. "I appreciate that, Billie. The baby's asleep, I take it?"

"Yes. Be nice if you'd call him by his name sometimes."

The softly spoken censure stung but he didn't push back because she was right. His son's name had yet to cross his lips. He supposed it was his way of distancing himself from the truth. "You're right. I'll do better."

"Not for me, but for him."

He nodded solemnly. "I don't know much about children."

"He doesn't know much about fathers either, so you can learn together."

That made him smile even as he wondered what the future would hold for the three of them. Deep down inside he wasn't as angry as he'd been the day they married and he was having difficulty putting a finger on the reason as to why not. "Has Alanza had a chance to take you two shopping?"

She shook her head. "No. I've been too busy saving ranchers from bears and planting rose-bushes all over the county."

"Tell me about that."

"Do you really want to know?" she asked eyeing him.

He nodded and listened as she filled him in on

Alanza's original request and how she'd come to know so much about the flowers and their care.

"Tom Foster sent me a slew of them this past week, but when one of his hands brought eight this morning I had to put my foot down."

Drew was confused. "Where's he getting them?"

"He's been sending his men out into the countryside to dig them up. He found out how much I enjoy them when he was recovering here after the bear attack. He was too injured to go home, so the doc treated him here for the first couple of days."

Drew wasn't pleased hearing Foster knew something about her that he didn't. He told himself it wasn't jealousy, but didn't delve into his reaction any further. "So are you done with your planting?"

"I am."

"Then maybe in a few days the three of us can go to Sacramento and pick up some things."

"Your mother and I can make the trip, you don't have to concern yourself."

"And if I want to?"

Her eyes met his. "You gave your son your name, Drew, it's enough. I know you have better things to do with your time."

"Such as?"

She shrugged. "I don't know. Lawyer things."

"And suppose I want to go shopping for my family instead?"

He enjoyed the way she studied him as if trying to discern what he was about. Truthfully he didn't know either. *And you will love her until there is no tomorrow . . .* He pushed away the old woman's words.

"Are you being nice because you want sex, Drew? Because if that's all this is about then we can go in the bedroom now."

His jaw tightened. "This isn't about sex, Billie." Although his body begged to differ. Seeing her earlier and being near her now reminded him of the tastes of her breasts and how her soft hips felt against the skin of his palms. He wanted her mouth, and to dally in the silken heat between her thighs, fit himself there and stroke her until she screamed with rapture. Realizing he'd made himself harden, he shifted his position to accommodate the awakening in his loins

She was watching him. "Then what is this about?"

"Can I not just sit with you?"

"I suppose, but we didn't exactly part on friendly terms when you left for San Francisco, so I thought maybe you coming here was about something else."

"And whose fault might that have been? After

our wedding night, I didn't expect to wake up and find you gone."

"What reason did I have to stick around? You were still going to leave, weren't you?"

He looked away.

"My point is made."

The hard look he flung her way didn't seem to faze her at all, because she said, "You're angry. I'm angry. I'm going to bed. See you in the morning."

She stood and waited.

That she was dismissing him had Drew hovering somewhere between laughter and fury at her audacious, maddening, and, yes, beautiful self. He didn't know whether to spank her sassy little behind or drag her into his arms and kiss her in order to give that smart mouth something better to do. In truth, he wanted both. Instead he rose and studied her through the shadows. He finally inclined his head. "Good night, Billie."

"Good night."

When the men Prince sent to Yates's office hadn't returned by sunset, he assumed they'd failed the task and had fled the city to escape his wrath. First, Billie and now the Ruiz girl. Even though he knew where Billie was he was still furious that the girl had slipped through his fingers, too, so he'd taken it out on the illustrious Emmalina Ruiz and to eliminate witnesses, the servant, too. Both were lying dead in the parlor—their throats cut. While ransacking the house to make it appear like a robbery, he'd searched for valuables, because even in death, Senora Ruiz owed him, and he'd left the house with a few pieces of jewelry and some gold doubloons. The booty didn't equal the loan, but it was better than nothing.

Now, seated in the back of his well-sprung carriage, he was headed for the docks. There was one last loose end to snip, then he'd call it a day.

Addy knew her death was coming, so she'd prepared herself by taking a bath and putting on a white gown. Earlier in the day, she'd given away her small cache of valuables to longtime customers and what little money she possessed to friends. Nothing else in the house was likely to survive, so she didn't worry about the rest. Now as the sun set, she knew it wouldn't be much longer. Taking a seat in the center of her bed, she waited.

As night fell, she heard footsteps making their way around the perimeter of the house and smelled the kerosene being splashed around its base. She knew the men were there on Prince's orders because her death would come not by his hands but from his words.

A big whoosh sounded as a match was tossed into the kerosene and she sensed the spreading flames. Smoke filled the small house, stinging her eyes and lungs. After a short while, fire crept into the bedroom, tentatively at first, and upon finding no resistance grew strong and tall. The flames crawled up the walls feeding greedily on them and the thin drapes with shimmering tongues of red and orange, bringing with it a tremendous heat and a desert-hot wind. They jumped to the bed and moved up her body and crawled up her arms raised in praise. The flames embraced her and danced over her with a joy she and they both shared. She was finally going home to the River of Life to stand beside her mother, grandmother, and her precious Chassie. As the firestorm burned away her last breath, she smiled.

Outside a crowd gathered and a bucket brigade formed in a desperate attempt to save the structure, but it was too far gone. Watching the blaze from the interior of his carriage, Prince smiled too as the house began to fall into itself and the towering flames stood bright against the night. The men he'd hired to do the job had long since melted into the darkness, and his day was now complete as well. He tapped the head of his cane against the roof, the carriage pulled away, and he settled back against the seat. The burning of the witch pleased him on myriad levels. Now, she'd never be able to implicate him in her daughter's death, and although he had no direct proof, his gut told him she'd not only played a role in Billie's escape, but also was the reason his mother was near death. Pearl DuChance was no longer the famed beauty she'd once been. Her gums and tongue were black, her teeth had fallen out, and her ivory skin was now the color of piss. The doctor he'd brought in to evaluate her failing condition said it appeared as if she'd been poisoned over a long period of time. Other than making her comfortable by giving her opium for the pain there was nothing medically he could do. It was his opinion that she wouldn't live much longer: maybe a day or two more and then Prince would bury her. Nothing would assuage his fury and grief, but watching the old woman burn helped immensely.

Chapter 15

"**I**f the scowl you're wearing gets any uglier, Alanza's going to send you to your room."

Drew cut his brother a look and groused, "I thought this was supposed to be a children's party. Why are there no other children here, and why are all the men circled up around my wife?" He swore if another man came up and told him how lucky he was to have such a fierce and beautiful little wife he was going to start throwing punches.

"She and Tom are telling the bear story. First time many people have heard the full details."

Drew rolled his eyes and took a small sip of his sangria.

"Feeling neglected, are you?" Logan asked, sounding amused.

Drew watched Billie laugh in response to something Tom was saying. "She thinks I only want her for sex."

"Why wouldn't she?"

Drew's scowl deepened.

"Personally I'm still trying to figure out what you see in her. She's life smart, has a backbone, and is way too mouthy for my liking."

"That's right, you prefer your women to kick and throw rocks."

Alanza walked by carrying a grandchild in each arm. "Drew, stop scowling. You'll scare the children." She moved on.

He shook his head and took another sip.

Logan asked, "Do you want some brotherly advice?"

"No."

"Surrender."

"To what?"

"Billie. Your feelings. Love. Whatever you want to call it. But it's got you by the bullocks and the longer you fight it, the more miserable you're going to be."

"Are you done?"

"Almost. Remember the hard time you gave me last summer over Mariah? It's your turn." Leaving him with a pat on the back, Logan walked across the room to join his wife and the others listening to the bear story.

Drew spent the rest of the evening nursing his sangria and mulling over his wife. She met his eyes a few times across the room, but he supposed his impassive response wasn't encouraging so she ignored him from then on. He made an effort to mingle and to speak with a few people but they kept pointing out how charming and witty Billie was, so he eventually made his way outside to the patio.

To his surprise, Mariah stepped out to join him. "Are you unwell?" she asked.

"I've been better."

"The cure is to let her know how you feel."

"You sound like your husband."

She laughed softly. "If it's any consolation, she does care about you, but she doesn't think her feelings are reciprocated."

"She's doing a good job of hiding it."

"And you aren't?"

He didn't reply.

"You might want to dust off that legendary Spanish charm you're supposed to be so famous for and start using it, otherwise we may have to put you down."

He laughed. She gave him a kiss on the cheek and left him outside alone.

Lying in bed, Drew thought back on the advice he'd received. He didn't deny he had feelings for Billie, but Logan had called it love. Having never been in love, he wasn't sure if his brother was correct or not but one thing he had gotten right. Whatever was going on inside did have him by the bullocks and was growing more and more pronounced.

Drew slept in the following morning and by the time he came downstairs the household was well into its day. He found his mother in her study. The cousins were playing with toys on the carpeted floor. He nodded at his niece and said to his son, "Good morning, Antonio," which brought on a blissful smile, followed by the raising of his little arms.

Drew picked him up. Because he didn't live on the ranch he'd had only minimal contact with his niece, so what he knew about babies would fit on the head of a pin. Drew was amazed at how light he was in his arms. Father and son eyed each other just long enough for Tonio to begin his usual stream of chattering. "What's he saying?"

Alanza shrugged. "Only he knows, but the idea is to respond. It's how little ones learn the back and forth of conversing."

Drew assumed she knew what she was talking about and apparently his son thought so as well because he kept up his part of the conversation, complete with gestures for emphasis. "What should I say?" He was finding this very amusing.

"Doesn't matter. Just say anything. Agree. Ask him to tell you more."

"But he doesn't understand."

"*Dios*, Andrew. That isn't the point. The point is to play. Enjoy. Loosen the lawyer's vest and be silly with him. He won't be little for long. Soon he'll be talking back and chasing women."

He shot his mother a look, which she met with a smile.

Little Maria was observing all this. Drew leaned down and asked, "Do you know what he's trying to say?"

She chattered a moment as if to offer a translation then resumed trying to eat a wooden block that was as large as her head.

"Where's your mama, Antonio?"

Alanza answered for him, even though Tonio was chatting away. "She's over at Tom's giving gun lessons to Amanda and the other ladies. She'll be back later."

Drew noticed his son was wearing miniature denim trousers. "Where'd he get these denims?"

"Mariah made them. Little Maria has a few pair, too."

Traditionally children of both genders wore clothing that resembled dresses or jumpers. Only when boys were much older did parents dress them like little men. Drew himself had grown up wearing the same kind of apparel, but he was glad that times were changing so that boys could stop being mistaken for their sisters. "Do you think Billie will mind if I took him for a ride?"

"Probably not, he's ridden with me a few times, but be sure you ride slow and hold onto him. He's wiggly and quick. You don't want to have to come back and explain to his mother how her son fell off your horse."

No, he didn't. So with a wave good-bye, father and son left for the stables.

They rode to the portion of the Yates land Drew had been dreaming of building his house on since he was fourteen. It was on a rise above the river and had a magnificent view of the mountains. "You think you'd like to live here, Antonio? We're a pretty good piece away from your *abuela*, but close enough for her to ride over to visit, and for you to ride to see her once you can sit a horse."

The open land spread out around them was in bloom with the wildflowers of May and there were dragonflies darting and in and out of the cattails and tall grasses down near the water. Seeing two eagles soaring overhead, Drew pointed them out, but Tonio was focused on trying to put the end of the reins in his mouth. "Don't eat that."

Laughing and appalled at the same time he pried the leather loose. "We need to have your mama feed you better. Leather is not something little boys have for lunch."

The boy giggled as if he understood the joke and in that beaming smile Drew saw Billie's face for the first time. The realization stopped his heart and swelled it with an unnamed emotion. Their eyes were shaped similarly and the smiles were nearly identical. Why had he never noticed the resemblance before? *Probably because you've never bothered to get close enough before,* a sarcastic voice inside pointed out. Tonio reached up and attempted to put his fist into his father's mouth, but Drew kept his lips sealed. For a few moments they played the silly game and there were no words to describe how it made him feel. From that moment forward Tonio ceased to be just the "the baby" or "Billie's son." In the blink of an eye he'd become Antonio Andrew Yates, their son. His son. The certainty was overwhelming. He wondered if Logan felt the same connection to his daughter. He could only guess that he did. "You're not supposed to make your papa want to tear up like an old woman, son."

They dismounted and Drew tossed Tonio into the air, which the boy enjoyed immensely. The toss was repeated and upon catching him this time, Drew looked down into the sparkling black eyes and his heart was full. "Let's go see the water."

Leaving the horse behind, Drew carried his son down to the river's edge then set him on his feet. He made a point of holding on to his hand. Tonio strained against the hold, so Drew let him go but kept an eye on him. The boy soon found a stick and used the end to poke at the muddy bank. Drew wondered what the world would be like when he reached maturity. Would it be a fairer one where his son could achieve whatever he put his mind to without being hindered because of his race or the language he spoke? Drew glanced up at the eagles still soaring overhead. He wanted his son to be able to soar in much the same way, but most of all he wanted him to have what life had denied Drew, a father. He turned back to Antonio, but he wasn't there. His heart pounded as he hastily looked around.

"Antonio!" He fought to remain calm even as the fear climbed up his chest. "Antonio!" Panicked he reasoned the boy couldn't've gotten too far. There'd been no sound of a splash so he hadn't gone into the water. "Antonio!"

The bank was lined with cattails and equally tall grasses, so he began to move through them while praying aloud for the first time in a very long time. And then, a dragonfly appeared and out of the grass toddled his son. He wanted to weep with relief. Scooping him up, Drew held him against his pounding heart and whispered a fervent prayer of thanks. He glanced down at his smiling son, who was squirming to be free because the dragonfly had flitted near again. "*Dios!* Are you trying to kill me? Please don't ever do that again. You almost gave me heart failure."

Drew hugged him tightly again and only when he was sure that he was unharmed and in one piece did he carry him to the waiting stallion. "Time to hand you back over to the womenfolk. They're obviously much better at taking care of you than I am. I need a drink."

Once they were mounted, Drew turned the horse towards home. "And this is not a story to share with your mama, remember that, okay?"

Billie was behind the reins as she and Mariah were heading home. "Do you think I'll ever be able to shoot straight?" her sister-in-law bemoaned.

"Takes practice. At least you keep your eyes open. I have no idea how Amanda Foster plans to shoot anything if she closes her eyes every time she squeezes the trigger."

There'd been six ladies at the lessons today. Now that they'd conquered their initial fear of the guns, bullets and the sound of the guns firing, their aim and skill had much improved.

"There's Logan," Mariah pointed out at the sight of her husband riding in their direction.

Billie had to admit he cut a fine figure mounted on the big black stallion.

When he reined to a halt beside them, Mariah asked, "Where are you headed?"

"To pick up Eli. He's coming in on the afternoon train."

Billie had no idea who Eli might be so she concentrated on the scenery. Her brother-in-law continued to be cool towards her and she didn't want to draw his attention, but apparently she failed.

"Billie."

She looked over into his stern eyes.

"I want to apologize for not believing your story about DuChance."

She was surprised by that. "None needed, but thank you."

"You're welcome."

She wondered if his attitude towards her was beginning to thaw. Mariah was wearing a pleased smile that lingered even after he offered her his good-byes and rode away.

Billie got Duchess moving again. "Did you put him up to that?"

"No. He's a lot like Alanza in that sense. No one can make him do anything. He rarely apologizes because he's rarely wrong, but in this instance he was. I'm proud of him."

"I doubt we'll ever be close, but I do appreciate the gesture."

Upon entering the parlor, Billie was caught off guard seeing Drew sitting on the floor of the parlor with both children in his lap. He was reading to them in Spanish. Alanza looked on from the sofa.

Mariah asked, "What are you reading?"

"*Las sergas de Esplandian.*"

Billie grinned. "Aren't they a bit young to be hearing about Queen Calafia?"

"You remember," Drew replied quietly and her insides fluttered in reaction to his tone and knowing gaze.

"I do."

She saw Mariah and Alanza exchange an arched glance. Little Maria wriggled out of her uncle's lap, wobbled to her mother and raised her arms. Mariah picked her up. "Thanks for watching her, Alanza. I'm going to take her home and put her down for her nap."

Tonio scrambled off his father's lap and reached up for his mother, too. Billie obliged him. "Have you been good for your *abuela* and papa while I was gone?"

He placed his head against her shoulder as if

ready for a nap of his own, and she was very confused by that. Getting him to nap willingly was
akin to putting a bear in a bottle. "What's got you
so tuckered out, little man?"

The explanation came from his father. "We
went riding, we chased dragonflies, gathered
sticks. We looked at the land where we're going to
build our house."

She stared at him like she'd never seen him
before then over at the chuckling Alanza. *"You
took him riding?"*

"And brought him back in one piece."

Mariah interrupted. "We'll see you at dinner.
Bye, Billie. Thanks for the lesson."

"You're welcome," but her eyes were still on
Drew as Mariah departed.

Drew calmly closed the book and stood. "How
about I come learn how to put him to bed, that
way I can do it on my own if I want to."

Her jaw dropped. *Who was this man and what
had he done with the real Drew Yates?* She stammered, "Sure."

Alanza viewed their exit with a knowing smile.

Tonio was already asleep when she placed him
in the crib and covered him up. "Usually putting him down for a nap is a test of wills, so don't
think it'll always be this easy. I believe he thinks
he'll miss something if he sleeps." She ran her

hand lovingly over his head, then leaned down and gave him a soft kiss.

Most days, Billie used the free time to sit and catch her breath because he never slept more than an hour, but with Drew in the room, she wasn't sure what to do next. "Most of the time, he doesn't sleep for long."

"Then come sit outside with me for a moment or two."

Both wary and suspicious due to how'd they parted the last time they'd been on the verandah together and because of his distant manner last night at the party, she agreed nonetheless.

Outside, it was still a perfect May day. Blue sky. Gentle winds against her cheek. Not too hot. "So you two had a good day?" she asked him.

"We did. I enjoyed myself, he seemed to enjoy it as well. I want to get to know him, and so . . ." His voice trailed off.

"That was nice of you."

"When he gets up would you like to ride out and see where I want to build our house?"

He'd said *our*, which immediately grabbed her attention. Had he changed his thinking about not living with them? She wanted to ask but feared the heartache, so she didn't and replied instead, "I would."

"Then that's what we'll do."

She was rattled to say the least. A quick glance showed him watching her, so she quickly focused elsewhere. "How long will it take get the house built?"

"Depends on the size, how much land we need to level, the number of workers Max and I have to hire."

"Your mother's Max?"

"Yes, he's one of the best carpenters in this part of the state. Does good work."

"I see."

"How many bedrooms do you think we'll need?"

Was he rattling her on purpose? There was nothing in his manner or tone to suggest that but something in his eyes radiated suspiciously like mischief. "Whatever you think is best."

"We can decide when the time comes. We'll get Max to draw up some plans and talk about it then."

She thought about having a house of her own and fought down a sudden welling of emotion. "Never had a home before, not a real one. You've lived here all your life though, haven't you?"

"Yes, but the ranch was nowhere near as prosperous as it is today. After my father's death, life here sort of fell apart. My mother did her best, but she didn't really know how to run the place."

He quieted as if thinking back. "When things hit bottom, we had nothing, no food, no money. I remember her loading us into the wagon and driving to her uncle's home downstate. She'd always been such a rock, but after we arrived there, she got on her knees and begged food for us. I'll never forget it. I wanted to go to her, but Logan latched on to my arm and made me stand still. I remember crying for her."

"How old were you?"

"Eight, nine."

Billie'd always assumed he'd been wealthy since birth. The idea of Alanza begging for anything was sobering. "You love your mother very much, don't you?"

"We all do. She was both mother and father at one point. Max was my father's best friend, and he helped out around here as much as he could, but she raised us and made us the men we are today. We'd walk through hell if she asked us to."

Even marry a whore. "I wonder if Tonio will love me as much."

"From what I've witnessed he already does."

"That's a nice thing to say, Drew."

"You're an excellent mother, Billie, don't ever doubt that. I may not know much about being a father, but I know a good mama when I see one."

She saw an honesty in his eyes she'd not seen

since his apology for his cruel words on their wedding night. "Thank you for that, too," she whispered.

"You're welcome. What was your childhood like?"

She hesitated.

"If you don't wish to talk about it, I won't hold it against you." His eyes held that same honesty.

"You may as well know. It was hard and painful. After my mother left, I ended up in an orphanage, where the owners rented us out for day work from dawn to dark. If the employers didn't think we worked hard enough or if we accidentally broke something in their home, we were beaten or sent to bed without supper. Sometimes both. After about six months I ran away." She glanced over to gauge his reaction before continuing. "I lived on the streets. Slept in alleys. Scrounged for food wherever I could find it. Even in refuse cans sometimes." Her lips tightened as the awfulness of those days resurfaced. "Then I fell in with a band of street urchins and they taught me how to pick pockets and cut purses and steal fruit from the street vendors. We even stole some guns from a home one time, which is when I learned to shoot."

Drew now had the answer to the question as to when and how she'd acquired her skill.

"I practiced every night until I became very good at it. In the end, we wound up selling it off." She continued her story by telling him about living in a ramshackle cottage with an old confidence woman named Mrs. Bean.

"We'd give her our take at the end of each day and she gave us food and let us sleep on the floor. When I was about twelve, my body began to change and she introduced me to her son. I was too young to know it at the time, but he was a pimp. He promised me a dime if I'd lay with him, and back then that was a fortune to someone like me." She looked his way again. "And that's how it began."

"You did what you had to do to survive. There's no shame in that."

"I know, but many people think there is, so I keep my past to myself."

"What gives you joy?"

"Never had anyone ask me that before." She quieted and thought about her answer. "Our son. Being here. Planting roses. I can't wait until they all bloom. Why?"

"Just curious. It's one of the things a man should know about his wife."

She was rattled again. "What brings you joy?"

He seemed caught off guard so she pointed out. "Turn around is fair play."

"I suppose you're right. Had you asked me a year ago, I would have given a ready answer."

"But now?"

"Life's different and so am I. Antonio gives me joy. Watching the two of you together does, too."

Billie held on to her racing heart.

"And on that, I'm going downstairs and see what Bonnie will let me steal from the kitchen. You relax and I'll see you when he wakes up."

He stood, inclined his head and left her alone to wonder what it all meant.

Had she asked, Drew would've told her it meant he wanted to move forward, to do away with the thorns separating them and try and make something of this marriage of theirs. He also wanted Billie in the myriad ways a husband wanted a wife, because in the aftermath of all she'd faced, he was now willing to admit that she was still as special to him as she'd been before the baby. Yes, he wanted them to share a bed, but he also wanted to read to her, hear her laughter, and enjoy the awe on her face when he gifted her with a surprise. She was feisty, proud, and had a backbone as strong as some men he knew. Her strength was reminiscent of Alanza's and he'd be a bastard to continue to lay all the blame at her door. They'd both given life to Antonio and it would take them both to make sure his life was a good one, so, he planned to use that legendary Spanish charm Mariah teased him about to woo her and court her, and if he had to employ his son as his second in command, he would. It wasn't going to be an easy undertaking. She could be skeptical to a fault, and truthfully he'd armed her with enough ammunition to withstand a year-long siege, but he loved a good chase and was counting on her to give him a run for his money.

Chapter 16

"**T**his is beautiful country," Billie said. She had the awake and squirming Tonio on her lap as Drew drove them away from the house. The vastness of the ranch always filled Billie with awe and she hoped she'd always appreciate its richness.

"That it is."

They rumbled over the open grassland. Off in the distance to her left were the orchards and corrals and the workers who maintained them. Up ahead were the mountains, and the closer the wagon got to them the more majestic they became. After a few more minutes, he finally stopped the team and pulled back on the brake. The quiet was like a thing alive. "So, what do you think?" he asked.

"Is this the spot?"

He nodded.

Her eyes swept the river below and the tall pines lining the far side of the bank. They were sitting in a wide open meadow that was backed by a large stand of pines a few hundred feet away. "I like this."

She saw his smile.

"Then let's get unpacked," he said.

"Unpacked?"

"Yep. Thought we'd spend the rest of the day here—have dinner, talk, let Antonio get tuckered out."

"Did you bring food?"

"Of course. That's why I went down to see Bonnie."

To say she'd not been expecting this was an understatement. Once again she wondered at his intent. His kindness made her want to surrender and enjoy it, but inwardly, she was still wary.

He climbed down and came around to take the baby. Once Tonio was secured, Drew held out his hand and guided her to the ground. His grasp was firm and warm and she fought off the way his nearness singed her hand.

Leaving her there, he carried his son to the back of the wagon. "Let's see what we have in the bed, Antonio."

He handed her the baby, and unloaded a couple of blankets to sit on. Out next came a crate filled with a skillet, plates, tableware, what appeared to be a fishing pole, and lord knew what else. He even produced three good-sized potatoes and an onion. Crate in hand, he said, "Now to find a spot. Let's get closer to the river."

She set Tonio on his feet and let him follow his father. Carrying the blankets, she brought up the rear.

"How about here?" he asked.

They were just a short walk above the river-bank and had a clear view of their pristine sur-roundings. "Perfect," she told him.

After laying the blankets out, and setting the crate down, and while she sat and basked in the sunshine, father and son went looking for sticks and branches to make a fire. They returned a short time later with an ample supply.

"So, what are we having for dinner?"

"Those potatoes, and"—he pulled his pole free—"salmon maybe, or for sure some bass. You ever fished?"

"No. How about I handle the potatoes?"

"That's fine."

He spent the next little while readying the sticks for the fire, a task made more difficult by the curi-ous toddler who kept claiming the sticks as his own. "Would you go away." Drew laughed while attempting to block the sticks with his body. "Go see your mama."

"Tonio. Come here."

But he wasn't paying her any attention. He was dead set on the sticks. She got up to move him away but paused when Drew handed him one of the smaller twigs. "Here, this is yours. Now let me do this."

Looking at the stick in his fist, he smiled and babbled and pointed it and moved off to poke at the rocks in the bank. But of course, the peace offering didn't satisfy him for long and as soon as Drew was done, Tonio was back.

Drew gave up. "Okay. I'm going to let you wreak havoc here, and I'm going to fish. We'll make the fire when I'm done."

"That might be a good plan."

Tonio was now hunched down and removing the underpinnings of the carefully erected pile.

She shook her head and kept an eye on him while Drew walked to the water's edge, which of course drew his son like a magnet. Billie got up to retrieve him. Otherwise there'd be no fish to go with the potatoes, and the oranges he'd also taken out of the crate.

In hindsight, she could've allowed Tonio free rein because his father caught nothing. Not salmon. Not bass. He did manage to snag a turtle but it wasn't on the menu so he let it go. Finally, after nearly an hour or more of frustration and Tonio's wails of hunger, the grumpy Drew surrendered. They ate the potatoes and onions she cooked in the skillet over the fire and a few slices of orange for the inaugural dinner on their future home site. Billie hid her smile.

Drew was silent driving back. *What kind of a man am I?* Couldn't even catch one lousy fish to feed his family? He could tell Billie wanted to crow, but she blessedly remained silent, hopefully out of respect for his pierced pride.

"Maybe you should teach Tonio how to fish."

He cut her a look and she turned her smile to the passing landscape.

"And here I was just silently praising you for not making fun."

"It's just refreshing to know that underneath all that wealth and charm you're human like the rest of creation."

"You think I'm charming?"

"You're fishing for compliments because you couldn't fish for fish?"

"You're a cruel, cruel woman."

"Be glad this cruel woman knew how to cook potatoes or your son may have starved to death."

He chuckled in spite of his mood and felt better.

She told him in a voice that was both gentle and honest, "Your son doesn't care if you're perfect, Drew."

"What about his mother?"

"His mother knows you aren't perfect, and it's okay."

Their gazes held and lingered. Something arced between and more than anything he wanted to stop the wagon and pull her into his arms. Instead, he simply nodded. "Good to know."

He dropped them off at the door and drove around to the stables to hand the wagon and team off to the hand on duty. With that accomplished, he hurried up to Billie's room and spent the rest of the early evening hours learning how to give his exuberant son his bath. After the drying and the dressing for bed, Drew tried to read him more of the adventures of Queen Calafia but Tonio was too wiggly to sit in his lap for more than a few minutes, so Drew closed the book and watched him toddle away. He never knew a child could instill such joy. He looked forward to spending every evening with him from then on.

When it was finally time for Antonio Andrew Yates to end his day, Drew watched with love in his heart as Billie placed him in the crib. "Come say good night," she beckoned to him softly.

He walked over and looked down. His son was having trouble keeping his eyes open after his exciting day, but then, Drew reckoned every day was exciting for someone his age. "Night, mister. Get some sleep. More worlds to conquer at sunrise." He ran a hand over the small brow and although he was a bit self-conscious placed a kiss on his cheek.

Billie said her good night, gave him his final kiss of the day and led Drew out of the room.

"Thanks for your time with him today, Drew."

"He's my son. It's the least I can do. Maybe next time I'll even provide fish for our dinner."

She walked over to the closed doors that opened onto the verandah and looked out at the gathering dusk. "That's the second time you've used the word, our—first *our* home, now *our* dinner. Is there a meaning to that, or am I just reading more into it than I should?"

Taking in the seriously set features evaluating him from across the room, he heard: *You will love her until there is no tomorrow.* "What if said I want us to be a family in every sense of the word. That I want us to try and work things out so that our son will grow up with parents who care for him and for each other."

She searched his eyes.

"That when we get the house built, we share a bedroom so I can make love to you until sunrise and wake up with you beside me." He saw tears. "Why are you crying?" he asked with concern.

"Because if you are pulling my leg, I swear I'll shoot you dead."

He crossed to where she stood. Come here," he whispered and took her into his arms, and held her tight against his heart. "We started out on a rocky road but I'd rather work on making it level and have some fun doing it." He tilted up her chin and brushed a tear from her cheek. "Don't think I've ever seen you cry before."

"Nothing to cry about before."

He eased her back in against him. "And hopefully, there'll never be again. Unless they're tears of happiness." He enjoyed the feel of holding her close.

"Are you sure about this?" she asked quietly.

"I am."

She gazed up. "You won't come to me tomorrow and say you've changed your mind?"

"No. Promise."

They resumed the embrace and savored each other's nearness. "I'd like you and Antonio to move into my room, if you want."

"I do."

"Tonight?"

Her soft chuckle ruffled the silence. "You aren't wasting any time, are you?"

"No, I've wasted enough. I have a verandah too, you know. We can move him in and sit out under the stars once it gets good and dark."

"Can I take a bath first? It's been a long day."

"Tub's big enough for two."

"Such a tempting man, but you always were."

"I'll take that as a compliment."

"Still fishing, are you?"

He gave her a playful swat on the behind. And before either of them could think or speak, they were drowning in a slow kiss that reignited a passion so familiar and longed for they groaned from the pleasure it gave. Hands roamed and desire began its siren call. His mouth set fire to the skin of her throat while his palms moved over the tightened buds of her breasts and played until she moaned lowly. Lowering his head, he bit each pleading nipple through the thin cotton of her dress and she melted like butter in the sun.

"Let's go move Antonio."

Billie thought that a good idea but his hands and lips were so potent she didn't want to move.

He captured her mouth again. "Come on. Let's go."

But he couldn't seem to turn her loose. Her dress was rising up her legs and his hands were slowly mapping the bared length. He lovingly squeezed the flesh on the back of her thigh then circled a warm palm over the drawers encasing her hips.

Dazzled by this opening prelude, Billie followed blindly as he took her hand and led her back into her room. They kissed their way over to Tonio, then paused long enough for her to pick up their sleeping son and carry him out while Drew followed with the crib. They settled him in one of the smaller rooms and left the door ajar so they'd hear him if he cried.

Only then did they start their kiss-filled journey to the bathing room and his tub large enough for two.

For Billie the night was as memorable as their wedding night, only this time, there'd be no parting at sunrise. He brought her to her first orgasm while they waited for the tub to fill. "I plan to make you come for the rest of the night," he husked out against her ear while she stood shuddering in the steamy room with her back against the wall. Her dress was pooled at her waist, her bared nipples damp, and his wicked hands between her thighs made her hips rise greedily in scandalous delight.

"The next one will be in the tub . . ." he promised.

And the promise was kept. After washing her with an erotic slowness that nearly drove her mad, he coaxed her to stand and fit himself against her back. She raised her arms, braced her hands against the wall. He slowly introduced his splendid readiness from behind and she died and went to heaven. Later, she realized they could have slipped and broken their necks with their spirited intertwining, but at the time, she was too busy enjoying the decadent rhythms set by his powerful thrusts to worry about safety or the water that lay in puddles on the floor. Her entire existence was focused on being pleasured and giving him pleasure in return. When they finally collapsed, they slid into the tepid water remaining in the tub, then he dried her, carried her to his bed and the lovemaking continued.

As on their wedding night, he loved her tenderly. His kisses made her feel adored and his touch moved over her as if she were born of the finest silk. Their couplings had always been uninhibited and that coming together was no different. It was hot, raw, and filled with positioning lusty enough to make the Kama Sutra blush— positioning that had her panting one minute and him growling the next. Needless to say they enjoyed themselves.

Hours later, the sated and pulsating Mr. and Mrs. Yates slid into sleep, and when Tonio awakened at sunrise, Billie was still by her husband's side.

Struggling awake, Billie sat on the edge of the bed and willed herself to open her eyes. Nothing in the room seemed familiar and it took a few seconds for her dulled brain to assist her memory. Once it did she glanced over her shoulder at her gloriously nude husband entangled in the sheets and she smiled. *Lord what a night.* Tonio was in the other room talking to the sunbeams as he did each morning. She ran her hands over her still sleepy face. "Time to get up, Drew."

He didn't move. If anything the soft snoring became more intense. She chuckled. "Hey. You. Father. Our son's awake and it's time for his parents to report for duty."

He didn't move. She now understood where his son got his sound sleeping habits, but she'd be damned if Drew was going to be allowed to loll around until noon, as was his habit, while she got Tonio washed up and ready for the day. They'd only been asleep a few hours, and she refused to suffer alone. "Morning, Drew!" she yelled. Leaving the bed, she padded nude over to his armoire. The last time she saw the dress she'd worn last night it was lying on the wet floor of the bathing room. She looked through his things for a robe to cover herself. "It's a glorious day, Drew!"

From behind her, she heard a sleepy male voice grouse, "Woman, if you don't stop all that screeching."

"Your son's calling. Time for us to get up."

"What time is it?" he mumbled.

"Seven."

"In the morning!"

"Yes."

"Tell him to go back to sleep," and he huffed back beneath the sheets. Billie stuck her arms into a black velvet robe that was many sizes too large and tied the belt. Crossing her arms she studied his sprawled form. Truthfully, she couldn't force him to join her, and by society's standards it was her job as Tonio's mother to shoulder the lion's weight of his care, but being as untraditional as a woman of her times could be, she wasn't happy. "Fine," she said quietly and left him in the room.

Lying there, Drew wondered how one word could make him feel so damn guilty. *Fine.* Sighing with frustration he threw back the sheet and struggled up to a sitting position. It took several minutes to will himself to move and once he felt reasonably able to do so, he snatched a robe from the armoire and followed in her wake. That she and the baby were nowhere to be found made him even more testy, so he went down the hall to her room. His surly mood immediately melted under the smile Tonio shot him from his perch in his mother's arms. He kissed Billie on the cheek. "I'm not at my best in the morning, sorry."

Tonio seemed excited to see him, so he placed a kiss on his small brow. "Morning, son. You think you can let the roosters crow *before* you make us get up?"

Billie said to her happy son, "And I agree. Are you listening to your papa?"

There was a knock on the door. Drew turned to it in confusion. "Who is that?"

"Bonnie probably. She brings breakfast." He must have looked even more confused because she laughed. "This is what goes on while you're sleeping away the day, my lord."

He gave her a mock quelling look and walked over to open the door.

After breakfast, Billie took Tonio down for his morning visit with his *abuela* and Drew sat outside with a coffee and a cheroot still trying to recover from the early rising.

"What are you doing out here?"

It was Logan.

"What's it look like I'm doing?"

"Did I somehow lose track of the morning? No one ever sees you fancy types until at least noon."

Drew exhaled a stream of smoke. "Is there something you want, big brother?"

Logan sat. "Nope. Just wondering why you're up with us common folk."

He gave a one-word reply. "Antonio."

"Ah. Wake you up with the chickens, did he?"

Drew sighed.

"Maria does the same thing. Luckily for me, I'm usually up anyway. Sometimes I even take care of her so that 'Riah can sleep an extra few minutes or two. Puts feathers in my cap."

"Really?" Drew had never considered that before, but then he'd never had a wife and early-rising child before.

"Really."

"I'll keep that in mind. What're your plans today?"

"Fences to repair. Eli and I have to deliver a mare later." He quieted for a moment and studied Drew's face. "How's the fathering coming along?"

"Better. My getting up so damn early was my attempt to show her that I can be a good one."

"And the husband part?"

"A bit more complicated but we're pulling in the same direction, so hopefully it'll be easier from here on out. Took her out yesterday to see where I want to put the house."

"So you'll know, I apologized to her for not believing her story."

"Thanks. I'm sure she appreciated it. I'd like for you two to get along."

"I know, but she's no wilting violet, that's for sure."

A smile played over Drew's lips. "No, she's not."

He thought about last night and then paused as he was reminded of the threat posed by Prince Du-Chance. "Hoping DuChance will leave her alone, but I know he won't."

"He'd be stupid to come here, so maybe he's figured that out."

Drew wasn't convinced. He was determined not to obsess over what the man might or might not do. They had their guard up so if a confrontation developed, they'd deal with it appropriately. "You mentioned Eli. Why haven't I seen him?"

"He just returned from a trip to Texas. Went home to bury his father."

He and his brothers knew all about that. "How's he holding up?"

"He's keeping it to himself."

Drew understood. Sometimes men had difficulty with heartache. "He and Naomi ever work out their differences?" Naomi was a diner owner. Eli had been after her for years to marry him.

Logan shook his head. "No, but she's going to have to make a decision. He's talking about selling his stake in the business and moving back to Texas. I don't want to lose him but I understand. He wants to take care of his mother."

Drew wished Eli the best of luck, especially in his quest to coral the indomitable Miss Naomi Pearl. He knew all about trying to tame a prickly woman. "So will you help me with the building of the house?"

"Sure will. Just let me know when."

"Once I get with Max, I'll let you know. Glad Mama finally surrendered. Maybe now she'll stop playing us like Punch and Judy," he cracked.

"Hell will freeze over first." He peered into Drew's face. "Are you still mad with her?"

"No, but at the time I was angry at her and everything else. I probably should talk to her about that."

"Yeah, you should. I can tell by the way she's been watching you that she's concerned about where she stands."

"I'll take care of it as soon as I can. I don't want her worrying."

Logan stood. "Okay. I brought Maria over so 'Riah can finish up a sewing order she's working on. I'll see you later."

"Thanks for the tip about the feathers."

Logan chuckled. "That's what big brothers are for."

After his departure, Drew thought about what he wanted to say to his mother, and then resumed adjusting his mental faculties to getting up with Antonio and the chickens.

His mother was in the stables preparing for her morning ride. She paused at his approach. "Good morning, Drew. Have you recovered from your early rising?"

"Just about."

"What are your plans?"

"Thought maybe you'd like some company on your ride."

She studied him for a moment. "I'd enjoy that."

"Can you wait while I let Billie know I'll be gone for a bit?"

"Sure. She's going to watch Maria until I return. Being an *abuela* is wonderful but sometimes I need time alone. I'm grateful that she allows me that."

After informing Billie of his plan, he saddled his stallion and he and his mother rode away. He knew without asking where they were heading—to the river and the benches Max built for her after their father's death. It was the place where she went to sit, think, and be alone.

They dismounted and turned the horses loose, then sat and watched the river flow by. "I brought Billie and Tonio to the river yesterday. My plan was to show off my fishing skills and catch dinner, but I caught nothing."

She smiled. "We plan and God laughs."

"Apparently."

The silence grew for a moment and she said, "The last time I asked if you were angry at me, you didn't want to discuss it. Can we discuss it now?"

"Sure. I was furious, but you were right for all the reasons you stated that day—Antonio's future being the most important one."

"Logan said I'd gone too far this time and I worried that I had."

"You wouldn't be you if you weren't pulling the strings."

They shared a smile. "And you and Billie?" she asked.

"Better. I came down off my high horse to meet her halfway. Best thing I could've done."

"In spite of who she was before coming to us, she's very special. She so wants us to be proud of her, and you especially."

"I know. I'm trying to make her proud of me as well."

"That's a worthy goal."

He agreed.

"So, where do you plan to put the house?"

"Up on the bluff."

She looked upstream. The spot was just visible from where they sat. "You've talked about a house there since you were an adolescent."

"I know and now I can. Looking forward to it. Your sons are also looking forward to giving you away."

"With the hopes that I'll never return, I'll bet."

He laughed, then turned serious. "Max is a very lucky man. Glad you finally came to your senses and said yes."

"So am I. We'll do well together I believe. I believe you and Billie will do well together, too."

"We're trying, is all I'll say for now. Your acceptance has gone a long way in helping her settle in, and there're no words for how grateful I am."

She patted his hand. "That's what mamas do."

And with that, they let the silence rise.

Chapter 17

For the rest of the morning, Drew hung around the house. He played with Antonio and Little Maria and lusted silently for his wife. Mariah appeared just before lunch and arrived bearing gifts.

"These are for you, Billie." While everyone looked on, the skeptical-looking Billie took what appeared to be a large stack of folded garments from her sister-in-law's arms. As she unfolded three new skirts and blouses, the skepticism melted under the emotion forged by Mariah's generosity.

"Thanks so much," Billie whispered while hugging her tight. Drew saw tears in her eyes.

"I know you haven't had time to do any shopping, so I made you some things to wear until you do," Mariah explained.

"Is this so I'll return all the clothes I've had to borrow?"

The women laughed. Drew could've kissed

his sister-in-law, and was glad she'd put up with Logan enough to marry him.

Billie caught his eye and pointed to her eyes. "Happy tears, Drew."

"I know."

The sisters-in-law shared a final hug and Mariah departed with her smiling daughter in tow.

Billie looked down at the bounty and said, "This was nice of her."

Alanza said, "It's what family is supposed to do."

"So I'm learning."

Max came by after lunch, and while he and Alanza visited, Drew went upstairs with Billie to put Antonio down for his nap. Just as she'd predicted, he didn't go willingly. He cried and wailed. He tried to climb out. She put him back in gently. "It's time for your nap, Tonio."

The crying continued. Finally, she kissed him on his wet cheek, covered him and walked out of the room. A startled Drew followed. She closed the door. Behind it Antonio wailed as if he were dying.

"You're just going to let him cry?"

"Yes."

The sound was breaking Drew's heart. He turned to the door.

"Don't."

The censure in her gaze and tone stopped him cold and he unconsciously released his hold on the doorknob.

"He needs to sleep," she explained. "His belly's full. His bottom's dry and nothing is hurting him. Let him cry."

"But—"

"Toughen up, Drew. At first, it killed me, too, when I began training him to sleep on his own, but it was either that or have a cranky whiney little boy on my hands for the rest of the day."

Wails continued to come through the door.

She added reassuringly, "He's gotten very good at falling asleep at night, but he still fights the afternoon. He'll settle down in a few minutes."

Drew wanted to ask how and where mothers learned such things, but he sensed himself on the verge of trouble with her already, so instead he stood there silently. A few minutes later: silence. Surprise filled his eyes.

"See?" she said softly. "He can rest, and now, so can we."

"Really?" Drew asked waggling his brows.

She laughed. "Not that kind of rest. I usually read while he's asleep."

"You're no fun at all."

"That isn't what you said last night."

"And you didn't tell me no last night."

Their amusement mingled. Drew surrendered. "All right. You read. I'll go and see if Max is done sweet-talking my mother so I can speak with him about the house."

She kissed him on the cheek. "Thanks."

As she headed for his library, he watched the sway of her skirts, thought about the silken hips beneath and shook his head. She was temptation personified. Lucky for him she was all his.

Billie took down the trove of magazines she'd borrowed from Alanza and Mariah and chose a recent issue of *Frank Leslie's Illustrated Newspaper*. The shortened name was *Leslie's Weekly* and she preferred to call it that. According to Alanza, Mr. Leslie died in 1880 and his second wife, Miriam, now edited the paper. Miriam was a suffragette and a celebrated writer in her own right who legally changed her name to Frank Leslie after her husband's demise in order to keep the paper afloat. Inside was a reader's delight of serialized fiction, illustrations, and articles on everything from news to sports to the latest stage plays touring the country. Billie found the offerings extremely helpful in her quest to refine her reading and they kept her abreast of the world's current events. Picking up an issue she hadn't finished during her last session, she settled in and began.

Over the next few days, Billie wondered how her life could be more perfect. Her roses were in bloom, filling the eye with their lovely colors and the air with their beautiful scent. Mariah was taken with the mauve damasks planted by her house. She made Billie promise to plant more for next year. Antonio was thriving under the spoiling love of his *abuela*, and she and Drew were thriving as well. She was enjoying this version of her husband; he was more like the Drew she'd known back in San Francisco and less like the angry man on their wedding day. The morning before he'd actually gotten up with Antonio to see to his needs which allowed her to sleep a blessed thirty minutes longer! He was attentive, funny, and stellar in the bedroom. Outside of the bedroom she was seeing less and less of him, however. Max worked up the drawings for their house and a crew of hired men were already at work leveling the ground. Drew was so busy ordering supplies and handling logistics during the daylight hours that the only time she saw him was when she and Tonio drove out to the site to check the progress.

Another perfect element had to with her reading. On the nights when Drew wasn't too tired from work or from making love to her, he'd taken up reading to her again—mostly the Queen Calafia stories, but she never tired of them or him taking the time to make their evenings special and help with her goal of self-improvement.

One morning, as she casually leafed through a week-old San Francisco newspaper picked up by Logan on his visit to town the day before, her life soured. "Have either of you read through this paper yet?" she asked Mariah and Alanza. The children were playing on the floor nearby.

Mariah shook her head. Alanza must've heard something in her voice. "Not yet. Is something wrong?"

"What's Rosaline's mother's Christian name?"

"Emmalina. Why?"

"According to this, she's dead. The police think she was killed during a robbery at her home."

"Oh, my. I never cared for her but I certainly didn't wish her such an awful end. May I see that?"

She handed it over and as Alanza read through the short notice, Billie saw her shake her head sadly. "Her servant was killed, too. It says no next of kin could be found, so her church took care of the burial. That's so sad."

Mariah asked, "Billie, do you know if Drew's heard anything from Rosa?"

"He hasn't and he's worried she and the others may have run into trouble." He'd shared his concerns the night before.

Alanza's lips tightened. "We'll pray that good

word comes soon." She handed the paper back to Billie and while the children alternately played and bickered over the wealth of toys at their command, and Mariah worked her embroidery hoop, she resumed reading. The stories about all the places and goings-on in the city that was so familiar made her a tad homesick. Although she'd come to enjoy the slow pace and the quiet the ranch offered, parts of her still dearly missed the hustle and bustle San Francisco was noted for. She turned the page. Nearly buried at the bottom beneath a bevy of advertisements for everything from tooth powders to prostitutes were two items that made her hand fly to her mouth.

"Now what?" Alanza asked.

"The woman I stayed with after I left Pearl's died in a fire. The police said there was a strong smell of kerosene so they believe it was arson."

"Who would want to do something like that?"

Billie knew of only one person, and her heart ached at the thought that she might have been the reason for Addy's untimely death. *Mine will come by fire . . .*

Alanza peered at her with concern. "Are you all right?"

Billie shook off the memory. "Yes. The news just took me by surprise. Addy gave me a place to live, and in return never asked for anything more than my delivering her medicines every now and then. She didn't deserve this."

Mariah said, "I'm so sorry, Billie. Maybe the police will find the culprit."

Billie hoped so even as the words in the second item screamed for notice.

Alanza's voice distracted her momentarily. "Do you think this DuChance may have had something to do with the fire?"

"I do. Now that he knows where I am, he's probably figured out she helped me escape. It's curious that both Addy and Rosa's mother died on the same day."

Mariah asked, "Is he that callous?"

Billie nodded. "Yes, Mariah. He is."

Worry filled their faces. Billie took in her son idyllically and knew she'd kill Prince without a thimble of guilt if he threatened the life of her child. "And then, there's this." She read the second item aloud and watched their eyes widen and their jaws drop.

In the bedroom later that evening, an outraged Drew looked up from the newspaper and into his wife's eyes. "Who would plant this?" Filled with disbelief he read it again:

PROMINENT LAWYER ANDREW YATES FLEES AHEAD OF SCANDAL SURROUNDING FATHERING CHILD WITH INFAMOUS BARBARY WHORE

"Only one person I know of."

"I agree. And reading that Emmalina and Addy died within hours of each other makes me think he may have had a hand in their deaths as well."

"Considering Emmalina owed him money and Addy helped me . . ."

He slapped the paper with his hand. "But this is bullshit." Drew noticed the distance and unhappiness in her manner and set the newspaper aside, eased her into his arms and held her tight. "We knew this smearing might happen."

"Yes, but I've been so happy lately I guess I was hoping it wouldn't."

That she'd confessed her happiness brought a small smile to his lips. "Are you happy?"

"More than I've ever been in my life."

He placed a soft kiss on her brow. "Then we'll not let this spoil things. We'll simply hold on until it blows over."

Emotion chiseled her jaw. "I will kill Prince if he harms Tonio."

Drew looked down into her deadly serious eyes and a chill crossed his soul. He pulled her close again and whispered against her hair. "Let's hope it won't come to that."

In San Francisco, Prince set his copy of the same newspaper aside and smiled. He could just about imagine Yates's reaction. Since most well-heeled members of society read the newspaper, and Yates considered himself part and parcel of that class, there was no doubt in Prince's mind that the short notice would come to his attention eventually. The reporter who'd arranged to place the item in print was a regular customer at the Pearl and always hungry for salacious gossip involving the well known. Granted, such stories about men and women of color were generally ignored by the city's white citizens, but Yates traveled in high places and a scandal tied to his name would draw at least a few raised eyebrows.

Prince removed his black bowler and gloves. His mother went to her death yesterday afternoon, and he'd just returned from the cemetery. She was no longer in pain and he was grateful for that and for the surety that all she owned would now become his to inherit. Adding her small empire to his many pies would only give a small boost to his Barbary reputation, but her money . . . Bordello owners were often extremely wealthy and his mother had been no exception. His meeting with her banker to get a full accounting was set for the next day. Once that was accomplished he'd pay a visit on an old friend. He needed pawns in the chess game he was playing with Yates and the person he had in mind was a perfect choice to aid his quest for the Yates queen and her child. It pained him to have to return the fee paid by the original couple but fortunately, he'd found another to take their place and he had no intentions of letting them down.

The next day, a messenger arrived at Destiny with a wire for Drew. It was the long-awaited news from Rosa and he tore it open excitedly. The contents made him breathe a sigh of relief. They'd made it safely to his great-aunt Felicity in Monterey, but hadn't been able to send word due to the telegraph wires being downed by a storm.

The messenger asked, "Is there a reply, Mr. Yates?"

"Yes, give me a moment to write it down." He hurried into his mother's study and his steps slowed to a stop at the sight of Billie walking the floor with a large book on her head.

"Your mother said this will improve my posture," she replied in response to his puzzled look.

"And it's a very simple method," Alanza added.

He had to admit he enjoyed the way her breasts rose into prominence due to the straightening of her shoulders and spine. He wondered if he could get her to practice that nude and for his eyes only. Shaking off the delicious imagery, he forced himself to remember his purpose in entering.

"That's wonderful," his mother gushed after he shared the news.

Billie took the book from her head. "Do you think she knows about her mother's death?"

He'd been so pleased with hearing from them, he'd totally forgotten about Emmalina. "I've no way of knowing. That's not news one should receive by something as impersonal as a wire."

"True, but she needs to be told."

"Billie's right," Alanza said. "And such terrible news might be better coming from us than, say, reading it in the newspaper."

He agreed. So he composed a short message. As he wrote, Alanza added, "Let her know that I'll send a wire to her mother's church and ask about the burial. She'll probably want to return to San Francisco and pay her respects at the gravesite, but she shouldn't. It's too dangerous for her there. I'll pay whatever monies the church is owed."

"Thank you, Mama. That's a grand gesture. Rosa has a sister somewhere. I wonder if she knows? I've not an inkling as to how to reach her."

"We'll concern ourselves with Rosa for now. Tell her we will wire her again as soon as we learn more, and that for her own safety she should stay with Felicity in Monterey."

"She might ignore that advice."

"That's understandable, but I hope she'll weigh

both sides and choose to remain out of Du-Chance's reach."

Billie added, "And Drew, you probably shouldn't mention that Emmalina was murdered. Knowing her mother is dead will be hard enough. Being told she was murdered will only break her heart all the more."

He was touched by her wisdom and whole-heartedly agreed.

After dinner, Drew drove his wife and son out to the construction site to view the progress being made on their home. Once they arrived, Tonio was being his wiggly self and wanted to get off the wagon and run around, but with all the bar-rels and wood piled everywhere, neither parent thought that a good idea.

Drew was still thinking about Billie's wise counsel. "Not many women would worry about the feelings of their husband's ex-*novia* the way you did. Says a lot about you, Billie."

"I figure she still holds your heart, and truth-fully what I said could be for anyone grieving. Why are you looking at me that way?"

"You think I'm in love with Rosa?"

"Aren't you?"

"No."

"But you were going to marry her."

"I was, but not out of love."

She adjusted their squirming son on her lap, all the while viewing Drew with confusion.

"I asked her to be my wife because she was of good family and we got along reasonably well."

"So it wasn't a love match."

He shook his head. "I was basically settling for her as a wife, to be truly honest."

"She was so lovely and elegant. I just assumed."

She looked away and he would've given every dime he had to know what was going through her mind at that moment. His feelings for her ran far deeper than they ever had for Rosaline. Much more complex as well. Did he love her? He was pretty sure he did, and looked forward to a future together that would be free of the looming specter of DuChance. And who knew, maybe the day would come when she'd love him as well. "How about we get down and I show you what we've done since your last visit."

"I'd like that and so would he." As always, Tonio wanted to be on his feet.

He came around to help her down. "Here, I'll take him."

She gave him over gladly and they walked towards the building site. They'd decided on three bedrooms, a large kitchen, parlor and an office for Drew. He was having difficulty getting her to agree to two bathing rooms, however.

"Two seems so extravagant, Drew."

"You won't think so when this one gets to be about nine and you're sharing that one room with him. I grew up with two brothers. As soon as Alanza could afford to, she added our wing and our own bathing room so she could take a bath in peace."

"Never thought about it in those terms. Okay, two it is."

The leveling had been accomplished. Support posts were in place and standing tall. "We'll be putting the roof on this weekend. Usually people here invite the men in area to help with that, and they bring their families and everybody visits, eats, and has a good time.

"Is that what you're planning to do?"

"Yes, but if knowing people that have probably seen the notice in the paper makes you wish to stay away, I'll understand."

"I'll be fine. As long as you're willing to face them, I can too."

"Good girl. I believe Mama's going to announce her engagement to Max during the gathering as well."

"Hopefully folks will pay more attention to that."

They continued their tour of the site and she asked, "What did Max say about the sitting porches I suggested?"

"Said he'd build one on the roof if it made you happy."

She liked Max and was looking forward to knowing him better. "Having one on each side of the house suits me fine."

Billie kept wanting to pinch herself to make sure she wasn't dreaming. She had a good man, his wonderful family, a thriving child, and now, a house of her own. Last year at that time, Tonio was still the infant she was supposed to be turning over to Prince on his first birthday. She never imagined this new life would be waiting instead.

"Penny for your thoughts."

"Just thinking how amazed I am by everything that's happened in the past year." She was also amazed by his admitting not having loved Rosaline. She wondered how he'd respond if she confessed her own true feelings. Not that she'd ever do something so dumb, for fear it would wreck everything they'd built so far, but still . . . "Thank you for everything, Drew—for Tonio, and this life you've given us, and your kindness."

"You're welcome and you don't have to keep thanking me."

"But you didn't have to do this—any of it."

He drew her into his arms as best he could while holding the baby and placed a kiss on her brow. "Thank you for coming into my life and giving me a son."

He slipped his hand around her waist and they headed back to the wagon.

That evening, as she sat on the verandah watching the blood-red dying sun, she let her mind drift back over the day. She was glad Drew finally heard from Rosa. According to all accounts the mother had not been a nice woman but no one deserved to be murdered. She hoped the young woman would find peace down the road. As for Drew's words on why he'd proposed marriage to someone he hadn't loved, she supposed she shouldn't be surprised. Arranged marriages were quite common especially among the wealthy, she just hadn't figured him for a man who'd settled. *Yet he'd settled for you* came the thought. Luckily for her, he stepped out to join her at that moment and her thoughts fled.

"Antonio is in bed and sound asleep."

"Hallelujah. His parents survive to fight another day."

He sat beside her. "He's a handful. Never knew babies could be so intense."

"Neither did I."

"He's already showing who he's going to be."

"Yes. *Quite* the handful."

He draped his arm over her shoulder and she melted into his side as if they'd been sitting next to each other in just that way their entire lives. The kiss he placed against her brow felt the same.

"Does a man tell his wife he loves her even if he's unsure whether she loves him in return?"

She sat up straight and her jaw dropped.

"Not the right thing to ask?"

"Um—I'm a bit speechless."

He withdrew his arm. "Sorry."

"Oh no you don't, Drew Yates." She leaned back against him and repositioned his arm. "We're having this conversation."

He laughed and looked down into her eyes. "My son's a handful because his mama is."

"Thanks for the compliment."

"Come here." He dragged her onto his lap. She settled in with her cheek against his heartbeat. "You were saying," she prompted saucily.

"You're going to be spanked in a minute, missy."

"Promises, promises."

His soft chuckle reverberated beneath her ear. He looked down at her, and in a voice as quiet as the gathering night, said, "I love you, Mina."

Tears sprouted out of nowhere at hearing his name for her, and she said, "Then I suppose now's the time for me to say I love you, too. And I have for a real long time, but I couldn't tell you though."

"Why not?"

"It would've mucked things up."

He nodded understandingly. "It won't muck things up now."

Then she was being kissed with an intensity that touched her soul. The past didn't matter and neither did the future, only the present where he tasted her tears with soft brushes of his lips and she held him close enough to breathe into her heart. Later, when they made love, it wasn't their usual spirited, bordering-on-acrobatic coming together. Instead they gifted each other with an interlude that was slow and sweet as a Spanish guitar. He worshipped her as if she were the most precious thing in his world. His kisses enchanted. His touch enthralled. The feel of him inside her— magnificent. And when they finally collapsed against each other for the last time, he pulled her close and whispered, "I love you, Mina."

"I love you, too, Drew."

It was a night Billie would remember for the rest of her life.

Chapter 18

To Billie's surprise when she and Mariah drove to the construction site early Saturday morning there were already scores of men moving over the house like ants. The air recoiled with the sounds of hammering and shouting. Lumber was being toted, ladders were everywhere and the workers were climbing up and down going about their tasks. She spied Drew up on the open spine of the roof working beside his brother Logan nailing in beams and Max walking around calling out orders and being in charge.

"How long will it take?" she asked Mariah, who'd gotten down from the wagon and stood waiting for Billie to pass her her daughter.

"All day. By the looks of it your place is going to be pretty good size, so it may be nightfall before they're done."

A multitude of people of all races—Black, Spanish, White, Native—were descending on the meadow driving buggies, wagons, and coaches, and unloading food, tools, children of varying ages. She even saw a man carrying a fiddle and another a trumpet.

"There'll be music, too?" the laughing Billie asked as she and Tonio walked with Mariah and Little Maria through the grass. Having never been to a community event such as this one, she found everything new.

"Yes, and ice cream, and sack races, and so much food we'll have to waddle home."

Billie saw eyes following their progress and wondered if any of them had seen the article in the paper. She and Mariah had discussed the possibility on the ride over.

"Are you ready?" Mariah asked.

"Ready as I'll ever be. For Drew and Alanza's sake, I'm hoping no one will be out and out nasty, though." Billie planned to ignore any slurs thrown her way, but anyone denigrating her child would be in for a fight.

"There may be a few who'll be unkind, but I doubt they'll have the guts to say anything within earshot."

The air was sweet with the smells of roasting pigs and beef, and alive with the high-pitched squeals of children's laughter. There were men shaking hands and women hugging and rocking as if reveling with an old friend. In spite of the way some people continued to pause to watch her pass, Billie was looking forward to the day.

Amanda Foster, with her pigeonlike shape, waved and beckoned them over. When they reached her side she gave both women a hug. "Billie, my roses are absolutely stunning."

"I'm glad."

"Was the notice in the paper the truth?"

Billie didn't hesitate. "Yes."

"Just wanted to hear it from you. Some of the women won't be continuing with their lessons."

"Sorry to hear that."

"Well, I hope they get eaten by bears. You saved my husband's life. I plan to call you friend until the Good Lord takes me home."

She drew Billie into another hug and said with fierce emotion, "Don't let anyone tell you you aren't a good person. You hear me?"

"Yes, ma'am."

"Good, now go have fun."

A buoyed Billie and Mariah walked on.

In the grass adjacent to the building site, but far enough removed not to be in the way of the workers, people had set down blankets and pallets to claim their spots for the day. Behind them were four long trestle tables groaning with food and a bevy of women buzzing around them. Billie spied

Bonnie standing with Alanza who, dressed in her ever-present divided skirt and boots, appeared to be spearheading the work. Seeing her daughters-in-law approach brought on a smile and she beckoned them to her side. There was curiosity in the eyes of some of the women. Others gave Billie a critical once-over. While Mariah shared a hug with a beautiful dark-skinned woman, Alanza announced, "Ladies, I want you to meet my newest *nuera*. Drew's wife, Billie."

The woman who'd shared the hug with Mariah stepped right up. "Welcome, Billie. I'm Naomi Pearl. Pleased to meet you."

"Thanks. Same here."

"I own the diner in town, so if you like pie I have a piece with your name on it." Naomi eyed Tonio, who seemed unsure about all the people and noise and was clinging close to his mother. "And who might this handsome gentleman be?"

"This is my son, Antonio."

Naomi stroked his cheek. "How many hearts have you broken just this morning, Antonio?"

He gave her a big smile and reached out.

"May I?" Naomi asked Billie.

"Sure. Just be careful of your earrings. He likes to grab."

So while Antonio conquered yet another woman's heart, Billie met the women around the table. Among them was Lucy Redwood, a Native woman who greeted her warmly. "So glad to meet you, Billie."

"Thank you."

"My daughter Green Feather is Logan's god-child. She's back East attending Hampton Institute in Virginia."

"That's a long way from home. Bet you're missing her."

"I am, but we're so very proud."

Alanza continued the introductions. There was Eliza Gail, the town postmistress, who used a cane to get around. She sniffed at Billie and stalked off, earning a glare from Alanza, who next introduced Jenna Lane, a cook at Naomi's diner, and then BiBi Crane, the new schoolteacher. The two women nodded a greeting. Next came tall, sneering, Felicity Deeb, who after being introduced offered no greeting, nor did she even pretend to be polite. "Alanza, surely you don't expect us women of high moral standards to break bread with an *adventuress*. I read the piece in the paper."

Billie tensed.

Alanza responded, "Then you should probably have Jim take you home, Felicity."

Felicity looked surprised.

"You will not slur my family to my face, on my

own land!" Alanza snapped. "Where were you raised?"

Billie saw muted smugness play across the lips of Mariah and Naomi.

Felicity sputtered, "Well, I just—"

"Go home, Felicity. Find your husband and spare the rest of us your high moral standards."

Billie certainly didn't need Alanza to fight her battles but she admittedly enjoyed the woman being put in her place.

Felicity shot Billie a glare of blazing hostility, which she met emotionlessly. The angry woman turned to the group as if seeking support, but when she didn't receive any, she stalked off. Billie wondered how many of the others shared Felicity's opinion and were simply too afraid of incurring Alanza's wrath to speak up, but she decided she didn't much care. This was her home now and they could accept her or not.

Alanza didn't seem to care either. "Where were we?"

The group resumed their tasks around the tables. Naomi walked over to Billie and handed Antonio back to her. "He is so precious."

Billie agreed and kissed his chubby little cheek.

Naomi asked, "Can you and I be friends, Billie?"

"Sure."

"Good, because with you as a friend, I may never have to endure Felicity's high moral presence again."

Billie laughed and Naomi sauntered away.

Having to keep a close eye on Tonio prevented Billie from helping with much, so Alanza took him for a bit and Billie jumped in. The woman who'd been introduced as Jenna Lane was at a far table alone setting out desserts so she made her way over there. "Can I help?"

"Sure. Can you put that cake there."

Billie complied and asked, "So, how long have you been working with Naomi, Wanda?"

She stilled, then added another cake to the table. "I wondered if you remembered me."

"I do. Been a few years, though." They'd worked together at the Pearl but one day, Wanda was gone. It wasn't uncommon for girls to drift away, but she'd given no notice as far as Billie knew and she remembered wondering if something had happened to her. Back in those days, Wanda Russell had been bright and brassy. Viewing her now in her mud-colored dress and pulled-back hair, one would never connect the two. Billie looked down at her own sedate garb and supposed the same could be said of herself.

"I've worked for Naomi about a year. Was real

surprised to see you. Thanks for not letting on that you knew me."

"You're welcome, but why a new name?"

"Started a new life. My man doesn't know anything about who I was before, and I want to keep it that way."

"He won't learn it from me."

"Thanks. You fell into some pretty high cotton—marrying into all this, I mean."

"Yes. Drew's a good man. Known him a while."

"I remember. We girls envied you back then."

"So, are you and your man married? Do you have children?"

"Yes. A son. He's almost four now. He's sitting over with a neighbor. Name's Benjamin, after my father. I had him after I left the Pearl. Was passing myself off as a widow when I met my husband, Curtis. He works for the railroad and he's gone a lot, but he's a good man."

Billie saw Alanza waving her back. "I need to go see what she wants. Take care of yourself, Jenna."

"I will and thanks for keeping my secret."

"You're welcome."

Billie retrieved her wiggly son and went to find Mariah. Bumping into Wanda was surprising but Billie would keep her word and not give her away. Everyone deserved a second shot at life.

As the morning wound down the number of people in the meadow seemed to have grown tenfold. Children were having foot races, tossing balls and carrying fishing poles down to the river. Some of the littler ones were in tears over injuries incurred, while older siblings were quietly scolded for inappropriate behavior. Billie was sitting with Lucy Redwood and trying to keep Antonio from wandering off when Mariah walked up toting Maria. "The baby jail is ready, finally."

Billie was puzzled. "Baby jail?"

"Yes. Grab Tonio and come on."

The baby jail turned out to be a wooden penlike structure where the mothers of little ones could deposit them. It was large enough to hold an army of toddlers and stocked with enough playthings to keep them happy until the new year. Several adolescents girls were being paid a few pennies to watch over them so the mothers could visit, help out, and not worry. Billie thought it was a splendid idea. Her only worry was whether Antonio would actually allow her to leave him there. The only other child in his world was his cousin Maria, so she wasn't sure how he'd do among so many others but she put him inside. He stood there looking around a moment at the half dozen children his size, glanced up at her for a second, smiled, and toddled off after a ball. Maria was right behind him. Relief filled her. She didn't plan to leave him for an extended period of time, just long enough to catch her breath and take a walk over to the construction site to get a look at her new home and her husband.

The hammers continued to ring. The roof was looking more complete and the house was now almost totally enclosed.

"Hello, Mrs. Yates."

She turned to see Reverend Paul Dennis standing beside her. "How are you, Reverend?"

"Doing well and so are the roses. Thank you so much for your charity."

"You're welcome."

For a moment he stood and looked at the work going on. "Quite the house."

"I agree. Although all this hammering is making my head ache."

"Be over soon." He paused for a moment then asked, "May I broach a delicate subject?"

She shrugged. "Sure. Is it about the piece in the newspaper?"

He paused again, met her cool eyes, and nodded. "Yes."

"Broach away then."

"I just wanted to let you know that you are welcome at the church."

"Are you trying to save my soul?"

He smiled. "Not too cynical, are you?"

"I am who I am, Reverend."

"Although we reverends are in the soul-saving business, I was extending an invitation just to let you know you're welcome."

"Appreciate that. Not sure how some of your flock's going to feel about it, but thanks for the invite, and having the guts to offer one."

He chuckled softly. "You're welcome." Inclining his head politely, he moved on.

She threaded her way through the blankets and families until she was close enough to the house to see her husband. He was on the ground huddling over the drawing with Eli, Logan, and Max. As if sensing her presence, he glanced up, and the smile he sent hit her heart like an arrow from Cupid. He said something to his companions and walked over to her.

"Having a good time?" The hammering suddenly stopped and relief flooded her ears.

"I am. Our house looks to be coming along."

He glanced up at it. "Yes it is, though we still have a long way to go still. Where's the son?"

"Baby jail."

He laughed.

"And while he's serving time I thought I'd come and say hello." She ignored the interest they were receiving from the people nearby.

"Folks treating you okay?"

"Yes. No one's been overly rude. Although your mother did ask Felicity Deeb to leave. Seems she didn't wish to break bread with an adventuress because of her high moral standing."

"She's a bitch."

"I figured that out." People were still staring. "All these eyes make me feel like an attraction at the circus."

"Me too."

They saw Logan waving at Drew. "I need to get back. I'll see you when we break for lunch, which better be soon. I'm starving."

He hurried away and Billie headed back to break Tonio out of jail. On the way, Eileen Jackson, one of the ladies who'd been taking the gun lessons, pointedly turned her back when Billie passed near. Billie ignored her.

Lunch was an orderly madhouse as people lined up to help themselves to the tables and tables of food. The workers were allowed to eat first, so wives took plates over to the site while other men like Logan and Drew got their own plates and sat down with their families. Naomi came over to join them.

Once everyone there had plates and seats, Alanza and Max stood up in the middle of the gathering and called out. "May I have your attention please. Max and I—"

Before she could utter another word, applause erupted and many people jumped to their feet cheering and hooting. It swelled, gained momentum, and someone yelled at them, "About time!" And "Who's wearing the pants!" and "How much did she have to pay you, Max!"

The laughing Alanza lowered her head as if outdone by all the teasing. Max was laughing as well. He then threw an arm around her waist, bent her back and kissed her long and hard. The meadow erupted. When he finally turned her loose, she looked stunned.

The laughing Drew said, "I don't think she's ever been kissed that way before."

Logan said, "Let's hope she doesn't take a bull-whip to him."

Mariah cracked, "She'll have to figure out where she is first."

"She does look pretty woozy," Naomi pointed out.

Billie had to agree. Her very formidable mother-in-law appeared to be a bit unsteady on her pins. She thought it wonderful that Alanza had found love at her stage in life. Max seemed to be just what she needed, and he obviously wasn't afraid of her at all.

When the crowd finally quieted and she'd gathered herself again, Alanza added that the wedding would be held during her annual birthday celebration later in the summer, and that everyone was invited.

Billie was stunned at the announcement. "She's inviting everyone here!"

Drew drawled. "May as well. She always invites half of creation anyway."

"No one gives a birthday party the way she does," Mariah added. "And it lasts at least three days."

She'd never heard of such a thing. She hadn't minded the small group of neighbors that attended Tonio's and Maria's birthday, but for Billie birthdays had never been anything to put on the dog for. She acknowledged it when she got up in the morning, then got on with her day. She wondered when Drew's birthday was.

A bit later, while people were enjoying their ice cream and other desserts, Eli Braden walked to the spot in the clearing Max and Alanza had occupied earlier and in a loud voice called out Naomi's name.

Everyone looked her way but her response was, "Eli Braden can kiss my grits."

Billie spit punch and grabbed a napkin to wipe her mouth.

Mariah said, "Now, Naomi."

"Don't now Naomi me."

Logan said, "You're bad as Alanza."

"Hush," she advised giving him a smoking glare.

"Hushing," he replied, grinning.

"How long are you going to punish him?" Mariah asked her. "Eli loves you, and quiet as it's kept, you love him, too." Naomi opened her mouth to dispute that but Mariah stopped her. "Lie, and lightning will strike you dead."

Naomi closed her mouth.

Billie sure wished she knew what this was all about but was having too much fun to interrupt and ask.

Logan said, "He's still waiting for you."

Lips tight, Naomi viewed the standing Eli as if weighing her decision. She finally let out an audible exasperated sigh and got to her feet. "Okay." She strode off.

"Will someone please tell me what this is about?" Billie asked.

Logan explained. "A few years back when Eli was courting Naomi, she found out he had a few other women he was paying court to as well, so she gave him the boot. He tried to get her back by making her jealous and brought another woman with him to eat at her diner."

"Didn't go well, I'll bet."

Mariah interrupted, "From what I heard from

Naomi, no. Apparently men don't think these things through real well."

"Hey!" Logan and Drew protested in unison.

She grinned but ignored them.

Logan took up the tale again, "Anyway, Eli's lady friend decided she'd gloat a bit, and when Naomi came to take their order, she said, 'Naomi, you might want to quit sampling your pies honey, otherwise you're going to have to widen the doors.'"

Billie's eyes went big. "What did Naomi say?"

"It wasn't what she said, it's what she did. She went in the back and got a pail of dishwater. She poured half of the dirty contents on the woman's head and the other half on Eli's."

Billie stared and then laughed.

Logan added, "He had on his best suit, too. Never was able to wear it again."

Drew chuckled. "The course of love never runs smooth, or something like that." He turned to his son sitting in his lap, "If you see a woman coming with dishwater, run, okay?"

Billie grinned.

Meanwhile, up in the circle, whatever Eli was saying to Naomi was too quiet for anyone to hear, but he was on one knee and Naomi's stern face was now soft with tears. He handed her a small box that she opened and then cried harder.

Mariah whispered, "Aww. So sweet. How come you didn't propose to me on one knee?"

Logan gave her a look. "Fooling with you, I only had one knee, remember?"

Drew laughed so hard at the comment Billie thought he might hurt himself. Once again she was left in the dark.

Mariah leaned over and whispered in her ear, "I kicked him in the knee the day we met."

"Ah."

However the smile he beamed at his wife was filled with love, so apparently the incident was now a source of amusement.

Next they knew Eli was imitating Max and kissing Naomi in front of God and everybody. Once again cheers rang out across the meadow.

"Now, who's looking woozy?" Mariah asked laughing. "Isn't love wonderful?"

Billie's eyes met Drew's. "Yes it is."

By the time evening rolled around people were packing up to head home. Hugs of good-bye were shared and children and families were rounded up. Billie saw Jenna Lane walking with a woman and a young boy she assumed to be her Benjamin. Jenna waved and Billie waved in return. She didn't know if their reconnecting today would evolve into a friendship but she wished Wanda well.

Drew and the workers were calling it a day, too, so carrying her worn-out son, she went to meet him. As she was walking, she ran into Bonnie. They stopped and spoke for a moment about what a good time everyone had. Bonnie then reached into the pocket of her skirt and withdrew an envelope. "With all the goings on, I forgot to give you this wire. Messenger delivered it earlier."

"Thanks."

While Bonnie walked on Billie opened the wire and read: **SOON.** P. DuChance.

A chill coursed through her and she was left shaken by the unexpected warning. It had been sent to both frighten and intimidate and had done its job well. She drew in a breath and stuck the warning in her pocket. With her hate for Prince rekindled she went to find her husband.

Chapter 19

After the departure of the workers and their families, Alanza sat with Max on the bench overlooking the river. He had his arm draped over the back of the seat. His nearness rendered her as nervously aware of him as a young girl with her *novio*.

"It was a good day," he said.

"Yes, it was."

"How'd folks treat Billie?"

"Very well for the most part. There were a few gawkers, and I had to ask Felicity Deeb to leave. She said her moral standards were too high to associate with an adventuress, as she called Billie."

"I saw her and Jim arguing, but didn't know what it was about, or much care considering who it was. Jim looked livid when she stormed off toward the road. I could tell he didn't want to follow, but he had no choice. She wears the pants and everyone knows it."

"He's going to be even more livid when he's not invited to the wedding because I don't want Felicity there."

"Fine with me."

Jim Deeb was the former head of the cattlemen's association. When he lost the office to Logan a bit over a year ago, he threw his hat in the ring for mayor. Alanza doubted he'd be voted in due to his penchant for taking bribes, the main reason why the cattlemen relieved him of his gavel.

"Speaking of choices: Where are we going to live?" Max asked.

"I assumed you'd move into the house with me."

"Did you now?"

"No?"

"I suppose I could. Be nice if we had a place of our own."

"Soon as Drew and Billie move into their house, it will be our own."

He glanced her way and then turned back to the water.

"What?" she asked.

"I'm building us a bed."

"I have a bed."

"And how long has it been in your family?"

"I'm not sure. It originally belonged to my mother."

"We're not having our wedding night in your mother's bed."

"Oh."

He chuckled softly.

"What's so funny?"

"You, my love. I feel like I'm marrying someone who should have a duenna nearby."

"I've had two children, Max Rudd."

"I know that and this is not a swipe at Abe but have you ever screamed in bed? From pleasure, I mean."

"Screamed? Of course not. I did my duty and Abe was very tender and respectful but there was never any screaming involved. Why would there be?"

"Because sometimes the pleasure can be so much you have to let it out."

She stared at him, confused. "What are you talking about?"

He traced her cheek. "Nothing, Lanz. We'll talk about it on the wedding night."

Alanza knew she was missing something but had no idea what it was. She sensed he was amused by her and she wasn't sure what her response should be other than storming off, but she set that aside.

"Didn't mean to get you upset."

"I'm not upset."

He leaned close and brushed his lips softly against hers. "Yeah, you are . . ."

Every inch of her body fluttered in response. She'd never had a man do to her what he was doing to her; never had her lips coaxed with such sweet softness, or had the corners kissed gently until they parted as if possessing a mind of their own. Only then did he press his mouth to hers and kiss her truly. The fluttering turned into tiny shooting stars and somewhere inside a presence awakened that she had no name for. When his mouth strayed over her jawline she lost touch with where and who she was, so she forced herself to back away.

He traced a finger slowly over her lips. "Come. I'll walk you back."

Later, alone in her bedroom, Alanza studied herself in the mirror. She touched her lips. Why was kissing him so different than it had been with Abe? *Abe didn't love you. I do. It'll make a difference.* His words came back to her as clearly as if he were standing at her side. Apparently it made a world of difference. She'd never lost herself the way she had for those few short moments. It occurred to her that she needed to have a talk with someone about all this, because apparently there was more to what went on between a man and a woman than she knew.

"The only parts of my body that don't ache are my eyebrows," Drew confessed tiredly while soaking in the tub. "Climbing the stairs just now nearly killed me."

Billie chuckled. "Physical labor not much called for in your line of work, eh, Mr. Lawyer?"

"Don't start. It was bad enough having to endure Logan's teasing."

"You poor thing." She stood behind him and slowly kneaded the muscles in his shoulders and neck.

After a minute or two of silence, he purred, "A good woman is worth her weight in gold." His eyes closed. "Think I'll just slip beneath the water and let drowning put me out of misery."

"Don't you dare."

"Have I told you I loved you today?"

"Not that I remember, no."

"Well I do, and not because you have the hands of a goddess."

She moved her ministrations higher up his neck. "Liking this, are you?"

"*Dios,* yes. I'd let you work on something a bit lower if I had the strength."

She peeked over his shoulder and saw him rising to the occasion. "I think it's jealous."

"I know it is."

Moving to the edge of the tub, she took a seat and reached down into the warm water. "Maybe . . . if we go very slow . . ."

He groaned with pleasure.

"Slow enough?"

"Oh, hell yes." He was moving sinuously to the decadent rhythm. Drew considered himself the luckiest man in the world. His wife was not only beautiful and a wonderful mother, she was absolutely scandalous behind closed doors—every husband's dream. "Don't ever leave me."

She laughed softly. "Don't worry. You're stuck with me now, Andrew Yates."

"Hmm. Not a bad idea." He lifted her and set her atop him.

"Drew!" she cried as she entered the water. "I thought you were tired."

"I was." He raised the hem of her nightgown and slowly pushed his way home. Watching her eyes flutter closed and her features soften in response to his own decadent rhythm made him harden even more. "We're going to wind up with more little conquistadores running us ragged if we keep doing this without a sponge."

She sighed. "As long as there are a couple of little queens too, I don't mind if you don't."

Her nightgown was drenched and clinging to her skin, throwing the tight buds of her breasts into tempting relief. Unable to resist he brought her closer so he could play.

She moaned. "There's going to be water all over the floor again . . ."

He didn't reply. He was too busy savoring the way her gorgeous breasts flexed in his hands and swelled in response to his tonguing and tender bites. Moving the sodden gown up to her waist, he cupped her hips to increase the pace and the water rippled and sloshed over the sides. "Let's make a queen."

By the time they were done and stretched out in bed, sated and dry, Drew was exhausted and Billie felt like they'd made a passel of queens. Lying side by side in the dark, she said, "Got a wire from Prince today."

"What did it say?"

"Soon."

"Soon?"

"Yes."

He sighed. "Can I kill him the moment I see him?"

"Be my guest."

He turned over. "Soon," he echoed sarcastically. A heartbeat later he was snoring.

But because Prince had already shown what he was capable of, Billie laid awake for a long time thinking and wondering when he'd make his move. She was glad she'd been holding the gun classes because her skills with her Colt were sharp as ever. If she had to defend herself she might only get one chance to save her life.

When she awakened the following morning Drew was dressed and putting clothes into a valise. She struggled up. "What are you doing?"

"Packing. I'm going to San Francisco for a couple days."

"Why?"

"To confront Prince DuChance. I'll not have us looking over our shoulders for the rest of our lives wondering when he's going to show his ugly face."

"Drew?"

"Nor will I have you terrorized, Mina."

Billie studied the hard set of his features. "I don't want you to end up dead, Drew Yates."

"Neither do I, but this has to stop."

She searched for a way to make him reconsider. "Will you at least take Logan with you."

"No, this is my fight, not my brother's."

"I suppose all I get to say is, okay?"

He paused and met her eyes. "I'm sure you and I will have plenty to fight over in the years to come, but don't fight me on this."

Her lips thinned at his tone.

With his clothes and toiletries in the bag, he set it aside and came and sat near her on the bed. He reached out and traced a finger slowly down her cheek. "Do you know how much I love you?"

"As much as I love you."

"And that's why this needs to be done. I don't want either of us walking around on eggshells because of a piece of offal named DuChance."

"I understand, but you have to promise to keep yourself safe and come back to me."

"Don't worry. I'm going to be the first person to hold Callie after she's born."

"Callie?"

"The little queen we made last night. We're naming her Callie after Queen Calafia."

Billie laughed. "We are?"

"Yes."

"And, I suppose all I get is say on this is okay, too."

"Yes." And he kissed her sweetly.

When the kiss ended, she placed a loving hand against his cheek. "Get yourself killed and I'll dig you up and kill you again."

"Understood." He got to his feet. "Going to go say good morning to our son, and then set out for the train. I'll leave you to tell Mama."

"Coward."

"Yes, I am. I'll be back soon as I can." With that he departed.

Billie sat in the silence he left behind and for the first time in a long time prayed.

Later, after breakfast, she let her mother-in-law know where her son had gone and why.

Alanza shook her head. "He's always been more hotheaded than he should. Are you worried?"

"Yes."

"So am I. But the fact that this DuChance had the nerve to send you a wire is infuriating. In a way I can't blame Drew. I do wish he'd taken his brother, however."

"Taken me where?" Logan asked walking into the parlor.

"To San Francisco to confront DuChance."

"What?"

So the story was told again.

Logan said, "If this wasn't so serious I'd say he left just so he wouldn't have to work on the house today. Carpentry is not his strong suit. However, were someone holding a sword over my family's head I'd be just as angry. Do wish he'd said something to me though. He knows I would've gone with him."

Billie wished he had, but there was nothing they could do about his decision now.

Logan looked to Billie. "My brother can take care of himself. He'll be back."

His assurances were appreciated.

"Going to go meet Max out at your place. I'm going to town later. Let me know if either of you need anything."

His exit left her and Alanza alone. Billie watched Tonio toddle over to one of the tables that held his *abuela*'s most prized vase. He eyed it then glanced at his mother as if gauging his chances of grabbing it, but his mother shook her head. "You're going to get in trouble," she warned. But knowing how determined he could be and the quickness he was capable of exhibiting, she walked over and picked him up. He wasn't happy, and as he cried, she asked Alanza, "Do you think I could get Max to build a baby jail just for him?"

Alanza laughed. "I'm sure he would, and speaking of Max, may I ask you something, Billie?"

Billie handed her son the little stuffed chicken Lupe Gutierrez made for him a few weeks ago. The tears ceased and he immediately put it in his mouth. "Sure."

"Have you ever screamed in bed?"

Billie's eyebrow rose. "Um." She had no idea what may have sparked the question or where the conversation might be headed, but she didn't wish to make her mother-in-law any more uncomfortable than she already appeared to be. Had she heard them making love last night? "How about you tell me what this is all about first."

"Max asked if I'd ever screamed in bed and I told him of course not. He said something about letting the pleasure out. I was hoping you could possibly explain it to me."

Billie held on to her smile. She was liking Max Rudd more and more. "So do you want the unvarnished version or a roundabout kind of explanation?"

"Unvarnished, I suppose."

"Then yes, I have screamed in bed with your son on numerous occasions. And if Max knows what he's about you'll scream, too."

Her eyes grew large.

"You asked me, Alanza."

"I know. I know. I just—go on."

"The screaming part usually comes when you have an orgasm."

Alanza's blank look made Billie ask, "Do you know what that is?"

"No."

She wondered how on earth that could be. "When you and your first husband made love, you never felt like you were going to fly apart?"

She shook her head. "No."

Billie sat back and reminded herself that Alanza

was part of an older generation and like many good women were discouraged from enjoying the pleasures lovemaking could bring. It wasn't something discussed or even whispered about. Drew once told her some men believed good women didn't have orgasms. "Okay. If the man you're with knows what he's about, as I said, the pleasure he gives you builds up inside, sort of like a pressure cooker or a boiler that has too much steam. When it blows, that's called an orgasm and you feel like you're flying apart."

"Is it painful?"

"Not at all. I think it's one of the best feelings in the world."

"And it makes you scream," she stated dubiously.

"Sometimes to the heavens. You lose your mind a little bit, too."

The doubt on her face was so precious, Billie wanted to give her a reassuring hug.

"And this happens, how often?"

"If you're lucky, it'll be every time you make love."

"Really?"

Billie nodded and waited as Alanza appeared to think that over.

"This is all very new," she confessed.

"But it's okay. Max seems like a good man. You'll figure it out together."

"Please don't tell Drew we discussed this."

"Don't worry. I won't, and if you have any questions, ever, about different positions—"

"Different positions? There's more than one way?"

"There are dozens. My favorite is astride. Orgasms are more intense."

Alanza looked so shocked, Billie thought her eyes would pop out and roll around on the parlor floor.

Billie added, "There's even a place on your body that the Good Lord made strictly for pleasure."

She scoffed. "That can't be true."

"It is, and hopefully Max will show you."

Alanza shook her head as if she were overwhelmed. "This is too much."

"You won't think so when that orgasm hits you. Anything else you want to know?"

She shook her head. "I think I may know too much already."

Billie smiled. "You'll be fine. Just remember there's nothing wrong with screaming when the time comes."

She still didn't look as if she believed that, so Billie said no more.

But apparently, Alanza wasn't done. "Explain what you mean by astride."

"You can ride a man the same way you do a horse."

She cocked her head Billie's way. "You mean with him beneath."

"And the woman on top. It's a very nice way, too."

"Okay. No more questions."

"That's fine."

Alanza rose to her feet and left the room. Watching her go, Billie chuckled softly.

Chapter 20

On the train ride to San Francisco Drew gazed out his window at the passing countryside and thought about his mission. He couldn't wait to confront DuChance. The man seemed to have no problem going up against women like Billie's friend Addy and Emmalina Ruiz, but when faced with an opponent of equal or superior strength he'd probably back down as he'd done the night Drew foiled the beating of the young woman in the alley. Drew's ire was still high over the wire and wondered if the man thought they'd hide beneath the beds in response. *Soon.* Be it an attempt to frighten, or intimidate, Drew felt neither and he planned to make that clear, just as soon as he got his hands on the bastard. Going to the police about the threat would be futile as Prince could claim the single word meant something different. Drew also couldn't point the finger at him as the murderer of Emmalina and her servant or Addy's arsonist because he lacked credible evidence placing the man at either scene. All he had was his anger, guns, and fists. Together and separately he was certain that would be enough.

When he reached the city, he hired a hack. His first stop was the Black Pearl. It was closed and shuttered. "Do you know how long it's been this way?" he asked the driver.

"Noticed it for the first time a few days back."

Drew thanked him, paid his fare, and walked the short distance to the brothel owned by Gertie Stiles.

"The place has been closed for a few weeks now," she informed him as they sat in her office. "Pearl's dead, you know."

"No, I didn't."

"The day after she was buried, the girls came to work and found the placed shuttered, and Prince nowhere to be found. They couldn't even get inside to retrieve their belongings."

"So he hasn't been seen?"

"Not in the Barbary." She paused and viewed him speculatively. "Saw the snippet in the paper about you. That whore wasn't Billie, was it?"

"Yes. She's my wife now."

"You married her?"

"I did. That a problem?"

"Of course not. Gives old whores like me hope.

Not that I was ever fortunate enough to be with someone like you. Congratulations to you both."

"Thanks." He brought her back to the matter at hand. "Any idea where he might be holed up?"

"Not a one. Sounds like he doesn't want to be found. Why're you looking for him?"

"Personal."

"He still after Billie?"

The question caught him off guard. "How'd you know?"

"Word on the street was he was offering a reward to anyone with information on her whereabouts."

"I see. Maybe I'll do the same for word on him." He stood. She'd given him all he'd needed to know. "You've been helpful as always, Gertie."

"Thanks, and I have great respect for anyone who has the balls to marry one of my kind. Give her my regards."

"I will and thanks again."

Back out on the streets he tried to decide what to do. Gertie knew the Barbary like the back of her hand and if she said Prince was nowhere to be found he believed her. *Now what?* He certainly had no desire to spend the next few days in a search that would be akin to chasing his own tail. Why had DuChance disappeared and seemingly so suddenly? Hoping he'd pulled up stakes in favor of life elsewhere was an opium dream in light of the wire Billie received. Prince was somewhere hiding and more than likely plotting his next move. With that in mind, he didn't want to find out the scum was somewhere near Destiny waiting for Drew to leave so he could strike. Not that Logan would let anything happen to her or Antonio, but he'd feel better being home, so he decided to take the first train back in the morning. In the meantime, he'd go to his apartment, retrieve his mail from Mr. Volga and get a good night, but first he needed to go back to see Gertie and ask a favor.

"Paint?" she echoed in response to his request.

"Yes. Do you have any? And a brush."

"Probably. Let me ask."

She returned with a can of red that matched the color of her front door.

"Thanks, I won't need much. I'll return this shortly."

He carried the can to the Pearl. Brush in hand, he left Prince a message of his own on the shuttered windows:

SOON YOU BASTARD! A. Y.

With that done, he walked past the small crowd of curious onlookers that gathered while he'd been painting and returned the can to Gertie. Thanking her again he hailed a hack for the ride across town.

His landlord was pleased to see him. "Back from Spain so soon? How's your grandmother?"

"She made such a miraculous recovery it wasn't necessary for the family to go at all."

"That's wonderful."

Drew was glad he'd remembered the lie. "Things been quiet here?"

"Very. No more surprise visitors."

"Good. May I have my mail?"

"Certainly."

Once it was retrieved, Drew thanked him and went upstairs to his apartment.

There were only a few letters. The first one he opened contained an invitation to a dinner Consuela and James Anderson were having at their home. He realized the date of the event was that evening. Knowing he wouldn't be attending, he set it aside. Next were two notices from the courts postponing his land claims hearings yet again. Frustrated, he set them aside as well. In light of the talk he'd had with Judge Ross he'd have to make a decision about what to do with those clients and soon. But the next letter he opened took that decision out of his hands. It was written in Spanish and addressed to Senor York. In short, it stated that due to the scandalous rumors tied to his having fathered an illicit child, his services were no longer desired. The families, and there were five of them who'd affixed signatures to the bottom of the letter, didn't wish to be associated with such indecency nor have their names or claims linked to a man who held such little regard for decency and the tenets of the church. They'd included a bank draft with the hopes it would cover what was owed and that they would undertake a search for a new lawyer on their own. He balled up the letter and threw it across the room. He'd been so worried about the scandal splashing on his mother, it never occurred to him that it might also impact his livelihood. Rather than spend the remainder of the day brooding, he took a short nap, then got up and dressed for the Anderson soiree. He hadn't planned to attend, but changed his mind. He needed the distraction.

Consuela met him at the door. "Good evening Drew. How are you?"

"I'm well. Just got back in town." As always the house was packed with guests.

"I've done my best to dispel the nasty rumors about you."

"Not rumors, truth. I have a son and I've married his mother. She's lovely and I can't wait to introduce the two of you."

"She isn't with you now, is she?" She glanced behind him in what appeared to be fear.

Drew studied her for a long moment. "No, she isn't. Why?"

She leaned in and said quietly, "I care for you a great deal, but you must know I can't entertain a woman like that in my home. At least not publicly."

Holding on to his fury, he said evenly, "I see, then I'll take my leave, Consuela. My regards to Jim." He bowed frostily. "Have a nice evening." Turning on his heel he went out the door.

"Drew!" she called.

He didn't slow.

Back home in his apartment, he paced in anger. A less-confident man might have questioned the decisions he made. Marrying Billie had people slamming doors in his face everywhere he turned, it seemed, but he loved her and he loved his son. If anyone thought he'd turn his back on either of them, they could kiss his arse.

Prince DuChance knocked at the door of his pawn. When it opened, the surprise on her face made him smile. "Hello, Wanda."

"What do you want you?" she asked angrily.

"Now, is that any way to greet an old friend?" He'd expected the anger. "Aren't you going to invite me in?"

"No. State your business and go."

"And here I came all this way to see my son."

She stiffened.

He gave her a smile that didn't reach his eyes. "How is he, by the way?"

"He's fine. How'd you find me?"

"I saw your mother the other day. She told me where you were living, so I thought I'd stop by to see him and have you do me a favor."

"No favors."

"Then you won't mind me telling your new husband who you really are. Fine, upstanding, hardworking man that he is, maybe he won't care that Jenna Lane is really Wanda Russell, the two-bit whore of a two-bit whore who'd spread her legs for any yokel with a dime in his pocket."

She slapped him.

He grabbed her by the throat and forced her against the door. "Listen to me, bitch. You are going to do what I ask because you don't have a choice. And if you do it well, maybe I'll let you and the brat live."

He ruthlessly tossed her aside and he went into her house.

Drew arrived home late the following afternoon. It was naptime and he found Billie reading in his library. "Drew!" she cried happily and rose from the sofa to meet him. He took her in his arms, savoring her smells, softness, and how perfectly she fit against him.

"So glad to see you," she whispered.

"Glad to see you as well."

She drew back. "I didn't expect you so soon."

"I know, but Prince is nowhere to be found."

He used the next few minutes to give her the details, but left out the parts pertaining to the letter from his now former clients and his visit with Consuela.

"I like the part about the paint."

He kissed her brow. "I knew you would. How's the little one?"

"Testy but fine."

"Things here been quiet."

"They have. I worried about you though."

"And I worried that Prince would try something while I was away."

"Do you think he's here someplace?"

"I don't know."

"If he is I'll fill his arse full of lead."

With a laugh he drew her back into his hold. "My bloodthirsty little wife." Drew had no idea what he'd do if he lost her. Go insane with grief, more than likely. "I didn't see Mama when I arrived."

"She and the Gutierrez family left for Sacramento a little while ago."

"That's right. Today is Saturday, isn't it?" His mother, Hector, Lupe, and their three boys attended the Catholic church in Sacramento. Because of the travel time involved they departed on Saturday and spent the night with Lupe's family members. They'd return to Destiny late on Sunday.

"Have you eaten?" she asked. "Bonnie left plenty in the kitchen."

"What I'm hungry for is not in the kitchen."

She grinned.

He kissed her and as they parted, Antonio came toddling in. Billie's eyes widened. "How on earth did you get out of the crib?"

He grinned and clapped happily.

"Oh my goodness." She walked over and picked him up.

Drew cracked, "Thanks for ruining my lunch, son."

"What are we going to do with him?"

"Not sure," Drew said smiling, but looked forward to all the surprises the future held.

That evening, after putting Tonio to bed for the night, Billie sat with Drew out on the verandah. She was happy that he'd returned home so quickly and in one piece, but the looming specter of Prince remained.

"There was a letter waiting for me at my office from the families I've been representing."

"The land claim families?"

"Yes. They no longer want me as their advocate."

She stared. "Why not?"

"They saw the notice in the newspaper and they don't wish to be tied to me and my low character."

She felt sick. "Oh, Drew no. I'm so sorry. Are you going to meet with them and try to change their minds?"

"No. It isn't going to matter." He told her then about the conversation he'd had with his judge friend and how the color line was affecting his practice and others. Hearing that made her angry.

"So even if my character weren't in question, I'd still be out of work."

"You'd think in this day and age—"

"I know darling, but we meet the challenge and keep going."

"What are you going to do?"

He shrugged. "We won't starve and there's plenty of money for Antonio's education and any other essentials, but I'm not cut out to be a man of leisure."

Billie felt so badly for him. She leaned into him and he eased her into his side. "I love you," she said sincerely.

"And that means more than anything." He kissed her brow and they sat and watched the moon rise above.

The next seven days were the hottest of the summer. Temperatures soared and the men building the house worked under a blazing sun. In spite of the searing heat, the construction stayed on schedule and according to Max's estimate, Drew and Billie would be able to move in before the wedding. Billie's gun ladies were no longer in need of instruction, so the lessons were canceled, and with the passing of the bloom season for the roses, she was free to enjoy chasing after her child by day and making love to her husband at night. Alanza had yet to hear from Noah, but stayed on track with the wedding plans with the hope that he'd show up in time for the festivities.

On the eighth day, the weather was not only hot but windy. Everything not tied down or weighed down blew away. With the outside framing done and the walls up and secured, the workers plied their skills inside.

That evening, just as the sun was going down, Eli came tearing up to the site on his horse. "Naomi's diner's on fire! She needs help! Soon as I grab a fresh mount I'm heading back!"

The men dropped everything and ran for their horses. Drew, Logan, and Max stopped off at the house to let the women know what was happening.

"Go on! Go on!" Alanza implored, "Bonnie and I will load up the wagon and follow. If anyone is hurt, we can help." She ran from the room to change clothes.

Mariah and Billie were forced to stay behind. Fires were no places for babies.

"Be careful," Billie said giving her grim-faced husband a kiss farewell.

Mariah mirrored the actions with her own husband and both women stood on the porch and watched tensely as the men rode off. A few seconds later, Alanza, Lupe, and Bonnie followed in the wagon.

"I hope Naomi's okay," Mariah said with concern.

Billie shared her hope.

"I'm going to take Maria home and put her to bed."

"Time for Tonio, too. Hopefully everyone will be back soon."

Mariah nodded, gave Billie a hug and set off walking for home.

Chapter 21

Drew, Logan, and Max pushed their mounts at breakneck speed to cover the hour-long ride to town, and as they neared the darkening sky ahead was red with flames. It wasn't a good sign. Naomi's diner, along with most of the other buildings on the main street, were made of wood. Due to the soaring temps of the past week, the wood would be dry as tinder. They'd not seen Eli but guessed he was somewhere up ahead. Unlike the larger cities in the valley, the town had no fire-fighting equipment, so a bucket brigade would have to be established. From the size of the blaze, such an endeavor might prove futile, but they had no choice but to try and put out the flames.

When they finally arrived, the town was fully engulfed and the air was hot and thick with smoke. Windblown cinders danced like fireflies. Every able-bodied male within miles was lined up passing buckets of water hand to hand from the pump behind the general store once owned by Logan's former mistress, Valencia Stewart, and from the pump nearest Naomi's diner. Drew dragged his kerchief from around his neck and tied it over his nose and mouth to keep from choking on the acrid smoke. He and his brother got in line to aid the efforts of the brigade, while Max headed for the second line formed on the other side of the street. From the looks of the raging inferno nothing would survive but the men kept the buckets coming.

Billie's mind was heavy with thoughts of the disaster in town. As she climbed the stairs to put Tonio to be bed, she heard the door pull. Wondering if Alanza or one of the men had ridden back because they'd forgotten something, she opened the door to find Mariah. "What—"

"Run Billie!" Mariah screamed.

But before Billie could make sense of the warning, she met the ghoulish eyes of Prince Du-Chance. Her heart pounded. He pushed Mariah inside with a hold on her arm. Two men entered behind him, one carrying Maria, who began wailing.

"Well, well, well, Billie. I told you it would be soon, didn't I?"

She ignored him for the moment. Her main

concern was Mariah. "Are you all right? Has he hurt you?"

"No," Mariah snarled while trying to free her arm.

"She's as feisty as you are. I like that. Had I the time, I'd see just how feisty she'd be on her back, but I'll save that for another time."

"Let her go."

"I will in a moment, but only because I want your husband to know exactly who's taken you and his son."

She froze. "Leave my son here and I'll do whatever you ask."

"You're going to do that anyway. Give him the baby."

"No."

The knife appeared at Mariah's throat. "I start with her and your son will be next. Give him the child."

She knew it wasn't an empty threat. Screaming with inner rage, she handed Tonio over and his wails joined those of his cousin. He tried to reach for her and her heart broke but she had to ignore him or she was going to cry.

"Tie this one up." He pushed Mariah towards one of the men, who produced a stout length of rope. He tied her hands and ankles and pushed her down to the floor. Billie turned to make sure she was okay when a hand slapped a cloying, sweet smelling rag over her face. She attempted to pull it away but the hand was too strong. A wooziness crept over her. Tonio's crying and Mariah's scream of "No!" were the last sounds she heard.

The bucket brigade managed to save the doctor's office and two other buildings on the eastern side of the street, but every building on the western side including Naomi's diner was now a smoldering pile of rubble. Making their way there, Drew and Logan passed their mother, Max, and the women helping the doctor with the injured. She gave them a terse nod of acknowledgment and they moved on. In front of where the diner once stood, Eli held his crying wife to be. Her parents founded the place during the height of the Gold Rush and when they retired she'd taken it over. It had been a place for the community to gather for good times and to savor her prize-winning pies. Now, it was gone.

"How did the fire start?"

She shook her head. "I've no idea. I was at home when Jenna rushed in and said the place was on fire." She lived in a small house a short distance outside of town. Luckily the flames hadn't spread that far.

Drew noted the heavy scent of kerosene in the

air nearby. "Do you smell that?" he asked his brother.

Logan nodded. "Yes. Kerosene."

Drew asked Naomi, "Was she using kerosene for some reason?"

"Not that I'm aware of. She was supposed to be finishing up the prep for tomorrow."

Drew didn't remember seeing her anywhere during the firefight. "Do you know where she is now?"

Naomi wiped her eyes with a wadded handkerchief and shook her head. "She said she was going to the doc's office to see if he needed any help, but I haven't seen her."

Drew got a terrible feeling inside. The arsonist who'd set the fire at Addy's place used kerosene. Maybe it was just a coincidence, but the sudden urge to ride back and check on Billie was strong. "I need to go home."

"Why?" Logan asked.

Drew explained and Logan's eyes widened. "I'm coming with you. I'll let Alanza and Max know we're leaving and why. You go on. I'll catch up."

Drew took off at a run. The livery owner had managed to get his stock out ahead of the flames, so Drew left his tired stallion with the man, saddled a fresh one and rode like hell through the dark for Destiny.

And while he rode he prayed. He tried to convince himself there was no way Prince could be clever enough to pull off such a scheme, but five hours had passed since they'd left the ranch to help with the fire. Anything could be set in motion given such a long span of time. *Just let them be okay. Just let them be okay!*

But the moment he arrived, he knew things weren't. The front door was wide open, and there were no lights on inside. Dismounting, he drew his gun and kept his eyes and ears open as he carefully made his way to the door and inside. An eerie silence greeted him in the foyer. He peered around the darkness for a clue as to what might be going on. "Billie!"

He thought he heard a sound. Gun in hand, he listened and heard it again. It sounded like a muffled voice. "Billie!"

Hoping he wasn't making a fatal mistake by lighting a match and exposing himself, he withdrew his match kit from his shirt and lit a match against the flint. The flare showed the gagged Mariah trussed up and lying on the floor. His heart pounded. "Oh, God!"

He hurried to her side, hugged her tightly for a moment while she sobbed through the rag between her teeth. "Hold on, sis. You're safe now. I have you." He undid the simple knot and hurried to light a nearby lamp. Seeing little Maria asleep behind her on the floor gave him added relief but where were Billie and Antonio?

"Where's Billie?" he asked while untying her ankles and wrists.

"DuChance has taken her and Tonio. The only reason he left me alive he said was so you'd know he had them."

Ice filled his blood the moment she spoke Du-Chance's name, but it melted under the force of his burning rage. "How long ago?"

"Not very much after you and Logan left for the fire. When they knocked on my door I thought it was Logan returning for something."

He listened as she told him of being forced to accompany him and his men and that they'd held a rag over Billie's nose until she slumped to the floor. Wiping at her tears she reached behind her and gently picked up her daughter. Drew was happy they'd been spared but he was worried sick about his wife and son.

"Do you have any idea which way they rode after they left here?"

"No."

"Okay. I'm going outside to take a look around. Logan's right behind me and should be here shortly. Will you be okay alone for a moment or two?"

"Yes, but be careful. He may be still on the grounds."

Drew doubted that, but having underestimated Prince's cleverness once, he took her advice to heart. The moment he stepped outside, fat, heavy raindrops began falling like coins from the sky. The ranchers and farmers had been praying for rain and those prayers were being answered. Too bad it had come too late for Naomi and the town's other shop owners. Too bad for him also because any tracks Prince may have left behind to be found once the sun came up were now being washed away.

Alanza and the others returned an hour or so later. Drew related the grim news. "I need to find them."

Alanza shook her head. "You're not going to find anything or anyone the way it's pouring outside."

Drew paced. He knew she was right. Leaving while it was still dark made no sense at all, but he was slowly going mad with worry over the fate of his wife and child.

Logan added. "And when you go, you're not going alone."

Drew didn't argue. Having Logan by his side would help him hold on to what sanity he had remaining and possibly keep him from killing

Prince in cold blood once he was found, and Drew vowed that the madman would be found.

"Mariah, do you know anything about this Jenna Lane?" Max asked.

"No more than that she's been working for Naomi for about a year. Keeps to herself mostly. Has a boy of about four. Why?"

Logan explained, "She was working at the diner when the fire started. The air around the place was thick with the smell of kerosene."

"Was she filling lamps?"

"Naomi said she was supposed to be getting the diner ready for tomorrow's opening."

"And no one's seen her since the fire began," Drew added.

"She isn't tied to DuChance, is she?" Mariah asked, looking around at the hard-set faces of the men.

Alanza replied, "No one knows. It would be nice if she could be questioned."

But unless she was found, the mystery would continue.

Logan came over and hunkered down in front of his wife. "Are you sure you're okay?"

"I am. Just worried to death about Billie and Tonio."

As was everyone else in the room.

At first light, Drew and Logan took the train to San Francisco and upon arrival immediately began their search. With no idea where Prince might be, their first stop was Gertie's.

After hearing the grim tale, she promised to keep her ears open and help to spread the word.

"I'm offering a one-thousand-dollar reward," Drew added.

"So much?"

"My wife and son are priceless. The money means nothing."

"If I hear anything I'll let you know."

"Thank you. Send whatever you hear that may be helpful to my office. If I'm not there leave the information with my landlord, Mr. Volga."

"Will do. I'm sorry you're having to endure this. Good luck, Drew."

Their next stop was the police station. Drew's having lived in San Francisco for many years and having cases that sometimes involved the police, some of the men on the force knew Drew on sight, but that didn't seem to matter.

"Are you sure she didn't just take off?" he was asked by the man on duty at the desk.

"I know she didn't just take off. My sister-in-law was there when DuChance took her and my son away."

"This is Billie Wells, right? Didn't she work for him?"

Holding on to his temper, Drew nodded. "Yes, she did."

The man studied him. "Didn't I read something in the paper about you fathering her child?"

"Yes, and we're married. She's my wife."

"You married her!" He laughed. "You're pulling my leg."

Drew crossed his arms. He was getting angrier by the second.

The policeman grinned and shook his head. "Tell you what. Woman like that—who knows what's really happened, so if you haven't found her in, say, a week, come on back."

"A week!"

Logan grabbed him by the arm. "Let's go, Drew. We'll find her on our own. No sense in going to jail."

Drew knew he was right but he wanted to pull the man across the desk and pound a fist in his face. Instead he said icily. "Thanks for nothing."

The still chuckling officer nodded and went back to his newspaper.

For the next two days, Drew and Logan crisscrossed the city on foot and in a rented carriage.

They checked brothels and cribs all over the Barbary and talked to whores, their madams, and pimps. They spoke with the bootblack Mr. Arroyo, then drove up and down the wharves questioning dockworkers, fishermen, and anyone else who'd listen. They greased palms with coin, tequila, and in one instance a man promised to spread the word in exchange for an on-the-spot legal consultation with Drew. Drew didn't care. He just wanted to find his family. Driving by the businesses Prince reportedly owned were also dead ends. Throughout the search, Drew forced himself not to imagine their fates because the horror in that would dull his focus. So he looked for Billie in the face of every woman he passed and Tonio in every baby. One occasion during the afternoon of the second day, he spotted a woman on the walks carrying a little boy with curly black hair that was Antonio's size and color, and he jumped from the carriage. Running through traffic and the crowds on the walk, he came up behind her and spun her around. The baby wasn't his son. Apologizing profusely to the wide-eyed woman, he backed away feeling like a fool, but he didn't care. He wanted to find his family.

As dusk fell that second night, and the brothers returned to his apartment, he was at his wits' end.

"Keep your spirits up," Logan offered encouragingly. "We'll find them."

Later while Logan slept, Drew stood in front of the windows looking out at the street. Over a year ago, he'd stood in the same spot asking then as he did now, *"Where are you, Mina?"*

Billie came back to full consciousness seated on bare ground in a dark space. She was immediately sick. Once her stomach gave up all its contents, she wiped her hand across her mouth and sat back breathing heavily. She fought to remember how she'd come to be in the place, then the terrible turn of events rushed back and she began feeling beside her in the darkness. "Tonio!"

Terrified, her movements turned frantic. "Tonio!" *Lord, please let my baby be here.* "Tonio!" Her attempt to stand and move away was brought up short. Her arm was tethered. Her fingers ran over a length of stout rope knotted around her wrist. Still calling his name, she clawed at it but the knot was fashioned so tightly and so well, it wouldn't come free. There'd been no response from her son. She was alone.

Swallowing her panic, she listened for voices or anything that might aid in determining her location or help an escape. The lapping sound of waves soon drifted to her ears followed by the distant groan of a foghorn. Was she back in San Francisco? On one of the wharves? There was no way of knowing. Her eyes began adjusting to the gloom. She was enclosed. A shack apparently, but the darkness prevented her from seeing if there was a door. She knew that room-sized shipping crates were sometimes used, so was she inside one of those? Her rope was long enough to allow her to feel the sides of her cage. Her fingers grazed over wood. She traced the length of rope she was tied with to its source and touched metal. *An anchor?* Her thoughts were interrupted by the soft scratch of metal against metal. She tensed as a door opened, allowing in windswept fresh air and the shadowy shape of a man. The lantern in his hand illuminated the ghoulish face of Prince DuChance.

"Where's my son, damn you!"

He smiled. "With his new family."

"No!" She launched herself at him but the rope wasn't long enough.

His laugh filled the shadows. "You've been a thorn in my side for quite some time, Billie, and now it's time to pay."

"Where's my son!" she screamed again.

"No need to worry about that. You'll never see him again."

"If I don't kill you, Drew will. Where's my son, you bastard?"

"Yates may or may not, but you won't because I'm going to kill you first." The knife appeared in his hand. The long blade caught the glow from the lantern and gleamed sinisterly. "I'll enjoy sliding this across your throat even more than I did Emmalina Ruiz."

"Did you set fire to Addy's house, too?" she demanded.

"Since you'll never live to point the finger at me, yes, I arranged that. The witch deserved to burn. She'd been poisoning my mother for years."

"Because you murdered her daughter Chassie, and Pearl refused to intervene when Chassie asked for protection from you."

He shrugged. "Oh, well."

Billie's mind quickly searched for a way out of this nightmare alive, but nothing surfaced that might put her safely past him and the knife.

"I owe you for many things." He set the lantern down on the dirt floor. "For my face, and for eluding me the way you have. Had you let me fuck you that night, none of this would be necessary."

"Had my derringer done its job, none of this would be necessary."

"Cunt. First I'm going to have you and then I'm going to kill you."

He advanced and she drew in a quivering breath. "Where's my son!"

"You just worry about pleasing me so I'll let you live a little while longer."

He placed the sharp tip of the knife beneath her chin and she forced herself to stay calm even as she gathered her strength. Grinning like something truly out of a nightmare, he squeezed her breast, then slid the hand down to her waist. She let him grope between her legs. Looking up into his face, she closed her eyes as if enjoying his touch and let herself go slightly limp. When the top of her head exploded beneath his chin with the force of her outrage, he screamed and the knife went flying. She quickly grabbed his lapels and kneed him viciously in the groin. The agony doubled him over and she brought her closed fists down on his spine. As he collapsed she launched her knee again, this time into his already shattered chin. He cried out, hit the ground, and she kicked him in the ribs evoking a sickening crack, then stomped on his spine as hard as she could. Heaving with rage, she picked up the knife, cut herself free, and grabbed the lantern. For a moment he lay there moaning. Very slowly he lifted his head and the blood-covered face turned her way. He spit out teeth and the tip of his tongue bitten off by her first strike. Eyes glowing like hell spawn, he made a move to rise, but she slammed the lantern down hard on his shoulder blades. The glass shattered with a whoosh, spreading oil and flames that licked at the fuel saturating his clothing and heavily pomaded hair like something alive.

Bellowing, he frantically slapped at the blaze rising from his shoulders and hair and got to his feet staggering back and forth and bumping against the walls in a blind, desperate attempt to escape the gruesome inferno he'd become.

Seething, and deaf to his screaming, she watched and waited.

Again and again he stumbled into the walls while the putrid smell of burning flesh rose and filled the shack. Around and around he went, twisting, screaming, and aflame. His weight finally broke through one of the wood walls, and as if sensing the water nearby, he zigzagged away, his howls piercing the night.

She didn't follow. Seconds later, a splash melded with a tortured wail, followed by silence. *Prince will go by water because that was my daughter's gift.* She wondered if Addy'd known he'd die by her gift of fire as well.

Gathering herself, Billie finally cried and ran shaking hands over her face. Certain he wouldn't be returning, she stepped through the broken wall and into the night. Walking past the small knot of people staring curiously at the water and then at her, she headed towards the city. She knew Drew was tearing up creation trying to find his family, and now that she'd freed herself she needed to aid in the search for their son. She headed for the Barbary.

Gertie's was bright and gay with the sounds of laughter and music when Billie walked through the doors. When those inside got a look at her disheveled hair and clothing, the flecks of blood staining her face and hands, the place went silent as a tomb.

"Billie!" an alarmed Gertie cried.

The long journey from the docks had used up the remaining dregs of Billie's adrenaline-fueled strength. The scene before her eyes became hazy and she wanted to tell the madam to send someone to tell Drew where she was, but she crumpled to the floor instead.

Chapter 22

A knock on the door drew Drew's attention away from the window and to the clock on the wall. It read ten o' clock, and he wondered who it might be at such a late hour. Walking over to answer the knock he prayed Billie would be standing on the other side, and if not her, someone bearing good news. Instead he met the eyes of a short woman carrying a young boy asleep on her shoulder. He recognized her immediately. "Jenna?"

"Hello, Mr. Yates. May I come in?"

He studied her for a moment but stepped back so she could enter. "What are you doing here?"

"To tell you where your son is before I leave town."

His heart pounded with the excitement and hope. Dozens of questions competed to be asked first but she confessed, "I was the one who delivered him for Prince."

He searched her face again even as he yelled for Logan asleep in the bedroom. The boy in her arms stirred but didn't awaken. "Why don't you lay him down over there so we can talk."

She shook her head. "I'll only be here a minute or two. I'm on my way to the train station and hopefully to a place where Prince will never find me again."

"Where'd you take my son?"

When she told him, his knees buckled.

"Prince threatened to murder my son if I didn't help him."

Ignoring for the moment the implications surrounding the name she'd revealed, he asked, "How do you know DuChance?"

"He's my son's father."

A sleepy-looking Logan arrived dressed in his denims but still pulling on his shirt. He froze at the sight of Jenna Lane and cast quizzical eyes his brother's way.

"I have to go," she said. "Please tell Naomi I'm sorry for the fire. Was anyone hurt?"

"Not physically, but people lost their livelihoods."

"If could undo that I would, but he left me no choice. Tell Billie I'm sorry, too. If things had turned out differently maybe we could've become friends this time."

"This time? You know my wife?"

"Yes. We both worked at the Black Pearl. It's where I first met Prince."

Drew was too shocked to speak.

"Good-bye."

And before he could ask her anything else, she was gone.

Drew pulled up in front of the big house. There were a few lights on inside, so the residents were up. He sat there for a moment trying to decide how best to go about this heartbreaking task, but they had his son, and they were going to have to give him back.

"Do you want me to come with you?" Logan asked.

"No."

His knock on the door was answered by a surprised James Anderson. "Drew? How are you? What brings you here at this late hour?"

"May I come in?"

"Certainly."

James stepped aside. Upon entering Drew heard a baby crying and his eyes immediately went to the stairs leading to the home's upper floor.

James smiled. "That's our new son. We just adopted him a few days ago. It's taking him a bit to get used to his new home."

The cries were so familiar, Drew had to close his eyes and draw in a deep breath. *Antonio.* He sent up a prayer of extreme thanks, but at the same time, in spite of his last visit, he'd called the Anderson's friends for years. This would not be easy.

"So, what brings you here?"

"My son. The baby DuChance arranged for you to have is mine."

James's eyes widened and he searched Drew's face with wonder.

Drew continued, "His name's Antonio Andrew Yates. He was stolen along with my wife by Du-Chance two days ago."

His eyes grew even larger and his hand went to his mouth. "No!" he whispered. "The woman who brought him here said the child was hers but she couldn't afford to keep him."

"It was a cruel ruse, Jim. I know how long you and Consuela have wanted a child of your own and I wouldn't come here with such an accusation if it weren't the truth."

"But—"

"He has a birthmark on his back. I have one that matches it in the same place. He's my son, Jim. I've come to take him home."

Jim dropped down into a chair and his head fell into his hands. Stricken eyes met Drew's.

"Consuela's been so happy. This is going to break her heart. I didn't want to deal with DuChance but 'Suela said he'd handled similar arrangements for a couple she knew and that everything turned out well. How will I tell her?"

"I don't know but I've been turning over the world trying to find him."

"I won't ask you if you're sure. As you said, you wouldn't have come on just a whim. And she and I both noticed the mark."

He sat there for a moment but finally got to his feet. With shoulders slumped as if straining under the weight of the world, he climbed the stairs. Moments later, Drew heard Consuela's tortured cry ring out, "No!"

Wanting to kill DuChance for the pain he'd caused them all, Drew waited tensely.

The couple descended the stairs together. Consuela carried Antonio. Tears ran unchecked down both their faces. Upon seeing him, Antonio literally jumped into his father's embrace. Consuela stood and watched silently. Drew's own tears flowed as he kissed his son and held him tightly and rocked back and forth and gave silent thanks again and again for his safe return. "I'm so sorry, Consuela."

"No more than I, Drew." She ran her hand lovingly over the babe's head in a solemn farewell, and her glistening eyes shed more tears. "Take your son home," she whispered.

He nodded, and father and son made their silent exit.

Logan took the reins, and Drew held his son, who kept peeking up at his face. "Yes, it's your papa. Uncle Logan and I are pretty pleased to see you."

He snuggled close and Drew kissed his head. "Now, we have to find your mama."

When they returned to the apartment, Mr. Volga came running out. "A messenger left this for you. Said it's very important." Drew tried to hand Antonio to Logan so he could read the note but Antonio pitched such a fit, Drew kept him close.

"I don't think he's going to let anyone else hold him for a while," Logan said, observing his nephew with a smile.

Antonio burrowed into Drew's chest as if trying to get beneath his skin.

Logan touched his head gently. "Can't much blame the little fella."

When Drew looked up from the note tears stood in his eyes. "Billie's with Gertie," he said softly.

Logan yelled happily.

Drew said, "I've never cried this much in my life."

"You are a bit of a mess. Let's go get your wife."

While Logan sat in the carriage, Drew and the baby entered the bordello, and for the second time that night, the place went ghostly quiet. Few babies patronized Gertie's. Drew nodded at the staring crowd. Gertie, draped in a low-cut, flowing red velvet gown, stepped forward. "Follow me." And to the staring crowd, she snapped, "Is this a funeral or a whorehouse? Go back to having fun."

So the piano player began banging on the keys and the drinks and laughter resumed their flow.

Following Gertie through the shadowy hallway, he asked, "Is she hurt?"

"I don't believe so. Exhausted though. She may be asleep."

They entered a small room anchored by a huge brass bed. Billie was asleep in the center. He walked over carrying the baby. Drew's heart swelled with so much emotion he thought it might burst. *You will love her until there is no tomorrow.* Antonio looked down at his sleeping mother and did his best to wiggle free of Drew's arms.

Gertie said, "He's going to be quite the looker when he grows up."

But Drew was looking at his wife. He wanted

to wake her, and apparently so did her son. Drew sat on the edge of the mattress and set Antonio down on the quilt. He immediately crawled close. He looked back at Drew, who shrugged. "You can wake her if you think you can."

So the little boy, who'd recently learned to give kisses, kissed his mama on the cheek and just like in a fairy tale her eyes opened, and she screamed with joy. "Tonio!" Grabbing him, her face glowing with happiness she hugged him to her and rocked and rocked. "Oh, my baby! My beautiful baby! I've been so worried! Where were you?"

And then she saw her husband. "Drew!" she screamed and launched herself from beneath the quilt and into his arms. Poor Tonio, squeezed between the bodies of his parents, began to cry.

Billie drew away with a teary laugh. "Oh honey, I'm sorry," Billie apologized. "We get reunited only to crush you to death. Mama's sorry." Her eyes went back to Drew. "I'm so glad to see you."

"Same here." He turned to Gertie, who was wiping her eyes. "Thank you from the bottom of my heart."

"You're welcome. Now take your family home. You're making this old whore cry."

Drew took in the revealing nightgown his wife was wearing. "Where're your clothes so you can get dressed?"

"They have to be burned. They're covered with blood and—"

"Blood?" His eyes filled with questions.

"Prince's blood," Billie explained quietly. "He's dead, but let's get out of here first. I can tell you about it later."

She ended up throwing Drew's suit coat on over the gown. "Not much of a cover," he decided.

"This is the Barbary, they've seen worse or more, depending upon how you look at it."

They gave Gertie hugs. She kissed Antonio, got a smile for her trouble and the reunited Yates family climbed into the waiting coach.

Logan smiled at his sister-in-law. "Welcome back, sissy."

She chuckled. "Thanks, Logan. Good to be back." She glanced lovingly into the eyes of her son, who couldn't seem to take his eyes off her either. "So, where was Tonio when you found him?"

"With Jim and Consuela Anderson."

"Aren't they friends of yours?"

"I suppose."

Both she and Logan looked his way. "Why suppose?" she asked.

"Consuela and I had a difference of opinion the last time I was at her home." He wondered how she was recalling that conversation now after tonight.

"Was it something you can talk about?"

He scanned her face in the darkness softly lit by the moon. "It had to do with you. I mentioned how anxious I was to introduce the two of you, and she told me she couldn't entertain a woman like you in her home, at least not publicly."

He was angered all over again.

"And?" Billie asked.

"And what?"

"And was that all she said?"

He half turned to get a better look at her. "Yes, that's all she said."

She placed her palm against his cheek and leaned over and gave him a kiss. "Thank you for getting all riled up on my behalf, but what did you expect her to say? She's a society lady. Women like her don't let women like me in their homes, not even when we're married to wealthy, gorgeous, rancher lawyers such as yourself."

On the far side of the wagon, Logan chuckled softly.

"Billie?" Drew cried with disbelief.

"It's okay. My life has been fine not knowing Consuela Anderson and it will continue to be. Besides, I have a very thick skin from fending off acid looks from woman like her, so back to Tonio. How did you know he was there?"

"Jenna."

"Lane?"

"She set the fire on Prince's order so he wouldn't kill her son, who Prince fathered, by the way."

He saw the surprise. "You didn't know."

"No. But that maybe explains why she just seemed to disappear into thin air when I knew her before. One day she was at the Pearl, next day we were told she was gone. Never saw her again until the day we had the gathering. My goodness."

Drew explained the rest and she shook her head. "She doesn't have to hide now that he's dead. I wonder if her husband knows about this."

No one knew.

When they entered Drew's apartment, the familiarity of the surroundings and the memories she'd made there washed over Billie like a balm, and she was finally able to convince herself that being back with her son and husband wasn't a dream. She'd only gotten a few hours of sleep at Gertie's, and after the excitement of the reunion was even more exhausted, but sleep would have to wait so she could have some time to be with her husband. Antonio had fallen asleep on the ride so they put him on the sofa because neither parent wanted to let him out of their sight. Over their protests Logan left to find him a room at one of the nearby hotels so they could have some privacy. He'd be back in the morning.

While their son slept peacefully, Billie savored being held in her husband's arms and wanted to stay there for the rest of her days.

"When I came back and found you gone . . ." he said against her hair.

"I know."

"Tired?"

"Extremely."

"Then let's move to the bedroom so you can lie down."

He carried Antonio. She carried the sofa cushions and placed them on the floor beside the bed. Drew eased him down and covered him up. While he slept on unawares, Billie watched her husband put fresh sheets on the bed.

"I love my brother, but I'm not sleeping on the same sheets."

"Drew, that isn't necessary."

"For me it is."

She was impressed by his skill and proficiency. "You do that pretty well for a wealthy ranch-owning lawyer."

"Haven't always had servants. My brothers and

I can make beds, cook, wash dishes, sweep floors. Thanks to Mama we could've hired out as house-keepers."

Once the bed was ready, she slid between the fresh, crisp sheets and sighed with satisfaction. "You're right. It did matter."

"Told you," he pulled her close and wrapped her in his arms. "*Dios*, I missed you."

"Missed you, too." She ran her eyes over the man she loved more than anything in the world. "I thought I'd never see you again. And if Prince had had his way, I wouldn't've."

"Do you want to talk about it now, or after you get some rest."

"Let me just tell you how he died and then to-morrow I want to hear about the fire and all."

"Deal."

So she told him all: how she regained con-sciousness, searched in vain for Tonio, and about coming face-to-face with Prince. "He boasted about setting Addy's house afire. Apparently, she'd been poisoning Pearl for years, and it was his way of seeking revenge. I suspected she was doing something like that when I lived with her, but I guess I didn't want to believe it."

She then related the moments leading up to his fiery death.

Drew raised up and his eyes were wide. "You took down a man almost a half size larger."

She nodded.

"Where'd you learn how?"

"Had a customer when I first started in the business. A boxer named Tom. We were talking one night about his being in the ring and he asked me if knew how to defend myself. I said no, so he showed me. And Drew, his words came back to me as clearly as if I'd heard them yesterday. Tom said, 'and when the bastard hits the ground, try and kick his heart out,' and I did."

She could see him studying her and wondered what he might be thinking. "I was a bit woozy after the head butt but I guess I was too mad at the time to let it bother me. I have a knot there, too."

His fingers gently touched the tender spot hidden beneath her hair. "If I knew where to find this Tom, I'd give him ten acres of Destiny land and a thousand dollars."

"He saved my life."

"Yes, he did."

Billie drifted back on the memories. "I wasn't going to let him kill me. Not him." She met his eyes. "I felt nothing watching him burn. No guilt, no regret. Is that wrong?"

He shrugged. "You did what you had to do to stay alive, *corazon*. That's all that matters."

She agreed and burrowed closer. "How about we finish this tomorrow?"

His lips brushed hers. "You go ahead and sleep. I'll be right here when you wake up in the morning."

Chapter 23

Contrary to the promise, he wasn't, but Logan was. He knocked on the closed bedroom door. "Are you up, sis?"

"Yes?"

"Decent?"

"Just a minute." Wondering where her husband and son were, she hurried over to Drew's armoire and quickly grabbed down one of his robes. Once she tied the belt, she padded to the door and opened it. There stood Logan, holding a tray laden down with breakfast.

"Oh, Logan. You shouldn't've."

"I didn't. Mrs. Volga did. Where do you want me to set it?"

She pointed him to an empty area on the short, mirrored vanity.

He obliged and after setting it down, caught his reflection. "Only Drew would have a mirror this large and ornate."

"Has to be big enough to see all that pretty face."

Logan laughed, then quieted. "I like you, Billie."

"I'm glad. Things began pretty rocky for us."

"I know. My brother loves you more than Queen Calafia and I'm beginning to see why."

"I'll take that as a compliment. Since we both love him—you as his brother and me as his wife, be nice if we got along."

"I agree. Never had a sister before."

"And I've never had a brother before."

He stuck out his hand. "Pax."

"Sure. Whatever that means."

He smiled and said seriously, "Means—peace."

"Ah. Then pax it is."

She removed the silver tops from the plates and saw bacon, scrambled eggs, hot biscuits running with butter, apple butter and slices of orange. "Do you want some of this? Mrs. Volga always cooks for twelve."

"No thanks, I ate earlier."

"So where is my pretty husband and my even prettier son?"

"Out shopping. He said you needed clothes. He also told me about DuChance."

"Ah. He'll never hurt anyone again—that's the most important thing."

"Yes it is. I want you to teach Mariah to fight that way."

"Really?"

"Yes, and when my daughter is old enough, I want her to learn too. I don't ever want them to be in a situation like the one you were in and not be able to defend themselves."

"You're a good man, Logan Yates."

"Not as pretty as my brother but I have my own charm."

For a moment, Billie studied the man she knew to be as arrogant as a god on the outside but soft as his brother underneath. "Thank you," she said softly and tears stung her eyes.

"What for? Why the hell are you crying?"

She dashed away the water. "I don't know why. Maybe because you didn't have to come in here and have this conversation with me and teach the meaning of the word *pax*."

"I hate when Mariah cries and this isn't any better."

"I think sisters are supposed to tell brothers what's in their hearts."

"Good to know. Now stop it. Eat."

And he left.

Billie's pretty husband and even prettier son returned a bit later with a strange young man carrying so many packages he appeared to be hiding beneath them.

Drew explained, "I couldn't carry the baby and all the purchases, so the store lent me Bradley here."

Bradley nodded. "Morning, ma'am."

Drew directed him to set the packages on the sofa.

"Morning." Billie took Antonio out of his father's arms, freeing him to pay Bradley a nice tip. Beaming, the young man exited.

Logan said, "Going to go take a walk to stretch my legs. You still want to take the two o'clock train?"

Drew looked to Billie and she nodded.

"Good. I'll be back. Enjoy yourselves."

He departed and Billie said, "Logan is rather nice."

"He's good at pretending."

She laughed. "Show me what you bought."

There were three walking suits and three beautiful blouses to wear beneath. There was underwear. "You bought me underwear."

"Do you have any?"

"Well, no."

"Well, there."

She said to Tonio, "Your papa's not supposed to buy my underthings."

"Billie, I bought you underthings for years."

"That was then. I'm your wife now."

"What difference does that make?"

"Society says husbands aren't supposed to buy their wives underthings."

"Antonio, cover your ears."

Laughing, she covered the baby's ears.

"Then remind me to strip them off the moment I get you home."

"Scandalous man."

"Damn right."

Dressed in her fancy new clothes and underwear, Billie and her men boarded the two o'clock train for home. As it chugged out of the station, she glanced out at the receding city, thought back on how she'd come to be there, and savored the prospect of going home.

Alanza greeted them as if they were a gold strike. There were tears and hugs and kisses and more hugs. Mariah got in her share as well, and Billie had never been loved so well by any family of any kind.

Over her groaning protests, she was ordered to bed.

"You need sleep and rest," her mother-in-law declared. "For the next few days you are to do nothing but play at princess."

"Princess?"

"Princess."

"Andrew, take her away."

Laughing, he did as he was told.

In the days that followed, she rested, refused to let her son out of her sight, and let herself be waited upon as if she had royal blood. When word got around about how Billie bested Du-Chance, she received numerous requests to pass the knowledge on.

"I'm going to be giving more lessons," she told Drew that evening as they sat out on the veran-dah.

"What in this time?"

"Self-protection. Thanks to Logan, a lot of the men want their wives and daughters to learn what Tom taught me. Mariah has taken to calling the take-down method the 'Billie.'"

"Not many women have a fighting style named after them."

She shook her head. "I suppose I should be flat-tered."

He pulled her into his side. "While you've been lying about, Max finished the house."

She straightened. "Truly?"

"We can move in tomorrow if you like."

She threw her arms around his neck in joy. "Oh, Drew! That's wonderful! Can we really move in tomorrow?"

"Yes, ma'am, and maybe once we do, we can finally make the trip to Sacramento I've been promising you."

She snuggled back into his side. "I don't care about that. All I want is for us to be together and to be happy." She looked up into his eyes. "I love you Andrew Antonio Yates."

"And I love you, Mina. Forever."

Billie decided she'd wait until they moved in before she shared the news that they had another baby on the way. It would be a perfect housewarming gift.

Epilogue

Noah Yates made it home three days before the wedding. He'd met Mariah last year during his mother's birthday celebration, but he hadn't met his niece, Maria, nor had he any idea that Drew of all people was not only married to a beauty named Billie but had a son. In spite of the turmoil swirling in his own life, Noah was glad to be home.

"So, Noah, how's the seafaring business?" Logan asked at dinner his first day back.

Noah shrugged. "Fine, but it'll be better once I get my ship back."

Everyone at the table went still.

He'd been dreading this moment.

His mother looked puzzled. "Is it in dry dock being repaired?"

"No. A pirate woman stole it from me a few months ago off the coast of Spain."

Drew snorted with amusement. "You let a girl take the ship named after your mama?"

"Is her name Calafia by any chance?" Logan asked with a laugh.

Noah smiled. He'd been expecting the teasing. "I've no idea what her name is, but I'll be leaving just soon as the wedding is over to hunt her down. Sorry I won't be able to stay longer, Mother."

His mother was still staring at him with confusion on her face.

"I'll get it back." And he would, if he had to track the she pirate to the bottom of the seven seas.

Dear Readers,

And so ends our second visit to the Destiny Ranch. I hope you enjoyed Drew and Billie's story. Billie was one of the most unconventional heroines I've ever created. It was a pleasure getting to know her. For those unfamiliar with the series please pick up the first book, *Destiny's Embrace*—the story of Logan and Mariah—to catch up.

Up next. Noah. How on earth did he lose his ship to a lady pirate, and who is this mysterious woman? Stay tuned dear readers for the next trip to *Rancho Destino,* for a swashbuckling tale of pirates and passion on the open seas.

Until next time,

B